MW01139813

I'll Die at Your Wedding

A Belly Dance Mystery

Rebecca Wolf-Nail

The Belly Dance Mysteries

Like murder? Curious about belly dance? For fun links, random author's thoughts and Susan's Big-Ass Glossary of Bizarre Belly Dance Terms, visit:

www.BellyDanceMysteries.com

This book is a work of fiction. All events, organizations and characters featured in this book are figments of the author's deranged imagination

Dedication

To my mother and father, who supported me in all my artistic endeavors—no matter how weird.

You've been the best parents anyone could have.

Thank you.

Chapter 1

My glutes were screaming. My legs shook as I tried to hold the squat. Looking over at my friend Susan, I could see her face turning beet red. I realized that I was experiencing one of those strange psychic moments you get when you know you are thinking exactly the same thing as every other woman in the room.

"Holy crap, this is just the warm-up!?" Susan said through gritted teeth.

Yep, that was it.

The only person who seemed unaffected by tormented muscles was Tara Erickson—police officer, belly dance troupe director, and currently, our workshop instructor. With her lithe figure in perfect alignment and not a single blond hair escaping from her pony tail, she held the deep plié without apparent effort. She gently pulsed up and down as she bent forward, bringing her upper body parallel to the floor with a straight back, then held her arms out straight in front of her to increase the move's difficulty.

"Backs flat, people! Keep your belly button pressed against your spine and *reach*!" Her voice rang out loud and clear, and I could well imagine her barking orders to felons or shouting to her partner, "That perp's slowing down, Dufresne! Get him!"

"You just had to take this workshop, didn't you," hissed Susan. "Tara's our friend and you like her group, Nile Rising, so we both had to take her workshop. You are *so* going to pay for this!"

Despite her accusation, it really was all Susan's fault we were doing the endless squats. Susan Barry, my best friend since our school days, was the one who got me into belly dancing in the first place. What started out as her wild idea for getting more exercise had quickly turned into an obsession for both of us. If she hadn't dared me (double-dared, actually) to take that first class, we would never have performed at the Arabian Nights Bellydance Festival, never have seen the amazing dance troupe Nile Rising, never have met Tara, and I would never have signed us up for Tara's "Bootie Buster" workshop. But try telling Susan that? Huh.

"...six, seven, eight!" Tara placed both hands on her knees and smoothly rolled up to a standing position, instructing us to do the same. We all rose shakily, moaning as our tortured thighs were finally able to release. "OK, take a breath and now let's do that again!"

We obediently sank back into the bent-over squat position. This time even Susan was too tired to complain.

§

"So, what did you think?" Tara's blue eyes looked quizzically at us over a tall nonfat latte. Tara, Susan and I had met up at Georgio's Café after the workshop for some much-needed refreshment.

"I think I may never walk again," Susan whimpered. "You are an evil, evil person."

"Hear, hear," I said, massaged my aching quadriceps. "How often do you have to do those squat things before they stop hurting?"

Tara laughed. "Never happens! But it's a great way to strengthen your legs and develop your core muscles."

"My core muscles are dead," Susan declared. "They must be nourished immediately." She took a large bite out of a gooey cinnamon roll. "I sure earned this the hard way! Here you go, core muscles, have some food."

I eyed her choice critically. "I'm pretty sure cinnamon rolls don't build muscle. You should eat something with protein, like me." I waved a bite of pecan pie under her nose.

"Good idea." Susan snapped her jaws at the fork, but I pulled my pie back just in time.

Tara winked at us over her salad with grilled tuna. "Look at it this way, ladies: you'll be in better shape for the wedding if you do a few of those every day. I hear we're all going to be dancing a lot! You have three whole weeks to build up those glutes and thighs."

Temporarily distracted from our pain, Susan and I grinned at each other. In just three weeks our friend and award-winning dancer, Kalina Romanko, would be getting married to the handsome Middle Eastern drummer Harun Basarah. The belly dancing community was abuzz with anticipation, as it promised to be an unforgettable event.

"A June bride," Susan smiled dreamily. "I can't wait to see her dress."

"Ours are certainly nice," I said. "I can't believe she found a color that actually looks good on everyone!"

Kalina's wedding colors were white and periwinkle blue, and our bridesmaid dresses broke every tradition in the book by being absolutely lovely. The dresses' clean blue suited everyone (a major concern for a redhead like me) and their simple sleeveless tops and softly-flaring tulip skirts complemented every figure.

Susan broke me out of my reverie by poking me in the ribs with her elbow. "So, Ms. Maid-of-Honor, how are the bridal shower plans coming along? Are we getting the Chippendale dancers or what?"

I had been deeply touched when Kalina had asked Susan and me to be her joint maids of honor. We had divvied up the responsibilities more or less equally, with the bridal shower ending up on my plate. It would be held the weekend before the wedding.

"Or what," I said firmly. "The bride and groom agreed that there will be no strippers at either party. It's going to be nice and tasteful!"

"Bo-riiiing!"

"Not necessarily," argued Tara. "When my mom got remarried we had her bridal shower at the new civic center and it was just beautiful!

4

I lured her there by pretending I had to drop in for some police business after our dress fittings."

"It's going to be even easier to get Kalina to *her* party, because we're having it at Daniela's," I said.

Daniela Romanko-Nickleson, Kalina's mother, lived in a spacious house on Lilac Hill, one of Redvue's most affluent neighborhoods. It was it the perfect place to have a party, and all it would take to get Kalina there would be a summons from Mom.

"That will be nice," Susan conceded. "What a house! I guess being the daughter of the owners of Viva Technologies has a few perks." We nodded, knowing that as joint owners of one of the largest medical software companies in our area, Kalina's mother and stepfather had the means to spare no expense on the nuptials.

"What have you got planned?" Tara asked eagerly.

"Kalina's mom will get her there at about four o'clock. That means we want to get there about an hour beforehand. That will give us all a chance to chat before dinner. Dinner is being catered by Sound Seafood, by the way."

"Yum!" cheered Susan. "After that we'll do presents and a few games with prizes, a wishing tree, cake, aaannnnnd..." here she paused for dramatic effect.

"A hafla?" Tara guessed.

"A hafla," Susan confirmed. "We're hiring Arabica for the night—with a substitute drummer, of course."

Arabica, the Middle Eastern band in which Kalina's fiancé was the drummer, was a favorite with all of the local dancers. They would be providing live music for our hafla, which is basically an Arabic word for 'dance party.' Many of the guests would be either professional or amateur belly dancers who simply couldn't get enough dancing, especially to the music of a great live band. We all whooped with delight.

"Now that's going to be a party!" Susan declared.

"I can't wait," said Tara, "but what's a wishing tree, Susan?"

"It's like one of those things you see at Christmas." Susan said, running a finger around her plate to make sure no crumbs had escaped her fork. "You know, where you can buy presents for underprivileged children or people in nursing homes."

"That's pretty close," I said, pushing my empty plate away. "Except that at weddings and showers, it can be a tree where people write notes to the couple, giving advice or saying what they wish for them."

"How sweet," said Tara. Then she laughed. "I bet some of the advice could get a little spicy, especially from some of the older dancers we know."

Susan and I chuckled. We knew, alright.

"That reminds me, Susan," I added, "we need to pick up the wishing tree the week before the party. Don't let me forget! It'll be at Deerborne Florist."

Susan thought for a moment. "That name sounds familiar. Why?"

"It should," Tara said, "Harry Deerborne is Camellia's brother. Camellia's real name is Gina Deerborne."

Susan smacked her forehead. "That's it! I always forget most dancers have 'real' names too! So Kalina's having him do the floral arrangements as a favor to Camellia?"

"Oh, it isn't just belly dance nepotism," said Tara. "Harry's great! I can't wait to see the arrangements he'll be doing for the wedding—I was over at Camellia's for lunch the other day and she showed us some pictures of other events he's done and they're just amazing! You should see the arrangements he did at the wedding for Mayor Vick's daughter."

"It looked like something out of a fairy tale," I agreed, remembering pictures in the papers.

Our 'lunches' finished, Susan and I contemplated the difficulties of rising from our chairs.

"Oof, my behind hurts!" As she rose, Susan vigorously massaged her posterior. Nearby diners eyed her warily. She ignored them. "Everything stiffened up while we were eating!"

I was about to make a smart remark about this when my own legs seized up. "Ooh," I moaned. "Not good, not good! Too many squats!"

Tara, drat her, sprang out of her seat like a gazelle. "I keep telling you guys, a few of those squat sets every day can work wonders!"

"What's the penalty for strangling a police officer?" Susan asked in a stage whisper.

"Dunno," I whispered back. "She's off duty, so maybe it doesn't count!"

Tara assumed a martial arts stance. "Try it." She wiggled her fingers in a 'come and get it' manner.

"I don't like the grin on her face," I said.

"Cheese it," Susan laughed, "she's onto us!"

We strolled out of Georgio's into a rare day of May sunshine.

"Omigod, what's that big yellow thing in the sky?" Susan held her hands in front of her eyes, pretending to be blinded. In the Pacific Northwest, and especially in the Seattle area, a sunny day even in late in spring can be rare. This spring had been especially cold and wet, making the local farmers nervous about their spring and early summer crops. People across the area were desperate for sunshine.

"Aliens!" I yowled, joining in the spirit. "Git the shotgun, Grandpa!"

Tara shook her head at us, laughing. "Watch out, or I'll have to take you both in for being drunk and disorderly!" Her voice took on a mock growl.

"We didn't drink!" Susan protested. "You saw us."

"We only drank coffee," I said virtuously. "The waitress will testify in our defense."

"For some people, coffee is all it takes," Tara said darkly.

Before getting out her keys, Susan stretched her arms luxuriously up to the blue sky. "Oh, this sun is nice! I sure hope the weather is this good for the wedding."

"It's brave of Kalina to plan an outdoor wedding," I agreed, knowing that even in June, Seattle weather can get dodgy. "I'm sure the arboretum has a contingency plan for rain, but it'll be so nice outside with all the roses starting to bloom!"

Kalina's wedding would be held in the Redvue Arboretum, a lovely spot that had wild flowers and native plantings alongside formal rose gardens. The ceremony would take place in the main rose garden, and then we would proceed to the arboretum's exquisite Rose Hall for the reception. The procession would be led by Ruth Bingham, a local belly dance instructor.

Ruth would be balancing a shamadan, or large candelabra, on her head, and both Susan and I were looking forward to seeing our first live shamadan dance procession.

Wedding processions are a common tradition in many cultures, and Egypt has a long history of wedding parties in which a winding procession led the bride to her new home. The procession was often led by a dancer, and accompanied by musicians, more dancers, and even acrobats! The dancers lit the way by carrying lanterns and candles.

Early in the 20th century, it had become popular for a dancer to lead the way with an elaborate shamadan balanced on her head. Wedding receptions had begun to take place in hotels and clubs, so a procession into and around the reception room replaced the winding street dance. In some cases, once the wedding couple had been led to their seats, the dancer would perform an intricate candelabra dance to show what she could accomplish without knocking the candelabra off her head.

Susan and I had once tried on a friend's shamadan to see what it was like, and had been shocked to discover just how heavy and hard to balance it was. After that, we held anyone who could actually do a shamadan dance in high respect!

Susan and I both sighed happily, thinking about sunshine and weddings and dance. Then Susan had to go and spoil it.

"How's that giant rat of yours doing? Has it given anybody the plague yet?"

"Nutria," I corrected. "It's a nutria, and they don't carry plague." My day job is being assistant manager at a wildlife rehabilitation facility called Wild in Redvue. Although she has two dogs, Susan takes a dim and suspicious view of the assorted wild animals with which I spend my time.

"Looks like a rat to me," she said with a shudder. "And those orange teeth! Eeeew."

The Monday before our workshop, Susan had dropped in at WR to show off the new Sharif Wear dance pants she had just purchased. We were admiring the dramatic flair of the pant legs and the attached skirt when a shaggy-haired young man burst through the facility's front entrance. In his arms was a large cardboard box.

"Trey!" he shouted. "Is Trey here? I've got a total casualty!"

Trey Folkner, a young intern who was studying to become a wildlife veterinarian, swept his own sandy brown hair out of his eyes and rushed forward. "Rocky? What have you got there, man?" He peered anxiously at the box.

As we all gathered round, the young man whose name appeared to be Rocky looked at Trey with wide eyes. "I don't know what the hell it is! I was biking on the Sammamish Trail, and it came barreling out of the bushes and ran across the path, and I just couldn't stop! It bounced off my wheel, and I wiped out, and I went to check on it and it wasn't moving! It's breathing, though, so I don't think I killed it. Oh, geez, I hope I didn't kill it!" His voice took on a tone of awe. "I think it's some kind of mutant, dude. I've never seen anything like it!"

I decided it was time to take charge. I cautiously opened the box, having learned early on that an injured wild animal that appeared to be near death's door could suddenly spring to life and wreak havoc when its cage gets opened. I learned this the hard way when, as a young college student, I had been driving an injured squirrel to our nearest wildlife facility. Hoping it was still alive, I had opened the box at a red light. Several minutes of mayhem occurred before I had been able to recapture the patient, and my parents' station wagon had ended up with a number of large bites taken out of the upholstery.

The animal inside Rocky's box would certainly appear exotic to someone who hadn't encountered one before. About the size of a large housecat, it had the face and fur of a beaver, a long rat-like tail, webbed back feet and large, orange buck teeth. I couldn't see any obvious injuries, but it did appear to be stunned. At least it was breathing.

Susan came up behind me and stuck her own nose into the box before I could stop her. She sprang back with a loud screech. "Giant rat! Giant rat!" she yowled. A low growl began to issue from the box. Apparently our new patient did not appreciate the noise.

"Giant *mutant* rat," added an enthusiastic Rocky. "Is it making that weird noise?"

"Wow!" Trey was putting on the protective gloves we use when handling wildlife with large teeth. "Maybe we've found a whole new species! Dibs on naming it!"

"I hate to burst your bubble," I commented, nudging Trey aside, "but it's just a nutria. They're pretty common, but they spend most of their time in the water so a lot of people never see them." Donning my own pair of gloves, I carefully lifted the animal out of its box and put it on the examining table.

"Eeeee!" Susan squealed as the nutria lifted its head in alarm and began to struggle.

"Out!" I ordered Susan, seeing that she was adding to the creature's panic. "You're not helping!"

As Susan scooted out, one of our vets came in to examine the nutria. Thankfully, it didn't appear to have any broken bones. "Lucky little guy," she said, "he only seems to have some shock, bruising and perhaps a strained hip. We'll hydrate him now and get him into an enclosure to rest. Hopefully, he'll be back on his feet in a day or two."

Trey, Rocky and I breathed a sigh of relief. Even Susan, peeking around the door, had seemed glad about the outcome.

§

She wasn't looking so sure about it now. She shivered as she unlocked her car. "It creeps me out to think those things are swimming around our waterways. Do they ever come up people's

12

drains like the rats in New York? If they do I'm never going to feel safe on a toilet again!"

I have to admit, I was tempted to let her believe it. Alas, my position as a wildlife rehabilitator makes it my duty to educate the public, no matter how funny it would be for them to imagine a 20-pound nutria sneaking up the pipes to feast on their unprotected behinds. "Nutria don't live in sewers," I said patiently. "They live in wetlands—that's swamps and marshes to you. They're vegetarians, and the only harm they do is through burrowing and eating too many plants."

"I suppose they're OK as long as they stay out of my pipes," Susan said dubiously.

"They have no interest in your pipes," I assured her. "See you in class Monday, and don't forget that we need to pick up the wishing tree and find wedding shoes this weekend!"

"Let's make it Saturday. I have a client meeting on Sunday."

We got into our cars and went our separate ways.

Arriving at home, I discovered that even the short ride in the car had caused my legs and back to stiffen up. I was limping as I came in the door. My husband Michael glanced up from his computer as I passed his home office, where he spent most of his time doing freelance programming.

"Have a good time?"

I groaned in response, dramatically rubbing the small of my back.

"Very subtle." Michael's blue eyes twinkled. "I suppose if you ask *really* nice, I could be persuaded to give you a massage."

"You are the best husband who ever walked the Earth. The handsomest, smartest, most charming…"

"Flattery also works," Michael rose and rubbed my shoulders. Then he stepped back, wrinkling his nose. "But you'll have to take a shower first. No offence."

Later that evening, showered and massaged into bliss, I curled up in my favorite chair and sipped tea as I watched our beautiful Siamese-ragdoll mix cat Banshee demanding to be lifted into Michael's lap. This was a nightly ritual in which she would circle Michael's chair and look up at him beseechingly with her big blue eyes, and he would inform her that she was perfectly capable of jumping up by herself. She would continue circling, occasionally stopping to put her paws up on his chair and give a commanding yowl. Finally Michael would sigh, give in and lift her up and she would sprawl in his lap, kneading her claws into whatever part of his body was handy and purring loudly in triumph.

"Ow! Dang it, Banshee, that's my knee!" Michael looked over at me. "She needs a claw trim again."

I smiled, as always enjoying the sight of a full-grown man being dominated by a ten-pound cat. "Maybe later when she's a little sleepier."

He nodded sagely. Grooming Banshee usually went better if we were able to catch her when she was asleep. This was especially true when it came to trimming her razor-sharp claws.

Michael gently detached a claw from his sweat pants. "Has the Great Wedding Commission considered the offer to have my band to play at the reception yet?"

"I'm afraid the verdict was 'no.' Bagpipes really don't go with the whole hafla theme."

This was putting it diplomatically. A few months ago, Michael and Susan's husband Jim had decided to learn how to play bagpipes. Their beginners' class had formed a band, calling themselves the Buckle Swashers and blasting the public's ears every chance they got. While they had improved greatly in the last couple of months, there were still many sour notes—and you have never heard a sour note until it is played on a bagpipe! They were also very, very loud.

"Besides," I added, "The Rose Hall is too confined a space for bagpipes. They belong in the wide open fields!" *Wide, wide open, with a lot of space for the sound to dissipate*, I thought, wondering how many battles in Scotland had been started by pipers who wouldn't shut up.

"Oh, well, we need to spend our time getting ready for the Highland Games in July, anyway."

"That's the spirit!" I set my empty teacup on an end table, stood, and stretched. "I don't know about you, but I'm beat!"

Michael also stood, getting an annoyed squawk from Banshee as he lifted her off his lap. He settled her on his shoulder instead. "That's right, princess, we don't want to be in a boring old wedding reception anyway, do we?" he murmured in her ear. Still unhappy about being disturbed, she grumbled and wrestled out of his arms. Then she stalked over to her food bowl in the kitchen and glared at him with a commanding air.

"Oh, the reception will not be boring, even without bagpipes," I promised Michael as he obediently filled Banshee's bowl with crunchies.

I had no idea how right I would turn out to be.

Chapter 2

"Closed? Why is the bridge closed?!" Susan glared in outrage over the steering wheel. In big blinking words, a freeway sign announced the weekend closure of the 520 bridge. Susan expanded on her theme. "I mean, what is the point of even *having* a new bridge if it's going to be closed all the time? They should just rent us all kayaks."

The institution of a toll on the 520 bridge had been a sore point with many commuters who needed to cross Lake Washington to get to their respective jobs and activities. Now, a new bridge had replaced the older one, and an even higher toll had been instated to charge drivers for the pleasure of driving across it. As the new bridge was being built alongside the old one, there had been endless bridge closures. Residents of the Seattle area had once placed bets on when—and if—the new bridge would ever be completed, and if it would help or add to the existing traffic jams that stretched for miles in every direction. It turned out to be a moot point, since the new bridge was often unaccountably closed, just like the old one.

"Dang it, how are we going to get to the florist place now?" Susan thumped the wheel angrily.

"We'll just have to take I-90 and figure it out from there," I said as we passed the exit we had planned to take.

Grumbling under her breath, Susan continued to head south to the I-90 Bridge, now our only other option for getting to downtown Seattle. "The directions I printed were for getting there from the 520," she said dismally. "I *hate* going downtown!"

I sighed. We both knew we were going to get lost.

There is no point in going into detail about the next 45 minutes. Suffice it to say we ended up in a part of Seattle neither of us recognized and we went in endless circles, doubling back, and once, after a quick check for traffic and police cars, making a mad wrong-way dash down a one-way street. "Don't tell Tara," Susan said as she gunned the engine and I shut my eyes.

After holing up in an unattended parking lot and consulting our phones and a battered map of Seattle that Susan dug out from under her seat, we managed to find the street that, supposedly, housed Deerborne Florist. "Watch for address numbers," Susan ordered as we approached it, "I can't see them and watch for traffic at the same time." A loud horn behind us proved that she wasn't doing a very good job of that, either.

"Which way?" Susan demanded as we approached the intersection.

"I don't know, none of the buildings are marked with numbers!"

"Well, pick a direction, I have to turn NOW!"

"OK, left!"

Susan turned right. We proceeded for nearly a mile before I saw enough addresses to determine we were going the wrong way.

"Told you," I said as Susan did a very illegal U-turn.

"You were just guessing."

"Guessing right, you mean."

"You said left, not right."

"Shut up."

"Where did you say this place was?" Susan looked up and down the street. "I don't see a flower shop anywhere."

"We're practically in front of it," I said, conscious of the impatient line of cars that was stacking up behind us. "Just park!"

Susan whipped the car around 180 degrees and backed into a tiny slot between two parked cars. My screech of protest blended with the horns of startled drivers on both sides of the road.

"Weenies," Susan said disparagingly.

I shakily squeezed out of my side, which was so close to the neighboring car that my door wouldn't open all the way. "Who taught you how to drive, anyway?"

"Somebody who wasn't a weenie."

"Well, here it is." I pointed to a sign that read 'Deerborne Florist' in fancy gold script.

"Wow! Schmancy place."

Susan wasn't exaggerating. Deerborne Florist's storefront looked more like a high-fashion art gallery than a simple florist. Centered in the window was a tree entirely made of glass, with glittering crystal drops hanging from its branches instead of leaves. Drapes of black velvet provided a strikingly simple background.

Susan eyed it with misgivings. "I hope that's not the kind of tree we're picking up. Even if we could move it without breaking it, it's not going to fit in the car."

"The wishing tree should be a lot smaller. And lighter," I added, hoping it was true.

Susan lifted her nose and sniffed the air. "I smell chocolate. Where's it coming from?"

I'd been smelling it too, and it was causing cravings. We looked up the street and identified the source: a small shop a few doors down from Deerborne Florist called Chocolate Noir. A sign beneath the striped pink and brown awning advertised gourmet chocolates that were handmade on site.

Susan's steps automatically drifted toward it. "Ohhh, that smell. We have to go there!"

I grabbed at her elbow. "*After* we get the tree." There was no telling how long we were going to spend drooling over chocolates, and I figured we'd better get our business finished first.

We entered the lobby of Deerborne Florist, which was just as impressive as the outside. The walls were painted a soft shade of rose and hung with gold-framed pictures that featured lavish floral designs at weddings and other special occasions. Artfully-arranged pedestals displayed silk floral arrangements in every color of the rainbow.

A handsome young man in a dark green jumpsuit moved forward to greet us. He was in his mid-thirty's, with dark curling hair and bright blue eyes.

"Good afternoon, lovely ladies, how may I help you?"

I dug a slip of paper out of my purse. "We're here to pick up a wishing tree for the Nickleson bridal shower," I said, showing him the invoice.

"Ah, you must be the two troublemakers Camellia told me to expect," boomed a voice behind the young man. A man in his fifties or early sixties appeared, wearing a formal dinner jacket but somehow looking casual and a little bit rumpled in spite of it. Beneath gray-streaked brown hair, his twinkling blue eyes bore an unmistakable resemblance to Camellia. He nodded to the younger man, who seemed taken aback by his informal greeting. "It's OK, Chuck, I'll take care of this one. They're friends of my sister's."

Once again a smile crossed Chuck's face. "Belly dancers?" he hazarded.

Susan gestured to her middle. "To the core," she joked. We all laughed, but I noticed Chuck giving both Susan and me a not-too-subtle appreciative once-over. Considering that we were there as customers, it seemed a bit inappropriate.

Camellia's brother looked irritated. "Chuck, why don't you go check on the delivery sheet for tomorrow? Make sure we have the *right* centerpieces this time!"

Chuck winked at us. "No rest for the wicked," he said as he left the room.

Harry Deerborne ran a hand over his head and gave an exasperated sigh.

"Problems?" Susan asked sympathetically.

He smiled ruefully. "Oh, just the usual. Nothing that couldn't be handled if some people paid more attention to their jobs than the ladies!"

Susan laughed. "Don't blame him too much, that's a good-looking assistant you have there. I'm sure the attention goes both ways."

For a moment Harry didn't answer, and a worried look crossed his genial face. Then he broke into a smile. "So, I have the wishing tree all ready for you. All you have to do to set it up is take the top off of the box." He bent behind a counter and took out a beautifully-packaged box about three feet high and two feet wide, in the florist's signature rose, gold and black. He set the box on the counter, and deftly unfastened four gold clasps on each side of the box's bottom, which appeared to serve as a base. Then he lifted the entire box off the base, revealing a glittering tree underneath. Susan and I gasped in unison.

"Oh, Mr. Deerborne," I said breathlessly, "it's beautiful!"

"Amazing," added Susan.

About two-and-a half feet tall, the little tree appeared to have come straight from fairyland. The base was swathed in black velvet, out of which rose a slender silver trunk. Impossibly delicate silver branches glittered with cut-crystal drops that seemed to catch every available beam of light, refracting them into rainbows. I couldn't take my eyes off it.

"It's like an upside-down chandelier!" Susan squealed. "Mr. Deerborne, this is beautiful!"

"Call me Harry," he said, obviously pleased with our reaction. "With a sister like Camellia, I figured I'd better pull out all the bling for this one!"

"Bling doesn't begin to describe it," I said, still mesmerized by the dancing crystal leaves. "Do you make costumes, by any chance?"

Harry shook his head. "Sorry, my skills don't extend to sewing. Don't think Camellia hasn't asked!" He raised a finger to stroke one of the glittering leaves. "I can hook you up with a wholesaler of crystals, though. If you and some of your friends want a big enough order, I can get you a good price."

Susan looked speculative.

"We can't sew either," I reminded her. "Remember when you tried to make that circle skirt? The dragging hem, the machine that ate holes in the fabric, all the swearing?"

Her gaze didn't waver. "But they're so…shiny!"

"Maybe I'd better put the lid back on," suggested Harry, grinning. "I'll have Chuck take it out to your car for you." He handed me a small box that matched the larger one. "These are the cards for people

23

who want to write their wishes for the couple," he explained. I admired the little box, which was closed by a miniature version of the gold claps on the tree's packaging.

The cards looked like little jewels themselves. Made of delicate gold paper, they had "Karina and Harun" engraved on one side. The other side was left blank except for elegant scrollwork on the edges. Each card had a loop of slender gold thread attached, so guests could hang them from the tree. I imagined how pretty they would look against the sparkling branches, and looked speculatively at Harry. It seemed Camellia wasn't the only artist in the family. I found myself utterly charmed by the tree, cards and boxes that matched right down to the little golden latches.

Harry secured the top of the tree's box down over the base. At that moment, a pretty red-headed girl appeared around the corner.

"Harry, Mrs. Davis is on the line with a question about her daughter's graduation party flowers?"

Harry glanced at us and sighed. "Sorry, but I'd better take care of this. She's changed her mind three times already!"

"No problem," I said.

Susan nodded.

Harry handed the tree to Chuck, who had just returned. "Chuck, ring these ladies up and carry the tree to their car for them."

"My pleasure!" Chuck lifted the tree without apparent effort and carried it to the front desk.

Susan produced her credit card. The wishing tree had originally been her idea. She had wanted it to match the general theme of

Kalina's wedding, so we had decided to use the same florist. Chuck swiped the card, Susan signed the receipt with a flourish and we were ready to go.

Chuck carried the box out to the car and strapped the box securely into the back seat, fastening it in by looping the seatbelt through the carrying handle on top. Susan grinned. "Is this how you'll be transporting the trees for the wedding?"

"Oh, no," Chuck patted the top of the box. "This is just a little guy. For the wedding, we're bringing in the *real* trees. We deliver those ourselves—it'll be all hands on deck to set those puppies up!" He flashed us another of his devastatingly handsome smiles and flexed an arm, which promised to be muscular under the sleeves of his uniform.

Chuck pulled a business card out of his jacket and handed it to Susan with a wink. The front of the card was designed with Deerborne Florist's logo and number. "Now, be sure you call if you need anything," he said. "The shop's number is on the front, but *mine's* on the back. If either of you want anything, night or day, just give me a ring!" Then, with another devilish wink, he strode off toward the storefront.

"That was kind of weird," Susan said, stuffing the card in her wallet. Then she forgot all about it as a breeze wafted chocolate smells toward us. She locked the car door and headed toward the chocolate shop. I followed close on her heels.

In its own way, Chocolate Noir was just as charming as Deerborne Florist. Artfully-placed tables displayed boxes of chocolates, ranging from simple chocolate drops to box after box of elaborate truffles. A glass case by the register held plates of fudge, each variety sounding more delicious than the others.

"I have died and gone to heaven," Susan declared. "I mean, these truffles!" She proceeded to read the labels. "Dark chocolate with pear extract. Cinnamon milk chocolate. Smokey sea salt and caramel. White chocolate raspberry." Her dazed expression met mine.

"I can't decide," I admitted helplessly.

"We'll just have to buy it all."

"Can I help you?" inquired a voice behind us. An attractive young woman had appeared behind the counter. In her late 20's or early 30's, she had dark curly hair, brown eyes, and a figure that must have been very difficult to maintain surrounded by such rich chocolates.

"We don't know where to start," Susan said in bewilderment.

The woman smiled. "Well, which flavors do you prefer most— sweet, salty, citrus or spicy?"

"Yes," said Susan.

A full half-hour later we had the counter stacked with our choices. "My treat," Susan offered grandly, handing her credit card to our new friend, who had turned out to be the shop's owner and whose name was Marla.

Marla deftly swiped the card and packed our chocolates into two large brown and pink bags. "Thanks for coming in," she said cheerfully as we left.

"Like we had a choice," moaned Susan, digging into her bag as soon as the shop door had closed behind us. "Mmmmm, ginger orange dark chocolate, come to Mama!"

"You didn't have to pay for mine, too," I laughed, digging into my own bag. "These were not cheap!"

"You can owe me lunch sometime. It would have taken too long to get separate tabs."

I appreciatively rolled one of the dark chocolate pear truffles over my tongue as we got back into the car. "Deal," I said.

Behind the wheel, Susan was arranging things in her purse while she stuffed more chocolate into her mouth. The business card Chuck had handed to her fluttered out of her wallet, and she grabbed it before it could land on the floor. "Wow," she said, giving the card a closer look, "Chuck really did give us his number!" She held the card out so I could see a handwritten message on the back. It said, 'For a good time, call me!' plus his phone number.

I stared at it. "I'll bet Harry wouldn't be happy about this," I said. "Heavy-duty flirting on the job isn't exactly professional."

"Do you think we should tell Harry?" Susan asked as she pulled out of the parking space, still looking at the card. "He might want to know that his assistant is tom-catting around with his customers."

"It sounded like he already knew," I said. "Hey, would you mind keeping both hands on the wheel?" I snatched the card out of her hand in the hope that she would concentrate on not getting us killed by the oncoming traffic. Why do I let her drive when we go places?

We managed to find our way back to the I-90 Bridge without too many near-death experiences.

"Next stop, shoes!" Susan exclaimed as we arrived safely on the other side.

We both needed to find white shoes to go with our bridesmaid dresses so we had planned to stop at Redvue Square after picking up the tree. Mindful of the fact that we would be dancing a lot at the reception, I picked out a pair of dressy white sandals with a low heel. Susan fell in love with a pair of high white pumps.

"You won't last the night in those," I warned. "Remember how much trouble those stupid kitten heels caused me last year?"

The year before, I had worn an extremely cute but impractical pair of kitten heels to the Arabian Nights Belly Dance festival, and had been forced to purchase a pair of flats because of the discomfort they had caused.

"Yeah, and if it hadn't been for those shoes, we might never have cleared Kalina," Susan reminded me. "Plus these shoes are gorgeous! Who knows what they might be able to accomplish? I'm keeping them!"

I gave up, shaking my head as the salesclerk swiped her card. Susan could always kick off her heels and dance barefoot if need be. I just hoped she wouldn't trip in them during the wedding!

After a quick stop for gas, Susan drove me home. We made plans to meet up at the Nicklesons' before the bridal shower so we could both set up the little wishing tree. With aching feet but a happy heart,

I carried my new shoes and what remained of the chocolates into the house.

"Everything going according to schedule on Planet Wedding?" Michael asked as I came in the door.

"Yes, and I survived going downtown with Susan," I said as I slipped out of my jacket.

Michael, who knew how Susan drove, whistled. "No small feat! I didn't know being a bridesmaid was so hazardous."

I rolled my eyes. "You have no idea. The 520 was closed and we got lost and she broke every traffic law in the book!"

"Sounds like an eventful day. Hey, are those chocolates?"

"Oh, yeah," I said, handing him the bag. "You have to try them— they *almost* made driving with Susan worth the risk.'

"Well, the rest of the festivities are on the Eastside, aren't they?" he asked, selecting an orange chocolate caramel. "Cheer up. The hazardous duty should be over."

Neither of us had any idea how wrong he would turn out to be.

Chapter 3

The week before the bridal shower was too busy for me to think much about the wedding.

First, the wildlife sanctuary received an emergency call from a woman who had looked out her back door to discover a small cougar curled up against her house. The fact that it had barely lifted its head at her presence indicated that all was not well with the wild feline.

I had immediately rounded up Trey and Nancy King, our on-duty vet. She carried a tranquilizer dart gun. George Trumann, a hefty African-American man who had owned a construction company before he retired and now volunteered a great deal of his time building enclosures for us, came along in case we needed extra muscle.

As it turned out, tranquilizers were not needed. The cougar was indeed in a bad state, nearly comatose. It was emaciated and had several obvious wounds, and Nancy suspected that it had been struck by a car and had a broken leg. Whether instinct or chance had guided it to seek refuge at a human dwelling we would never know, but he clearly needed immediate help. We brought him back to the sanctuary, where Nancy performed a successful surgery to set the leg.

"He's not out of the woods yet," she warned us. "The fact that he made it through surgery is a good sign, but he's dangerously underweight and we're going to have to watch him closely for a couple of weeks."

Still, we were cautiously optimistic, and celebrated the successful surgery with a round of soft drinks in the staff room. Trey named the cougar Buster because of his busted leg.

"It's going to be a few months before Buster regains full use of his leg," said Nancy, "but if he continues to improve and gains some weight, George, I think we might be able to move him to the Green Room in a few weeks."

George's face broke into a wide grin. The Green Room had been one of his latest creations, designed especially for the comfortable recuperation of larger animals. It was a roomy outdoors enclosure with a small pond, large boulders for climbing, shrubbery and shelters for animals that wanted privacy and, of course, a high fence. A man with a deep love of animals and a special soft spot for cats, George loved the idea that Buster would be the first inhabitant of his new enclosure.

Meanwhile, dance class was also busy. Anne, our instructor, was teaching us a new choreography featuring *raks tahtib*, a folkloric dance based on an Egyptian martial art.

"Most of you are familiar with *raks assaya*, the cane dance that is generally performed by women," Anne explained. We all knew that *raks assaya* meant 'stick dance,' but we didn't know the meaning of the word *tahtib*. Anne explained. "*Tahtib* is the name of the martial art in which the opponents use long sticks to strike and block strikes. *Raks tahtib* uses long sticks instead of the cane, and more closely parallels the actual martial art. The dance is often performed by men as well as women. Of course," she added with a laugh as she passed out long, solid sticks to the class, "when women dance it, it can be much more coquettish."

Susan looked disparagingly at her stick. "I just can't see this as being a serious weapon," she complained. "How can it be a martial art? Give me a good old-fashioned baseball bat any day!"

"Remind me never to join a baseball league with you," I said. "I don't like your automatic assumption that the bat is a weapon." I experimentally swung the stick, which could also have been called a staff because of its length and heft, over my head the way we had learned to do with canes. As it moved through the air it gave an ominous whistle. "Hmm," I said, quickly bringing it back to a standstill. "Remember the cane workshop we took at the Arabian Nights last summer?"

"Yeah, what about it?"

"Remember when you whacked yourself on the elbow with your cane?"

Susan rubbed her elbow, remembering. "Oh, hell, yeah! How could I forget?"

"These sticks are bigger." I gave mine another swing. "A *lot* bigger."

She eyed her own stick with renewed wariness. "You could be right about that."

By the end of class, there was no doubt in anyone's mind that a good solid stick can be a formidable weapon. Our choreography included spinning the sticks forwards, backwards, and over our heads. The class rang with the sound of sticks hitting the floor as hapless dancers lost their grips. I whacked myself hard on the shin, and Susan managed to hit the same elbow that had suffered injury in our cane class. Then in a move where the dancers spun, faced each other and hit their sticks together in mock combat, Susan and I ended up whacking each other's knuckles simultaneously.

"Ow!" Susan yelled. Unable to speak for a moment, I just sucked my knuckles.

Anne came over and reminded us that we both needed to angle our sticks down to the right and hit the sticks in the center to avoid mishaps.

As Anne turned to critique another pair, Susan moaned, "I know all dancers suffer for their art, but it seems to me that those of us who are absolute klutzes suffer more."

33

"Who are you calling a klutz?" I tried to adjust my grip and the stick clattered to the floor, narrowly missing my foot.

"Hah."

By the time class was over we all had a good assortment of bruises. Anne promised that we would improve with practice, adding that we had six whole weeks to learn the routine before our first performance at the annual Redvue Strawberry Festival.

"Six 'whole' weeks?" Susan whispered in my ear as we limped out of the dance room. "That's like saying we have six weeks to earn our freaking black belts!"

"It's not that much different from cane," I argued, "we just have to get used to the heavier sticks."

"The heavier, longer, more lethal sticks," Susan reminded me sourly.

"You sure changed your tune fast. If nothing else, you have gained more respect for an ancient martial art."

Susan raised her stick threateningly. "Don't make me go Kung Fu on your ass!"

"Tahtib," I corrected as I raised mine and gave it a twirl.

As luck would have it, a police car passed by just as we were squaring off. It gave a blip of its siren as it slowed.

"Oh, great, now look what you've done!" Susan scowled as the car pulled up to us.

"Me?!" I hissed. "You started it!"

"Is there a problem here, ladies?" a stern female voice demanded as the window of the car slid down. A policewoman in dark shades looked out at us, and for a moment I worried that we were going to be arrested for street violence. Then the officer took off her glasses and we saw that it was Tara.

"That's not funny!" Susan roared as Tara shook with laughter. "We thought we were in trouble!"

"Well, that's what happens when you criminal types go around brandishing weapons in public."

"I like that!" Susan feigned indignation. "Criminal types! After we went and solved a whole murder for you!"

"Which is why I'll let your suspicious activity slide," Tara's teeth flashed white in a chuckle. "This time." She looked at our weapons with interest. "Let me guess—*tahtib* class? I heard that's what Anne was going to do for the Strawberry Festival."

We nodded and Susan proudly displayed a bruise that was rapidly darkening across one shin. "We are serious martial artists now." To back Susan up, I waggled my bruised knuckles at Tara.

"Ouch!" Tara looked at our trophy injuries sympathetically. "Watch yourselves with those things. I've done *raks tahtib* before, and those sticks can really hurt!"

"We know," I said ruefully.

"So, is it a slow crime day or were you just looking for innocent citizens to hassle?" Susan quipped.

Tara ran a hand through her fair hair. "Unfortunately, crime has been anything *but* slow lately. Nothing violent, luckily, but there's been a lot of identity theft going on. We're all getting special classes in spotting credit card skimmers and preventing mail theft."

"That sounds nasty," I said.

"What happens when somebody's identity gets stolen?" asked Susan.

Tara gave us a slightly tired smile. "On the case again, detectives? It's mostly been duplication of credit and ATM card information. The criminals get the card information somehow, either with a skimmer at the point of a legitimate card use or by stealing statements in the mail. Then they can make unauthorized purchases, or, if they are able to get an ATM number and the password, they can even clean out somebody's bank account."

"Yikes!" Susan grimaced.

"Yeah," said Tara, "be really careful who you hand your credit card to, and check your ATM machine for signs of tampering, like a loose slot or wires. Always shield your PIN number by holding one hand over the other as you enter it—apparently the crooks have been installing a small camera along with the skimmer on some machines. We think that's how they've gotten several passwords."

"Double yikes," I said.

Tara sighed. "Unfortunately, crime does pay sometimes."

"Not for long!" Susan declared loyally. "Those bad guys don't have a chance against you!"

Tara smiled. "Thanks, and I hope you're right," she said. "Well, I'll see you guys at the bridal shower!" With a little wave, Tara pulled her car away from the curb.

Chapter 4

That Friday, the nutria (now neutered) was scheduled for release into a contained man-made lake at our local library, where he could enjoy the company of his fellow nutria without adding to the wild population of the invasive, although rather charming, species. He had become a favorite with the staff, who frequently gave him treats and were rewarded with delighted squeaks. Since the librarians regularly fed and monitored the nutria in their pond, we felt satisfied that he was going to a good home.

Buster had begun to eat on his own and was starting to gain weight. He also was tolerating his soft cast fairly well, and Nancy was optimistic about moving him into the Green Room soon. He had not been full-grown when we received him, but we were confident he would turn into a handsome adult puma. All in all, the end of the week seemed to be filled with good omens for the bridal shower.

§

Saturday dawned lovely, clear and warm. I drove over to Susan's house and helped her buckle the wishing tree box back into her car, which had a little more head room than mine. We planned to drive to the party together, and take advantage of the car service the Nicklesons' were providing to get people home if they indulged at the bar.

"I need to stop for gas, though—I totally forgot about it yesterday," Susan said as we pulled out of her driveway. "You would not believe the client I'm working with! Everything was ready to go to the printers' when he decided we needed to include his initials in the logo! I mean, that's a total re-design! I was up until two this morning!"

I knew that Susan's job as a graphic artist included many such challenges. Her clients, if anything, seemed more demanding than mine!

We pulled into a local gas station and Susan got out to fill the tank. She ran her card through the slot in the terminal. I waited, thinking happily about the upcoming bridal shower. In a little more than a week Kalina and Harun would be getting married! My mind wandered off into recollection of my own wedding to Michael—the insane bustle of the wedding, the trouble with the photographer, the teary good-bye to my family as Michael and I pulled away from the curb in our getaway car, the havoc and swearing that followed when we realized that Jim had somehow wired the brakes to the horn...

My recollections were rudely interrupted as Susan jerked the door open.

"There's something wrong with this credit card swiper," she griped. "It keeps declining my card. I'm going to have to go in and pay at the check stand." Card in hand, she stomped into the gas station.

A few minutes later, she stomped back out. "There's something wrong with their whole system here," she said in irritation. "The machine inside declined my card, too."

I grinned, not deeply concerned. "Sure neither of you has been buying yachts or something?" I said. "Jim might have forgotten to mention it."

"Very funny," Susan snorted. "I'll go to that place on Avondale. I'm sure their machines won't be out of whack!"

But the machines on Avondale also seemed to be out of whack. Since the tank on Susan's car was very close to the empty line, I talked her into using my card, which worked fine.

"Weird," Susan said. "I'll have to call the credit card people tomorrow to find out what's going on. What a pain! Plus, it was embarrassing, having that snotty little guy in the gas station swipe my card over and over, looking at me like I was some kind of criminal. I am going to give them SUCH a piece of my mind!"

I didn't envy Susan's credit card company's customer service representatives.

The gas tank full, we managed to reach the Romanko-Nicklesons' home in one piece. The large, elegant house looked especially charming now that the roses lining the driveway were starting to bloom.

Daniela came out of the front door to greet us. Dressed in a flowing green sundress and with a happy glow on her face, the mother of the bride looked much younger than her fifty-odd years.

"Susan! Ginger!" she exclaimed, "Thank you so much for coming! I'll have David bring the tree inside before he leaves."

"So, he's not brave enough to stay in a house full of party girls?" Susan laughed.

"Not on your life!" David Nickleson, Kalina's stepfather, came out and stood dutifully by the car as Susan opened the back door. To look at him you'd never guess he was a millionaire many times over. His casual khaki pants, denim shirt and laid-back attitude belied the fact that he was the brains behind Viva Technologies, a medical software company that was saving lives across the globe.

Once the car was open he deftly untangled the tree from the seatbelt, picked it up and carried it into the house. "Where do you want it?" he asked Daniela.

She guided him to a small mahogany side table in the gracious living room, and he set up the tree as we unpacked the cards. The room was decorated with streamers, and in the middle of it stood a table completely covered by delicious-looking seafood and sinful desserts. My mouth started watering just looking at it. When everything was arranged, we all stood back and looked at it admiringly.

"Oh, it's perfect!" said Daniela.

"Sure is sparkly," was David's comment. He kissed Daniela and smiled at us. "Well, I'd better go before the mob arrives. You ladies try not to get into too much trouble."

"Trouble? Us? We'd never!" Susan promised virtuously.

David made a snorting noise as he left.

Daniela offered us tea, and we sat and sipped as we waited for the first guests to arrive.

"What story did you use to get Kalina to come over?" I asked.

Daniela's blue eyes sparkled with mischief. "I told her we need to finalize the seating arrangements." She took a sip and added, "Which we do, of course, but not tonight!"

"Sneaky," Susan said approvingly.

"Very 007," I commented.

A few minutes later the guests started to trickle in, including Tara and Camellia. The band arrived and began to warm up. Daniela tried to arrange us all in different hiding spots behind sofas and chairs, but there were about twenty of us, plus the band. Susan and I had to squeeze into a coat closet.

"Kalina had better get here soon," Susan muttered. "You're hogging all the air."

"Well, you're standing on my foot," I hissed.

"I thought the floor felt squishy." Susan shifted her feet, and I squawked as she crunched her high heel into my other foot. "Dang! This whole closet's full of your gigantic feet," she complained.

I was about to defend my feet, violently if necessary, in the confined space. Just then a key started rattling in the front door. "It's her!" Tara whispered from a vantage point by the front window. "Places, everybody."

An excited hush descended over the house as Daniela greeted Kalina and steered her toward the living room. As soon as they were past the threshold, and before Kalina could notice any exposed feet or rumps, we all jumped out and yelled, "Surprise!"

We surprised her alright. Kalina leapt about a foot in the air and screamed so loudly it popped my ears. For a second I worried that we had overdone it—after all, a bride-to-be is under a lot of stress and a bunch of people yelling at her could conceivably put her over the edge. Then Kalina looked around the room and started to laugh.

"What is this," she asked, looking at the crowd and the table piled with food.

"Happy bridal shower!" cheered Pattie, an attractively plump dancer with piles of burgundy-colored hair.

The next few hours were filled with fun, food and dancing. The wishing tree was covered with happy thoughts and advice. Most of the guests had brought gifts, some practical and some a bit on the raunchy side.

"Have you ever seen underwear like that before?" Susan asked me as one of the service cars brought us home, well after midnight.

"That particular variation was new to me," I admitted.

Susan gave an earthy chuckle. "Sure made Kalina blush!" Then a speculative look crossed her face. "Hmm, I wonder if Jim would like that..."

"Ahhgh!" I protested, covering my ears. "Mental images, mental images!"

Susan kept chuckling to herself. "Yep, it's going to be some wedding!"

§

The following Monday, all hell broke loose at the wildlife center. Buster had developed a minor infection and stopped eating. Nancy was out of town, so we had to call in a vet from another shelter and ended up playing an endless game of phone tag as the message got relayed from volunteer to volunteer. A power line worker brought in a box full of baby squirrels whose nest had been disturbed. They had to be warmed, fed, examined and processed. Houdini, a raccoon who had been a previous resident, chose that day to stage one of his frequent break-ins to hunt for treats and to look for Trey, whom he seemed to regard as a special friend. Trey and I finally cornered him in the break room (where he had ransacked an entire box of doughnuts), nabbed him and dumped him unceremoniously outside. I was desperately trying to catch up on paperwork when my cell phone buzzed. It was Susan.

"You will not believe what's happened," she raged as I tried to fill out two charts at once.

"I'm kind of busy here, Susan," I said in exasperation, pinning my cell phone between my ear and my shoulder as I wrote the reports. "Is it an emergency?"

"I'll say it is! My identity has been stolen!"

For a moment, my brain spun in neutral as I tried to think who on Earth would try to pass themselves off as Susan. I made an inarticulate, questioning sound.

"Remember when my credit card got declined before the bridal shower?" Susan asked.

"Yeah?" I reached for an intake form for baby squirrel #3, signed it and handed it back to the intern.

"Well, I called the company, and some jerk has been charging thousands of dollars' worth of stuff on it!"

That got my attention. "What?! When?"

"Sometime last week, apparently. Between last Saturday and last, *last* Saturday when my credit card worked!"

This took some mental math on my part, but I figured out that she meant in between our shoe shopping spree and the declined gas charge. Then I got confused. "Wait, if somebody stole your card and charged stuff on it, how do you still have the card?"

"They think it got skimmed someplace where I used it before, or else somebody got our number by stealing our statements. It can't be that, though, because we've been getting our credit card statements online for ages!"

"Wow," I said, flooded with sympathy for my friend. "How much actually got charged on the card?"

"Well," Susan now sounded a little less frantic, "I'm not actually going to be charged for any of it. For one thing, they figured out pretty fast that I wasn't buying jet skis online, and that's when they put a hold on the card. I still had to go in, though, show my ID, cancel both of our cards that are on that account, and wait for new ones. That's pretty much been my day."

"Oh, geez, I'm sorry, Susan."

"I'm still mad, though!" Susan's voice nearly pierced my eardrum. "I can't *believe* anybody would be a crap enough person to do something like this! It was so embarrassing at that gas station, and now that card has to be cancelled and our new one will probably have a higher interest rate, and we have to look through all our statements to make sure nothing else happened on that account, and-and—I'm just freaking MAD!"

"I can tell," I assured her, "and I don't blame you a bit!"

From outside my office door came a loud crash and the sound of running feet.

"Trey!" shouted one of the interns, "Your raccoon got back in! We trapped him in here!"

"Oh, geez, not the supply closet, it's full of—" There was another crash and some high-pitched chittering.

"Aww, no! What a mess, man! Houdini, get back here!"

More footsteps followed by a bang and a yelp of pain from Trey. Muffled laughter from the interns.

"I have to go, Susan," I said quickly, "there's kind of an emergency here. Do you want to come over for dinner tonight to talk about it?

Susan sighed. "No, that's OK, but thanks for the offer. I just needed to blow off steam.

I sure hope they catch the guy who stole my number."

"From the sound of it, they'd better catch him before you do!"

Susan laughed. "No kidding. Hey, on the bright side, we have a wedding to go to tomorrow!"

Chapter 5

The day of the wedding dawned bright and clear, and those of us who had been rooting for an outdoor ceremony breathed sighs of relief. This did not include Susan, who had developed a bad case of springtime allergies.

"Whaaatchoo!" For about the fifth time, Susan's bomb-like sneezes made me jump out of my sandals.

"You'd better not do that during the ceremony," I said when my heart had stopped racing. "We have some old people coming, and they might have heart attacks."

"Ha, ha." Susan pulled a tissue out of her purse. "Talk to my nose. It's making the decisions today." She blew her nose with unnecessary vigor to make her point.

The two of us had arrived early to make sure all the preparations were going smoothly. Harry and his team of workers were there already, he in a tux and the workers in smart-looking deep green overalls. We watched in awe as they assembled two full-sized versions of the little wishing tree at the end of the aisle, beside a rose-covered arch. The circular seating area was flanked by rose bushes bursting with new, fragrant blooms.

"Aren't those something?" Susan temporarily forgot her nose as she lifted a huge digital camera, a recent gift from Jim. She aimed the camera at one of the trees and fired off a round of shots. Each picture was accompanied by a loud, fake "camera shutter" sound. I had been listening to the sound all morning, and it was getting almost as irritating as Susan's sneezes.

"Can't you shut that sound off?" I asked.

"I haven't found that feature in the manual yet. I'll figure it out someday. Hey, they've almost got that one all the way up! Isn't it gorgeous?" *Click-whirr, click-whirr* went the camera again as we watched the final tree being put in position.

"Harry's really outdone himself," I agreed. "The whole place looks like it was put together by a fairy godmother!"

A snort sounded from behind us. "Fairy godmother?!" We turned to see Harry laughing and wiping his brow. "I'll thank you to keep that opinion to yourselves, ladies. If Camellia hears you, she'll be

48

calling me 'fairy godmother' until I'm in my grave. Hey!" Harry suddenly turned toward the workmen, who were in the process of adjusting a tree that appeared to be dropping a limb. "Be careful with that!" With a brief nod of apology to us, he ran to direct the men, shouting "Bill! Where the hell is Chuck? He's supposed to be helping with this."

Bill Ellis, a short but powerfully-built man in his 40's, rolled his eyes as he steadied the branch. "Dunno, Harry," he replied in a raspy voice. "He was here a while ago, but I think he saw a girlfriend. You know our Casanova."

Harry's reply to this was salty enough to make me glad the minister wasn't present. With Bill holding the drooping branch in place, Harry whipped out a large spool of silver florists' wire and secured it to the trunk. Together, and with more colorful comments, they wrestled the heavy branch into the correct position. Then, after trimming the wire and stuffing the spool back into his pocket, Harry stormed off in search of his unruly employee.

"Well, I guess we don't have to tell Harry about Chuck's peccadilloes after all," Susan mused. "He seems aware of the problem."

"I wonder why he doesn't just fire the guy," I thought out loud. "It seems like that kind of behavior could backfire and seriously hurt the business."

"Oh, well, at least everything's just about ready for the wedding," Susan said. "The bridal bouquet and our nosegays are all arranged in the giant fridge, and Harry's going to arrange them on a table outside the dressing room right before the ceremony. After the bouquet toss, we're supposed to collect them and put them back in the vases in the fridge so Harry's can freeze-dry them later."

I nodded. I had been touched to learn that Daniella planned to preserve the bridesmaids' bouquets as well as Kalina's large wedding bouquet. We would all receive jewelry boxes with our flowers perfectly preserved in a glass dome on the lid.

At that moment Tara appeared around the corner, looking fresh and pretty with her fair hair in curls instead of its usual pony tail. "Everything's ready in the dressing room," she reported. "The bridesmaid dresses are all labeled and on the rack. Good thing, too, because Kalina and everybody else will be showing up any minute."

"Yikes!" I looked down at my watch. "It's later than I thought. We'd better get into our fancy duds so we can help people get dressed."

We went to the dressing room, a spacious room in the main building of the arboretum that was designed especially for the purpose. Lighted mirrors and continuous makeup tables lined two of the walls, with comfy chairs placed in front. There was a special section for the bride, with a pretty little cushioned couch in front of three full-length mirrors that were arranged so she could view herself from any angle. For privacy, the little enclave was closed off from the rest of the room by ornate Japanese screens.

"Can you believe this dressing room?" Susan crowed. "If only we always had this setup before a show!"

I fervently agreed. Belly dancers often have to change in and out of costume in cramped spaces and do their makeup in tiny, badly-lit mirrors that they're sharing with about five other dancers. I could hardly believe we were each going to have our own seats in front of the brightly-lit mirrors. It was absolute luxury.

As Tara had said, the bridesmaid dresses were hanging from a garment rack in the center of the room, each dress tagged with the name of the wearer. Tara, Susan and I found ours and had just gotten into them when the rest of the bridal party began to trickle in. Kalina and her mother arrived carrying a huge garment bag, a makeup case and other accoutrements. Giggling, they headed for the screened-off area despite our pleas to see the dress.

"Patience," urged Daniela, "the dress isn't half as beautiful without Kalina in it! You need to see the full effect." She pulled her daughter into the enclave. More giggles issued from behind the privacy screen.

Both the bridal room and the open dressing room had lovely flower arrangements supplied by Harry. Unfortunately, the fragrant flowers put Susan's allergies into overdrive.

"Are you *sure* you wouldn't like some antihistamine tablets? I have some in my purse." After suffering through three or four of Susan's earsplitting sneezing fits, Tara had a bit of an edge to her voice. An approving murmur ran through the assorted women in the room. We were all getting tired of Susan's nasal explosions, and the frequent whirring noises from her camera weren't helping.

51

"Antihistamines make me so sleepy," Susan complained. "I don't want to miss a single minute of this day."

I looked up at the clock. "We've got about half an hour. I'm going to go check on the guys and make sure they're on schedule," I said.

Susan grinned. "Make sure they're not wearing white socks."

"I'm on it!"

Susan and I had warned Kalina that our husbands might try to talk Harun into participating in what they called the Great White Sock Rebellion. It had started at Susan's wedding, when Jim complained about having to wear uncomfortable dress shoes in addition to an uncomfortable tux. His argument was that nobody would be looking at his feet, so why couldn't he be comfortable in his old brown loafers? The womenfolk had prevailed, however, and he had duly shown up at the wedding in his dress shoes. It wasn't until after the ceremony that he and all the groomsmen had lifted their pant legs to reveal the fact that, while they were wearing the prescribed shoes, they were not wearing the dark dress socks that came with them. All of them were wearing blazing white cotton socks. Michael had done the same at our wedding, in spite of a surprise sock check Susan had done just ten minutes before the ceremony. The rascals must have changed socks right before lining up at the altar!

I knocked at the dressing room and it was cautiously opened by Alex, a bandmate of Harun's.

"Almost zero hour," I said. "Is the groom about ready?"

"Ready as he'll ever be," Alex said with a snicker. "He's white a sheet and he's driving us all nuts going over and over his vows. We keep offering to help him run away to Timbuctoo, but he seems pretty determined to go through with it!"

"He'd better go through with it, or he'll have an army of belly dancers gunning for him."

Alex laughed. "I wouldn't wish that on my worst enemy! Tell Kalina we'll deliver him right on time."

I was about to turn away, but then I remembered my other duty. "Show me your socks," I ordered sternly.

"My socks?" Alex looked at me with an air of bewilderment, which *could* have been genuine. Or not.

"Yeah, I need to see your socks. Maid of honor's orders."

He obediently stuck out a foot and lifted his pant leg. The sock underneath was a plain regulation black dress sock.

"Very good," I nodded in approval. "Make sure it stays that way."

"O…kay?" His puzzled gaze followed me as I walked back down the hallway.

As I made my way back to the ladies' dressing room, I heard raised voices coming from around the corner. I skidded to a stop, but it was too late. I had already seen Harry and Chuck. They were too engrossed in their argument to notice me, though. For a few seconds I froze, hoping they wouldn't see me.

Chuck was laughing right in Harry's face, but Harry seemed to be maintaining a deadly calm.

"This is the last straw, Chuck! You're fired." Harry's words were spoken evenly, but his complexion was dark red and I wondered briefly if he had high blood pressure.

Chuck curled his lip. He suddenly looked a lot less handsome. "Like this job is worth having," he sneered. "After all, arranging flowers isn't really a man's job. Not a *real* man's, anyway. You should be grateful that you have somebody on your staff who can charm the ladies."

Harry's hand tightened around the spool of wire that he was carrying, but he still did an admirable job of keeping his temper. "Taking advantage of lonely women isn't anything to brag about, Chuck. I should have fired you a long time ago, but I kept giving you 'one more chance' because I felt sorry for your wife. Now I know what you were really up to, and it just disgusts me. Get out of my sight."

"You still owe me for today's work."

"You didn't put in a lot of work," Harry said, "but you'll get your check in the mail. It's worth it to get rid of you. I want you to turn in your uniform and leave. Now."

I had been slowly edging back around the corner, so I couldn't see them anymore, but I heard Chuck give a mocking laugh and heard his footsteps moving away down the hall. I also heard Harry's heavier steps walking towards me.

I didn't want Harry to think the whole unpleasant conversation had been overheard. Thinking fast, I backed up a few steps and then walked breezily forward as if I hadn't heard a thing.

"Hi Harry," I smiled as we passed each other. I think my voice sounded normal.

Harry's face was still red, but he managed to smile and say hello. "Is everything OK in the dressing room?" he asked.

I assured him that everything was fine. "Everybody loves the arrangements you put in there for us," I added. "And those trees are unbelievable. You're a real artist!"

Harry took a deep breath, and looked a little bit happier. "Thanks, Mrs. Connelly. I really appreciate that."

"Call me Ginger. After everything else we've seen you do, we can't wait to see the bouquets! Kalina wouldn't even give us a hint what they'd be like."

This time he really smiled. "I love doing weddings more than anything else," he admitted, "and of course I had to pull out all the stops for this one or Camellia would get me."

"I think you've done Camellia proud," I assured him.

We went our separate ways, and I thought he looked more cheerful than he had.

As I stepped back inside the dressing room, Susan hissed, "What took you so long? Did you get lost or fall in the toilet or something?"

"Or something." On such a happy day, I didn't feel like repeating the argument I'd just heard.

"Well you're just in time—Kalina's about ready. Do you have your gift?"

I nodded, the happiness of the moment wiping out all of the negativity I'd been feeling. "OK, ladies, here comes the bride!" From the screened-off section, Daniela led Kalina out for our inspection.

We gave a collective gasp. Kalina was positively radiant, her face suffused with a happy glow. Her dress had a sweetheart neckline with delicate jeweled straps, and was gathered around her slender waist with a jeweled belt-like appliqué. From there the dress flowed out into a full ball gown, with layer upon layer of lighter-than-air tulle floating over a satin underskirt. The tulle was lightly covered with gold-embroidered lace appliqués and sparkling crystals. The dress ended in an elegant train with richly-embroidered, scalloped lace edges. Kalina's long hair was done up in a simple French twist. To this, Daniela now added the finishing touch—a delicate tiara with an embroidered tulle veil attached to the back. It flowed behind her like those wispy clouds you see on summer mornings before the sun clears the sky.

"Do I look OK?" Suddenly shy, Kalina looked at us uncertainly.

The room exploded with exclamations. "Ok? Just OK?" "Are you kidding!?" "Oh, my god, Kalina, you're freaking *beautiful*!"

We surrounded her, hugging and crying and trying not to squish the dress.

Finally, Tara cleared her throat and recalled us to our senses. "Hey," she said in an unusually unsteady, gruff voice, "If you guys keep bawling, you're going to have to redo all the makeup you've been putting on your mugs for the last hour. We do *not* have that kind of time!" Her own eyes looked suspiciously moist and she took a tissue from a nearby table to delicately blow her nose.

As co-matron-of-honor, I took charge. "Tara's right," I said, clearing my own throat. "We still have some last minute details."

"OK, people," Susan ordered, "we need something old."

Stepping forward, Daniela fastened a small gold locket around Kalina's neck. "This was my mother's," she said softly, a single tear trickling down her cheek. "Now it's yours. I love you so much!" Mother and daughter embraced, and the entire bridal party would have started howling again if Susan hadn't interrupted.

"Hold the waterworks, everybody! Now we need something new." She held up a racy-looking lace garter in shocking pink. "To go with those new undies," she added wickedly. Amid laughter and Kalina's blushes, we slid the garter into place.

"And now, something borrowed," I managed between giggles. I tucked a dollar bill into the garter. I smiled at Kalina. "You have to give that back or it doesn't count."

"And now, something blue." Camellia came forward with a small box. She opened it to reveal a hairpin with a spray of blue and white crystal flowers decorating the end. It reminded me of the wishing tree, and I wondered if Harry had had anything to do with it. Camellia helped Kalina slip the little pin into her hair. She gently took Kalina by the hand. "You're all set now, sweetie," she said softly.

The bridal party fell silent, regarding the beautiful bride and feeling the same emotions women have felt down through the centuries. Our young friend was about to step from one stage of life into another. I felt a lump rising in my throat. Then *click-whirr, click-whirr* went Susan's camera, breaking the spell.

"I'd better put that someplace safe," Tara declared, snatching the camera away from Susan. "We wouldn't want it to get stolen during the ceremony."

Susan seemed about to argue, but at that moment there was a knock on the dressing room door. "Five minutes! Fiiiiive minutes everyone!" I thought I recognized the voice—either Justin or Jason, our teacher Anne's irrepressible twin teenage boys. This was confirmed by muffled laughter and a scuffle behind the door, followed by "Anybody in there need a bra fastened?"

The laughter was followed by a couple of yelps and Anne's hushed but authoritative voice. "In your seats, *now*!" More scuffling, and then Anne's voice continued, more loudly, outside the door. "Sorry about that, everyone. Hormones running amok, I'm afraid. Everything is ready—Harry's laid the bouquets out on the table outside your room and the guests are being herded into their pews. How's everybody doing?"

"Just fine in here," Susan replied, "how's the groom holding up?"

"According to reports, just this side of fainting," Anne laughed.

"You checked the socks?" Susan asked me in an undertone.

"Yep. They're black."

"Let's hope they stay that way."

We filed out of the dressing room and viewed the bouquets that had been lined up on a linen-covered table. Once again, Harry had come through beautifully. The bridesmaids' nosegays were large circlets of white rosebuds surrounded by tiny blue orchids. Diamond-like crystals had been interspersed throughout the circlets, reminiscent of the wishing tree. Blue ribbons embroidered with crystals cascaded from the arrangements. We ooh'd and ahh'd, and then caught sight of the bridal bouquet.

It was simply spectacular—a huge white orchid delicately sat amongst sprays of white rosebuds. The arrangement ended in a huge cascade of smaller white orchids, rosebuds and crystals. Harry had outdone himself, creating a fairyland bouquet that didn't seem to belong in the ordinary, everyday world.

Our contemplation of the flowers was interrupted by the appearance of an elderly woman who rushed by us, apparently in tears. Seeming not to even notice the bridal party, she continued down the hallway and into a ladies' room. We looked at each other in consternation.

"I know people cry at weddings," Susan said finally, "but that lady seems to be jumping the gun."

"We should go see if she's alright." Kalina's voice was all concern for the upset woman despite the fact that her wedding was going to start in a few minutes.

"Hey," Tara said, "Isn't that Mrs. Vick, the Mayor's wife? I wonder what's wrong?"

Anne stepped in. "Don't worry about this, ladies. I'll go take care of Eleanor. We've worked together on a few charity events and she knows me."

As Anne disappeared into the ladies' room, Mr. Nickleson came around the corner from the other end of the hallway. He made a beeline for his wife and stepdaughter. All other considerations were swept away as they exchanged hugs. Then Daniela slipped away to take her seat in the front of the audience. The bridesmaids filed out next, each taking the arm of a groomsman in preparation for the walk down the aisle.

I ended up being paired with Alex, and together we did the eternally awkward wedding hesitation step down the aisle. There were, I knew, supposed to be rose petals scattered on our path, but the little flower girl who had been chosen for the purpose had thrown a tantrum when she discovered that the basket full of petals was not hers to keep. A relative had spirited the howling child away from the festivities, and the procession had continued sans petals.

No pathway of petals was necessary for the bride, however. Coming down the aisle on her beaming stepfather's arm, Kalina made all the roses in the world pale by comparison. Harun, who had been looking pale and nervous under the rose arch as he waited for his bride, took one look at her and suddenly appeared to have been struck by a sock full of bricks. His dazed expression caused a slight wave of laughter to break out in the crowd of guests, but Harun and Kalina wouldn't have noticed if the skies had opened up and dumped hailstones the size of tennis balls. They had eyes only for each other.

As Mr. Nickleson placed Kalina's hand in Harun's, I heard a sniffle behind me that had nothing to do with allergies. Susan tried to discreetly wipe her nose on the hand that held her nosegay, which turned out to be a mistake. Her tears of joy turned into the tears of a desperately suppressed sneeze. The further the minister got into his wedding speech, the redder Susan's face became, until I was afraid she was about to have a stroke. At long last, the minister wound down and allowed the happy couple to get down to business. Vows and rings were exchanged, and finally the announcement was made, "You may now kiss the bride!"

The moment Kalina and Harun's lips met, Susan's sneeze exploded with an almighty bang. Mount Vesuvius couldn't have produced a more spectacular sound. Bride, groom, minister, guests, and probably everyone within a twenty-mile radius leapt about six feet into the air. When they came back down to terra firma, they indignantly looked for the source of the interruption. It wasn't hard to find, because Susan has never been able to stop at just one sneeze. A volley of sneezes followed the first one, until Susan ended up exhausted and leaning against the handy rose arch, her nose and eyes streaming.

For a moment, there was dead silence. Then Jim gallantly left his place in the audience, went to his wife, dropped to one knee and presented her with a handkerchief from his sport jacket.

Somebody in the audience started clapping. It caught on as Jim scampered back to his seat and Kalina and Harun, nearly doubled over with laugher, turned to begin their walk back up the aisle as husband and wife. Cheers and zaghareets erupted from the crowd.

"I guess it was going to be that or the camera," I said resignedly to Tara as we moved toward our escorts.

"If I could confiscate that nose of hers, I would!"

At this point Ruth Bingham appeared wearing a heavy gold caftan belted at the hips with a striped scarf. On her head she balanced an elaborate candelabra with real candles. Turning, she led the bride and groom up the aisle and down a path that led through the rose garden to the reception hall. Several musicians, including a drummer, flute player and a fiddler, fell into step behind them. The bridal party and guests followed, clapping and cheering for all we were worth.

The reception hall was enchantingly decorated. Two of Harry's crystal trees stood at the entrance, and every table had its own miniature version. At the far end of the hall was a raised platform that would serve as the stage. Strings of fairy lights draped the front edges of the stage and hung in swags from the back wall, ensuring that all the dancers would be well-lit in the soft glow. Ruth ascended the steps, followed by Kalina and Harun, who sat in big throne-like chairs that had been placed there for them. Guests were directed to their tables, and as everyone found their seats Ruth began to do the first dance of the evening.

Keeping time with the musicians, who had gathered at one side of the stage, Ruth did the traditional candelabra dance, starting with joyful steps and hip twists and ending on the floor in a full backbend. The candelabra stayed in place the entire time, evoking gasps and applause.

"Think we'll ever be able to that?" Susan whispered in my ear.

"Not without involving the Redvue Fire Department," I whispered back.

Ruth effortlessly arose from the floor and bowed to the new couple, who jumped up to give her a hug. There was a moment of uneasiness in the watching crowd as the candelabra teetered under the impact, but Ruth steadied it in time. Taking Kalina and Harun's hands, she presented them to the crowd, bowed to us, and left the stage. Kalina and Harun went to their table, and the big chairs were removed.

At this moment, Jim and Michael jumped up and took center stage. "Attention, ladies and gentlemen!" Jim announced in his powerful bass voice. "We would like to present to you the latest chapter of—" here he drummed vigorously on the closest table as the groomsmen and even Harun jumped up and lined up behind him— "...The Great White Sock Rebellion!!!"

On this signal they all raised their pant legs to display the infamous white socks. Cameras clicked as laughter and more than a few confused comments spread through the crowd of guests.

"Those sneaky—I can't believe it!" Susan fumed. She turned accusingly to me. "You said you checked their socks!"

"I did! You know how fast they can change."

"I wonder which of our husbands supplied the contraband?"

"Oh, the guys were probably indoctrinated a while ago and brought their own," I guessed as Michael slid into his seat beside me.

"I'll never tell," he said as I gave him a playful swat.

Jim got similar treatment as he took his seat next to Susan. Meanwhile, I could see Kalina dissolving in laughter as Harun proudly displayed his socks to everyone at the table. I suspected she had been in on the joke.

The reception passed quickly as we ate the delicious luncheon. Tara had reluctantly returned Susan's camera after the ceremony, and

Susan happily alternated taking bites of food and snapping photos of everything possible.

"I don't get it," I complained to Michael at one point. "The official photographer's camera doesn't make that much noise, and it's twice the size."

"I guess the manufacturers decided their amateur customers really needed to get the whole 'I'm taking a picture now' experience," he groaned. "If you can get your hands on it, I could attempt some sabotage."

"We barely got it away from her before the ceremony. Good luck getting it now."

After the luncheon Kalina and Harun then cut the cake, which was topped by a sculpture done by a friend of the bridal couple. It depicted a tabla like the one Harun played together with a blue and gold striped cane, like the one Kalina often used in her performances. Everything seemed perfect. Several bands took turns playing, and when guests were done eating they got up and danced. Before long, it was time for Kalina to slip away and get changed into her going away outfit, a pretty blue and white flowered dress.

A long black limousine pulled up outside the arboretum as Kalina prepared to throw the bouquet.

"Get up there, Tara," Susan urged, readying her camera to capture the moment. "You're single!"

"Don't make me put you in a sleeper hold," was Tara's reply.

The bouquet was caught by a giggling teenage girl with bright red hair, apparently a relation of David Nickleson's. She waved her trophy as the newlyweds dashed to the limousine under a shower of environmentally-friendly birdseed. We cheered until our voices were hoarse and waved until they drove out of sight. Daniela mopped up happy tears as she and Daniel embraced. Together they watched their daughter depart with her new husband.

Behind me, Susan sniffed noisily. "Stupid allergies," she mumbled into a tissue. "How can I take pictures when I'm sneezing?"

"You've been doing fine so far," I grumbled.

At this point, Tara came up to us holding a bundle of bridesmaid flowers. "You guys better rescue the bridal bouquet from that kid so we can get these into the fridge," she said.

I retrieved the bridal bouquet as Susan took mine and a few extra from Tara. Then the three of us made our way back inside, heading for the large cooler in the back of the kitchen.

"I hope none of these got too wilted," I said. "Most us remembered to stick ours in the water vases on the tables during the reception, but—"

My voice faltered as we rounded the corner. For a moment by brain refused to take in the ghastly sight in front us.

Chuck lay sprawled on the floor a few feet away from the refrigerator doors. His face was swollen and distorted, a bluish tongue protruding from his mouth. A length of silvery wire was wrapped so tightly around his throat that it had buried itself into the flesh of his neck. Blood pooled around Chuck's body. He was very, very dead.

Chapter 6

"I don't believe it," Tara said under her breath. "I just don't believe it." Unexpectedly, she spun around and pointed at us. "You!" She exclaimed. "You two!"

"What?" Susan demanded indignantly. "We didn't do anything."

"You don't have to! Bodies just stack up wherever you go"

This seemed a little unfair to me, seeing as how this body was only the third we had discovered.

"You're here too," Susan pointed out, "so maybe it's you that's the problem."

Tara had already whipped out her cell phone and didn't bother to reply. She started to give a concise report of our find to the authorities, pausing only to say, "Susan, Ginger, get away from there! Leave that body alone!"

The initial shock had worn off, and both Susan and I were overcoming our fear enough to creep closer to examine Chuck's mortal remains. It's possible that our recent forays into crime detection had hardened us—horror was quickly giving way to curiosity. At Tara's sharp order we jumped like guilty children and retreated, but not before I had noticed something that made my heart sink. The wire around Chuck's neck was exactly like the florist wire Harry had used to fix the damaged tree—and I had seen him put the spool back in his pocket.

§

It was this piece of glum news that I related to Susan as we made our way back to the dressing room. I also gave her a brief account of the argument I had witnessed. Tara had remained behind to guard the body until the homicide squad got there.

"So what are you saying?" Susan demanded. "Do you think Harry killed Chuck? I know we don't know him that well, but he still doesn't seem like the kind of guy who would strangle somebody. Anyway, it doesn't make sense."

"What do you mean, doesn't make sense? I heard them fighting less than three hours before we found Chuck's body!"

Susan pushed the door open and quickly checked to make sure we had the room to ourselves. "That's exactly my point. If Harry was mad enough to kill Chuck, he would have done it then, while they were fighting. You said yourself that he just fired Chuck and let him walk away."

Susan's words made me feel a little better. "You're right. I didn't think about that—Harry was mad, alright, but he didn't even throw a punch. If something violent was going to happen, it would have happened then."

"Still, it might be better if you don't say anything about this to Tara."

A throat cleared loudly behind us. "Say anything about *what* to Tara?"

"Dang, she's quiet," Susan muttered as we turned back to the door, which Tara had just entered. "Just like a damn ninja!"

"A ninja who's still waiting for an explanation," Tara said dryly.

And so I had to tell Tara the whole story of the fight I had witnessed between Harry and Chuck. She didn't share Susan's optimism, however. Worry spread across her face as I described the argument.

"This doesn't sound good," she said. "I hate to say this, but I think you're going to have to tell Detective Harris. He's on his way with the crime scene people."

"But we just told you how this means Harry's not guilty!" Susan wailed.

Distress showed in Tara's eyes and she cleared her throat. "Personally, I think you're right, but if Harry had an argument with Chuck right before the murder, we have to report it. You can't hold that kind of evidence back." She looked truly miserable as she said this.

"At least Harun and Kalina got away before all of this turned up," Susan grumbled as we walked to the office the police had set up as their temporary headquarters.

A smile flickered across Tara's grim countenance. "Yeah. And there's no reason why they should have to come back early from their honeymoon, since they were in full view of about a million witnesses the whole time!"

"I didn't even think about that," Susan shuddered. "After everything poor Kalina went through last year, it would be awful if her wedding got wrecked by another stupid murder!"

It seemed a little heartless to describe Chuck's death this way, but I had to admit I felt the same way. My main concern was not wrecking Kalina's wedding.

"I will personally make sure that doesn't happen," Tara said with a scowl. She must have been thinking along the same lines, and I knew she still felt bad for having suspected Kalina of murder in the last case.

"None of that was your fault last year, you know," I said awkwardly as we went into the office.

Tara gave me a brief smile of thanks. "I know," she said, "but I still want to make it up to her."

At Tara's suggestion, one of Harry's employees who hadn't been on the scene was called to take the bouquets away to be refrigerated.

With the body still in front of it, the arboretum's fridge would be inaccessible.

The next few hours passed tediously as we all gave our statements. Some of the guests had already left, but everyone who remained had to at least give their contact information in case they were needed.

The one bright spot was that Detective John Harris, the homicide detective that had been assigned to our last case, was apparently heading up this one as well. Even though he had temporarily latched onto the wrong suspect in the preceding year, Susan and I both liked the handsome, even-tempered man. Susan had already decided that as soon as Tara made detective, she and Detective Harris would be the next in line for wedding bells.

He rolled his eyes slightly at the sight of us. "Why does this not surprise me?" he quipped with a slight grin.

"Tara's here, too," Susan said defensively. "Why isn't somebody blaming *her*?"

"Since the time of death seems to have been be roughly during the time of the wedding ceremony, nobody's blaming anyone in the bridal party." He assured us. "It's just a coincidence that you two happen to be on the spot. Again." His lips twitched as Susan and I signed our statements.

Finally Jim and Michael were able to collect us, and they had a lot to say about our latest discovery.

"I can't believe you found another body," were the first words out of Jim's mouth.

Michael agreed. "It's like you two are the Typhoid Mary's of murder. It's amazing that Jim and I have managed to stay alive this long!"

"I'm ordering a bullet-proof vest as soon as we get home," Jim said. "Might as well play it safe."

Susan scowled. "Why is everybody blaming us for this? We had absolutely nothing to do with it. We didn't last time, either, except for solving the darn thing!"

"Which I assume you're *not* doing this time, considering how close you came to pushing up daisies last year," Michael said in a more concerned tone, putting a protective arm around me.

"No kidding," added Jim, also suddenly looking more serious. "The cops can handle it this time. I'm just glad you weren't around when it happened! Whoever did this must be a total nut job."

Susan gave Jim a squeeze as we headed out into the parking lot. "Don't worry, we are simple witnesses this time. No more detective work for us!"

Susan's tone was light, but her eyes were troubled. We exchanged doubtful glances, both of us thinking the same thing. We hadn't seen Harry since the discovery of the body, but we had heard enough through the grapevine to know that he was being taken to police headquarters for further questioning. Tara had tried to tell me it was just part of the investigation routine, but I could tell that she'd been worried, too. It looked like there was going to be trouble ahead.

71

Chapter 7

I slept badly that night. My dreams were a bizarre mix of happy wedding memories and Chuck's blue, swollen face. It was actually a relief when my alarm clock woke me up out of a particularly unpleasant sequence.

I showered hurriedly and dressed in my regular work uniform of jeans, a T-shirt and sweater. As I stuffed my feet into the work boots I keep by the back door, it suddenly occurred to me how different my work-a-day image contrasted with my belly dance persona. No glamor here, I thought ruefully as I pulled my still-wet red curls up into a scrunchy and swiped on some pink-tinted chap stick.

Maybe that was part of the appeal of belly dance, I thought as I grabbed my keys and headed out the door. It allowed ordinary women from all walks of life a chance to feel exotic and beautiful.

At the wildlife sanctuary, I was encouraged to learn that Buster had rallied and gained more weight over the weekend. The baby squirrels were settling into their temporary holding pen. Once they were big enough they would be moved into a larger enclosure with older squirrels, who would help them learn how to be squirrels before they all were released into the wild.

My co-workers were all agog to hear details of my latest brush with crime. "Is it true the guy's head was almost cut off by the wire?" Trey asked eagerly as we weighed and measured the squirrels.

I swallowed hard as I entered the data into a chart. "Trey, I really don't—"

Dennis Pilchuck, a young volunteer, regarded me with enormous eyes as he scooped up another squirrel. "I'll bet it was somebody in the military, like in Special Forces. They use garrotes to kill sentries and stuff when they're sneaking around."

Trey nodded wisely. "I had this history teacher that said garrotes were used for executions, too, like in Spain. 'Course in France they had the guillotine for that."

"Hey, I read this thing about the French Revolution," Dennis said with enthusiasm. "Sometimes the heads of French people kept living for minutes after they were chopped off! This old doctor guy was watching the beheadings, and he said their eyes could still move, and one of them even talked!"

"Dude! No *way*!"

"Oh, for Pete's sake!" Nancy King exclaimed as she came in to examine the charts. "Poor Ginger's just been through an awful experience and she might not want to talk about it or hear your ghoulish stories right now."

Trey and Dennis instantly looked abashed. "Geez, we're sorry Ginger," Trey said. "I guess we didn't think."

They looked so guilty that I assured them I was alright, even though the conversation had left me feeling a little green around the gills. One of the squirrels provided a convenient diversion by flipping around and biting Dennis on the thumb, fortunately through his protective leather glove. I knew from experience that he would have a nice purple thumb for a few days, though, and sent him off to ice it. Trey was laughing too hard to spend any more time thinking about murder, and I escaped back to my office.

Although the rest of the day passed more or less quietly, I felt drained by the end of the day and was glad to head home. A hot cup of tea, a relaxing dinner and a hot bath sounded like heaven.

It didn't turn out that way, of course. As I walked in the front door, Michael called to me from his office. "Hey, would you please call Susan? She called to say you're not answering your cell, and I told her you left it at home on the charger again. Ever since then she's been ringing up here every two minutes to see if you're home yet and it's making me nuts!"

"Sorry," I said as I pulled off my boots. Michael had installed a new phone charging station by the back door, but since I usually left

74

through the front I had been forgetting to grab it on my way out. I snatched up my phone and dialed Susan's number.

"About time!" Susan's voice exploded through the phone's tiny speaker and I held it away from my ear. "Where have you been and why don't you ever have your phone?!"

"What is it, Susan?" I asked, wearily filling up the teapot. "Michael tells me you've been making him nuts."

"That's because you didn't have your phone, dummy. How do you expect to know what's going on if I can't call you?"

"You're talking to me now and I still don't know what's going on," I pointed out.

"Well, here's the scoop: Harry's been arrested and Camellia's totally freaking out. So's Tara, for that matter. We're getting together tonight to come up with a strategy."

Try as I might, I couldn't imagine Tara freaking out. The news was certainly bad, though, and I couldn't imagine how Camellia must be feeling. I spooned extra sugar into my tea for energy. "Where are we meeting?"

"I was thinking your place, since the guys have band practice tonight and you don't have two spazzy dogs who'll be drooling all over everybody. We should have some peace and quiet there."

Peace and quiet seemed doubtful to me if people were freaking out and Susan would be attending, but I agreed to host the meeting. "What makes them so sure Harry did it?" I asked. "Just because of that one argument? Chuck was such a jerk, it seems like there would be more than one person who wanted him out of the way."

"There's more, alright! Wait 'till you hear the rest of the story. Tonight at seven."

§

Michael hesitated as he assembled his bagpipes and sheet music for the night's practice. "Are you sure you're OK with me being out tonight after everything that happened yesterday? The guys will understand if you need me to stay home. I don't like to think of you sitting here alone."

I gave him a peck on the cheek. "No worries there. Susan's coming over with—" I hesitated, not wanting to bring up the real topic of the evening, "some dancer friends. There's stuff we need to sort out."

Michael rolled his eyes. "Something to do with the million and one phone calls? Is there some dancer drama going on?"

"Yep."

"Then I'm out of here! This is no place for a sane man to be." He swung the pipes over his shoulder and fled, leaving me to wonder how sane a programmer-turned-amateur-bagpiper could be considered. It seemed to me there was plenty of insanity on both sides.

Chapter 8

Susan arrived shortly after six, interrupting my hurried dinner of microwaved macaroni and cheese. "So everything hit the fan last night, a couple of hours after we all left," she said, helping herself to a soda from my refrigerator. "How can you eat that stuff?" she added. "That color yellow doesn't occur anywhere in nature."

"I've seen you eat half a frozen cheesecake in one sitting, so you have no room to judge," I said. "Stop babbling and tell me what happened."

At the mention of cheesecake, Susan wistfully poked her nose into my freezer. Disappointed to discover only more microwavable dinners, she continued. "Well, the police were already talking to

Harry because of the fight you overheard, and apparently his other employees admitted that they had had arguments before. Nobody had a very high opinion of Chuck. He liked to slack off work, then try to blame the other workers if things went wrong. He was in charge of some delivery accounts that didn't quite square with the money that should have come in, and a few other things. Plus, we already knew he flirted with the lady customers."

"All of that seems like a good reason to fire Chuck, not kill him," I argued, "and that's exactly what I heard Harry do."

"Yeah, but you didn't hear what happened right before that. Remember how we saw Mayor Vick's wife crying right before the ceremony?"

I nodded.

"Turns out Chuck started having an affair with her while Harry was doing the flowers for the Vicks' daughters' wedding."

"What?" I exclaimed, choking on a piece of macaroni. Susan thumped me on the back, which made me choke harder. I waved her away and got a glass of water. "She must be at least thirty years older than he is! Not that it's wrong for women to date younger men, I mean it wouldn't have been wrong if they hadn't already been married, but I don't see the attraction for Chuck. He doesn't seem like the type to appreciate an older woman's better qualities."

"He appreciated her money," Susan said dryly. "The Vicks are stinking rich. That's how Mayor Vick keeps getting to *be* Mayor Vick, you know."

I knew. In spite of several scandals ranging from questionable campaign contributions to his involvement with a few pretty young secretaries, John Vick always seemed to be able to beat anyone who ran against him.

"Anyway, Mrs. Vick fell for Chuck, and since then she's given him some *very* nice presents and even gave him money when he claimed he wanted to start his own florist company. Of course his business plans 'didn't work out,' but she never asked for her money back. At least, not until she caught him putting the moves on one of the young female caterers at the wedding!"

"Oh, no," I said.

"Oh, yeah. They had a big blow up, which ended with Mrs. Vick running to the bathroom in tears, but not before she caught Harry and told him the whole story."

I whistled softly. "Geez! No wonder Harry was so mad. That kind of a scandal with one of his employees could really hurt his business."

"No kidding, especially if Mayor Vick heard about it. Not that he has any room to talk, if half the secretary rumors are true, but that doesn't mean he'd take kindly to his wife having an affair. Yee olde double standard and everything. Especially if she gave Chuck money."

I refilled the teapot and started to arrange a plate with snacks for the upcoming gathering. "So they think finding out about the whole mess made Harry so mad he tracked Chuck down *after* he fired him, and killed him? What makes them think it wasn't Mrs. Vick?" Then I

79

remembered how Chuck had died. "Oh yeah, she probably wouldn't have been strong enough."

Susan snuck a cookie off the plate and chewed thoughtfully. "Not her. She's a thin, frail old thing. A woman probably could have done it, given the element of surprise, but it still would have to have been a pretty strong one."

I glanced sharply at Susan. "Says who? You seem awfully well-informed."

"Says Tara. She called me when she couldn't get ahold of you on your cell phone. She's the one who wanted to set up this meeting."

I picked up the tray and took it into the living room. "That's funny," I said. "Tara sure didn't want us butting in on the last case. I wonder why she's getting us involved now?"

"Maybe she has more respect for our sleuthing abilities than she did last time." Susan looked out of the window. "Anyway that's her car pulling up, you can ask her yourself."

I ushered Tara in and hung up her coat.

"I came a little bit early so I could put you in the picture before Camellia gets here," she said. "I hope that's OK."

"No problem," I said. "We were just putting out snacks."

I handed her a cup of tea and motioned toward the cheese tray. Tara took a seat on the couch. Banshee, who had been hiding under the couch since Susan's arrival, gave an indignant growl at the disturbance of her refuge and scooted out from under it. With one fluid motion she jumped up on the coffee table, snatched a wedge of cheddar cheese, and jumped down again. She gave a cold, blue-eyed stare at the three humans in her domain and stalked out of the room, grumbling through the cheese clutched in her tiny jaws.

Tara watched her go with interest. "Your cat eats cheese? I've never seen that before."

I sighed. "She isn't supposed to, even a little bit can make her smell awful! It's too late now, though."

"That cat's got an attitude," Susan said, scowling. "You're lucky she sank her teeth into the cheese instead of you."

Tara laughed. "She's a biter? Growing up I had an orange tabby that nipped everybody! We called him Fang. He had to be shut in the bedroom if we had company."

"Banshee mostly bites Susan," I explained. "And," I added defensively, "if you hold a cat on its back while you wiggle your fingers in front of its face going, 'Are you gonna bite me? Are you gonna bite me?' you can't really blame the cat when it does!"

"Once. I did that once," Susan declared, "and she didn't just bite me. She wrapped her legs around my hand and got me with all four sets of claws! I bled for ages."

"Sounds like you were asking for it," Tara said with a grin. Then she sobered. "This situation with Harry is nasty, you guys. Thanks for meeting with Camellia and me. She needs support right now."

"We were just wondering why you wanted us to get us more involved instead of telling us to stay out of it," I admitted. "Is it really that serious?"

Tara's chin jerked up and down slightly. "It's about as serious as it can get. He's being charged with first-degree murder. It'll be official tomorrow."

Chapter 9

Susan and I were silent for a beat.

"So they're not even considering other suspects?" I asked finally. "That seems to be moving awfully fast."

Tara stared down into her teacup. "They have evidence. Lots of it: He had the argument with Chuck less than three hours before we found Chuck's body; he'd just discovered that Chuck was doing things that could ruin his company; and the murder weapon matched the florist wire he was carrying in his pocket and the wooden wedges they used in some of the table arrangements."

"Wedges?" I asked.

"Yeah, the ends of the wire were fastened around two pieces of wood to form handles. That way the murderer could hold onto the handles instead of wrapping the wire around his hand—which would have left some nasty cuts. The pieces of wood came from a box of wedges they were using to secure the arrangements."

"Scary," Susan commented.

"And evidence of premeditation," Tara said gloomily. "There's no question of somebody losing their temper and suddenly lashing out— whoever killed Chuck planned to do it and took the time to fashion a weapon."

I shook my head. "I admit we don't know him very well, but somehow I just can't imagine Harry doing that."

Tara ran her fingers through her fair hair. "It doesn't square with what I know about Harry, either," she said, "and I *do* know Camellia and Harry pretty well."

"How did you meet them?" Susan asked.

Tara smiled. "Camellia was my very first dance teacher. I met her about five years ago. She's been my teacher ever since. She's the one who encouraged me to start my own troupe."

"No wonder you're so good!" Susan exclaimed with a grin. She raised he teacup in a toast. "To Camellia!"

Tara laughed and raised her own teacup. "Camellia really does deserve the credit, especially for my technique. I was lucky to get such a good teacher right off the bat. It's important to get a good foundation in the movements early on."

She sighed. "It was a tough time in my life, though. I was a rookie cop back then, and I wasn't prepared for some of the things we have to deal with. I mean, you go through all the training and you think you're tough enough to do the job, but then you see accident victims or an abused kid and you just feel like you can't handle it!"

"Geez," Susan breathed. "I don't know how anybody 'handles' stuff like that."

Tara's eyes clouded. "I almost didn't. It seemed like all we were doing was picking up the pieces, not protecting people or stopping the bad things from happening. I wasn't making any difference."

"Baloney!" Susan exploded. "If you were out there helping accident victims or stopping a child abuser, I call that making one hell of a difference!"

Tara nodded, a bit of her smile coming back. "That's actually what Harry helped me realize. I was seriously considered leaving the police force for a while. I had a counselor, and she advised me to take up a hobby, but most of her suggestions just sounded boring to me. Then my friend Chloe, who had been taking classes with Camellia, bullied me into taking Camellia's class with her. I really went along to shut her up!"

I cut a sideways glance at Susan. "I know how that goes."

Susan snorted.

Tara gave a chuckle. "I'll bet." She took a sip of her tea. "Those classes turned out to be a lifesaver. It seemed silly at first, but I had so much fun! And Camellia sort of took me under her wing. As I learned more, she started having me over for dinner and we'd talk about the history of the dance, and famous dancers, and the direction I felt that *I* wanted to go with it. I met Harry then too, because he lives nearby. Harry was over at Camellia's a lot, and he's an absolutely amazing cook! He made us dolmas like you've never tasted."

"Mmmmmm," Susan rumbled. "I love those!"

My own mouth watered.

"Both of them were so good to me," Tara went on in a slightly choked-up voice. "They gave me such good advice, telling me not to quit the force until I'd given it more time, and helping me see that what I did really made a difference!"

"We could have told you that!" Susan smiled.

"It was Harry who really made me see it, though," Tara said, her eyes lighting with enthusiasm. "He told me how his own life was changed by a cop when he was growing up. When he was a kid, maybe eight or nine, he was in a bad car accident. He remembers the patrol officer who got there first talking to him, calming him down and telling him everything would be OK."

"Oh, poor Harry," Susan exclaimed.

"Yeah, he was hurt pretty bad. The car had hit them on Harry's side, and he was pinned in the wreckage. His mom was unconscious, and Harry thought she was dead. Naturally he was just freaking out, and trying to get loose to get to his mom. Then the patrol officer got there. This cop checked on both of them, called it in and had his partner control the traffic. Then he stayed with Harry, telling him that his mom was breathing, the ambulance was coming, and everything was going to be OK. He couldn't get Harry loose—the fire department had to cut him free."

"Oh, poor little thing," Susan breathed again. I looked down and found I was chewing my nails.

"But the cop was able to hold Harry's hand and he stayed with him, talking to him while the firemen were getting him loose, and staying with him until the ambulance took them away. Later, the rescuers told Harry's parents that if the cop hadn't been able to keep Harry calm and still before the fire department got there, he could have been hurt much worse, or even bled to death. He was pinned by several pieces of sharp metal."

"Wow," I said.

"So his mom was OK?" Susan asked.

"Yes, she had a mild concussion but she recovered pretty quickly. Harry actually had more injuries, like a broken arm and collar bone, and cuts from the broken glass and metal. He ended up spending a few weeks in the hospital. That police officer, an Officer Brownsen, came to visit him several times to see how he was doing. He gave Harry a big teddy bear with a police badge on it, and every weekend, he brought a fresh bouquet of flowers that his wife cut from her garden and arranged especially for Harry."

"Aww," Susan and I said, almost in unison.

Tara's eyes twinkled. "So," she continued, "there was Harry, lying there in the hospital room, and he especially remembers looking at those flowers—I think he said there were roses, daisies and some blue flower I can't remember the name of, but anyway they were something bright and cheerful. He remembers looking at the flowers and thinking about the policeman's wife picking them and arranging them especially for him each week. That's when he decided he wanted to spend his life doing the same thing for other people, to make them feel special and to help them through hard times."

"And now he's a florist! How cool," Susan exclaimed with a huge grin. "I hope Officer what's-his-name and his wife know how Harry turned out."

"Oh, yes, they stayed in touch with Harry and his parents. This was a much smaller town back then, and they even ran into each other now and then. Of course, Officer Brownsen retired years ago—as Captain Brownsen, by the way—and now he and his wife are living in Florida. Harry actually did the flowers for their going-away party!"

"Wow! Talk about making a difference," I said.

"I'll say," Susan chimed in. "Without Officer—sorry, *Captain* Brownsen, there wouldn't even *be* a Deerborne Florist!"

"I know," Tara said with a slightly misty, reminiscent smile. "That's exactly what Harry told me. I was in Camellia's kitchen, talking over some dance choreography with her before she had the other dancers from her student troupe over for dinner. We were just talking, while Harry was doing most of the cooking. Suddenly, I sort of broke down and told them both about all the doubts I was having, and how I was considering leaving the Force. Harry sat me down at Camellia's kitchen table and read me the riot act—wearing, if I remember it right, a big white lacey apron of Camellia's and two bright pink oven mitts!"

We broke into laughter at the image. "Oh ye gods, please tell me you got that on video," Susan choked.

"Sorry," Tara swiped at her eye with a napkin as we finished laughing, "I would have if I'd know it was going to happen." She gave a slight sniffle. "If nothing else, it was the best motivational speech I've ever heard for being a cop."

"You know," she added with tears in her eyes, "I decided I wanted to be a police officer when I was little, right after my Dad was killed in the Gulf War. He went over there, not just as an American soldier, but honestly wanting to help the people there to have freedom. He told me that they deserved to be free as much as we here in America do. I know that a lot has happened since then, and that innocent people have been killed and things aren't as simple as they seem, but I also know that my Dad went over there *wanting to make things better*. I was so sad when he died, but I also promised that I would help make things better too, especially since he wasn't there anymore to help people. I know the police have come under fire lately—and a lot of times justifiably—for using excessive force and for racial profiling and other things. All I know is that I joined the Force wanting to make a positive difference, and I don't care what race people are or what their background is. I want to help them. I want to make the kind of difference that Officer Brownsen did in Harry's life."

At this point Susan passed her another one of my paper napkins, because Tara's eyes were definitely streaming. I rose unobtrusively and got a box of tissues from the kitchen. Susan snagged several for herself before passing them to Tara. As I sat down I realized my own eyes and nose were dripping, but all the paper products were now out of reach. I tried to rub my nose on my sleeve without anyone noticing, but Susan gave a loud "Eeeeewwww!" and shoved the tissues in my direction.

"So," Susan said nonchalantly, "Harry managed to change your mind about leaving?"

"Yes," said Tara, gratefully swiping her own nose with a tissue. "He told me flat-out that if there is one thing the world needs, it's more good people in police forces, emergency services, and the armed services. They are usually the ones who get to people in need first, and by being compassionate and caring as well as authoritative they can make a huge impact on people's lives—even if they can't always stop the bad things from happening first."

At this point Banshee gave a loud, murderous yowl from the bedroom and we all jumped. "Ignore the beast," I said. "She's just mad because there are still strangers on her turf."

Tara continued. "Officer Brownsen's kindness didn't stop with Harry, because Harry made such a big difference in my life. And now," she said as her chin went up defiantly, "I'm not going to let him down. I *know* he didn't kill Chuck McKenzie! Even as a kid, Harry was able to take a horrible experience and turn it into a way to help other people. There's no way he'd deliberately go out and commit murder just because one of his employees turned out to be a jerk."

Susan asked the same question that I was about to. "How can we help?"

Tara leaned forward eagerly. "That's why I wanted us to meet with Camellia tonight. We need a plan!"

Outside, I heard the sound of a car pulling into the driveway. "Then I guess it's time to get down to it," I said as I rose and started toward the door. "That's Camellia now."

Chapter 10

Camellia looked exhausted as I greeted her and hung up her coat. She wore a beautiful outfit consisting a tunic and skirt that were tie-dyed brilliant red and orange sunset colors, but the strain the past two days had had on her was evident in her face. Even so, there was a gleam in her blue eyes that promised well for Harry. Camellia had come ready to do battle.

"There is absolutely no *way* Harry had anything to do with this," she declared as she accepted the cup of chamomile tea I poured for her. She set the cup on the coffee table and plopped down beside Tara. "Harry wouldn't hurt a fly. That would be a figurative term for most people, but I've actually *watched* him spend more than ten minutes trying to chase a fly out of his office. I wanted to smack it with a newspaper, but he wouldn't let me. 'It has as much right to live as we do!' he said, and then he finally chased it out of the window with a broom." Camellia paused to take a long drink of the soothing herbal tea. "What on earth is that noise?"

'That noise' was Banshee. Having heard the front door open and close, she had assumed the unwanted guests were gone and come out of hiding. Now she lingered at the end of the hallway, alternately growling and chattering feline obscenities under her breath.

"Oh, that's just Ginger's demon cat from hell," Susan said. "It wants to kill us all, but doesn't dare take on all four of us at once. Poor thing will just have to settle for making threats and smothering us in cat hair." Susan plucked a hair from her pants and held it up as an exhibit.

"I did vacuum the furniture before you came over," I said guiltily, noticing that by now all of my guests were sporting a few tell-tale Banshee hairs on their outfits.

Susan brandished another hair. "I think you might have missed a few."

"Oh, I don't mind cat hair," Camellia said with a smile. "Between my three cats, two dogs and the parrot, I'm always covered in some kind of fur or feathers."

I stood and scooped up my resentful cat, who squawked in protest. "I'll put her in the back room for now," I said. "Help yourselves to more tea." From the safety of my arms, Banshee treated my guests to a final hiss before we left the room. I heard chuckling behind me as I carried her away.

Once everyone had settled in with refilled teacups and plates, we got down to business.

"First of all," said Camellia, "I'd like to thank all of you for being willing to meet with me." Her voice faltered. "It hasn't been an easy time."

"Of course we're willing!" Susan exclaimed. "You're our friend."

"I just hope there's something we can do," I said doubtfully. "Except for Tara here, we aren't exactly detectives. I mean, we got lucky that first time."

"Lucky my foot," said Susan. "We solved the hell out of that case!"

Camellia smiled. "You're absolutely right. That's why I thought of you two."

Tara cleared her throat. "You did do a fantastic job, but I'd like to point out that you took some pretty big risks, too. That *can't* happen this time."

"I agree," Camellia said firmly. "Harry would never forgive himself if one of you got hurt trying to help him."

"Don't worry, of course we'll be careful." Susan's tone seemed a little offhand, seeing as how *I'd* been the one to save her by knocking the gun out of the suspect's hand!

"I'm serious," Tara said. "Any information we come up with needs to go to the police in charge of the case."

94

"Any chance you'll be on the team assigned to this case?" Susan asked hopefully. "We could use some inside information."

Tara snorted. "Not a chance, thanks to Mr. had-to-put-his-two-cents-in Detective Harris!"

"Oh?" Susan's expression was bland, but I knew she was hoping there wasn't going to be any trouble in the paradise she'd dreamed up for the pair.

"He advised the captain not to let me do any of the work on this case because I was 'too close' to the people involved."

Well, as the lead detective I could see his point of view, but with Tara already so upset I wasn't about to say so. Susan, of course, said so.

"It's understandable," she said in a soothing voice, "He's probably just trying to protect you."

"From what?" Tara blazed. "It doesn't matter if I'm close to them or not, or if I'm a woman—" she sputtered here for a moment, her cheeks bright red, "because that's the real thing, Detective Harris doesn't think I can handle this because I'm female!"

"Oh, I don't think that's his reasoning, Tara," Camellia argued. "It's probably just standard procedure not to allow police officers to be involved in an investigation if they're connected to the people involved—both for their own emotional well-being and to make sure everyone on the case is impartial."

"You don't think I can be impartial?"

Camellia smiled. "Well, no, since you just said that Harry is innocent."

"Of course he's innocent." Tara said. "I mean—I mean…"

"Would anybody care for some more tea?" Susan interrupted. I swear she said it in a British accent. Without waiting for a reply she jumped up from her seat, grabbed my arm and shoved me into the kitchen.

"What are you doing?" I hissed as Susan turned on the water faucet. Dead silence had fallen in the room behind us.

Susan ignored me. "Isn't this great?" she whispered, her face alight with glee. "She likes him! She really does like him!"

"What?! What are you talking about?" I stared at her while I automatically filled the electric teapot.

"Tara likes Detective Harris, dummy!"

"It sounds more like she's spitting mad at him."

Susan nodded, grinning like a maniac. "Exactly," she said. "Camellia's right, the whole thing probably *is* just standard procedure, and Tara should know that. If the captain himself had told her she couldn't work the case because those were the rules, she wouldn't care as much. The only reason she's getting so worked up is because *Detective Harris* said so, and that means she must have feelings for him. It makes perfect sense!"

The logic for this argument escaped me, but the kettle was boiling and we were running out of time for the whole ridiculous conversation. I filled a small plate with different flavors of tea and motioned for Susan to grab the kettle. We hurried back into the living room. Tara and Camellia both still had fairly full teacups, so I just set the plate on the coffee table. "For refills," I explained lamely.

Susan swooped in with the kettle, set it neatly on a coaster and resumed her seat. "Now let's get down to brass tacks," she said before anyone could ask questions. She fixed her gaze on Tara. "You're the only *real* detective here. Where do you think we should start?"

Chapter 11

Tara cleared her throat. "Well, I'm not actually a detective…"

"Yet!" Susan waved her hand, dismissing such unimportant details. "You have the training and the brains, you just need to get off your kiester and take the test. Pretend you already have, and take us through the case."

I was expecting an explosion from Tara, but after she opened and closed her mouth a couple of times, she furrowed her brows in thought.

"I guess," she said a little uncertainly, "we start with Chuck. I'm assuming," she added, looking around at all of us, "that we all agree Harry didn't do this."

We nodded.

"Then the argument Harry had with Chuck was just a coincidence. Somebody else was already planning to kill Chuck at that wedding, and the reason must be something in Chuck's past history and the people he knew."

"And maybe the people he took advantage of?" said Susan. "Especially women—he came on to Ginger and me pretty strongly at the shop, and we already know how he treated poor Mrs. Vick. Who knows how many other ladies he was working on?" An idea seemed to strike her and she looked over at Tara. "He was married, too. How much do you know about Chuck's wife? Her life couldn't have been very happy if he was always chasing after other women."

Tara sighed. "I checked into that. His wife Amelie is a harmless-looking creature from Idaho. She's a little older than Chuck was—maybe in her mid-to-late forties—but she came with an inheritance."

"That's probably why he married her," Susan interrupted her.

"But she couldn't have been at the wedding," Tara continued. "She certainly wasn't invited, and a stranger who wasn't part of the catering or florist staff would have been noticed. Most of the guests were either acquaintances of David and Daniela Nickleson or close friends of Kalina's and Harun's. There wasn't a lot of extended family on either Kalina's or Harun's side."

Susan looked thoughtful. "So the best suspects would be people who attended the wedding, either as guests or staff. We already know about the Mayor and his wife. How about other members of the florist staff?"

Tara nodded at Camellia. "This is your area. What did Harry tell you about his other staff?"

Camellia rolled her eyes. "Well, *first* he gave me all the reasons why none of his other employees had anything to do with it. They're all fine, hardworking men, completely trustworthy, yada, yada, yada. It wasn't until I said I just wanted to talk to them to get a better idea of how Chuck operated that he finally gave me the list of who was working there." She fished in her cavernous purse and came out with a sheet of paper.

"Hold on a minute," Susan interrupted, "what about employees who weren't working on that wedding? Could one of them have sneaked in? I mean, they all wear uniforms so they wouldn't have been noticed."

"The other employees would have noticed if someone who wasn't working showed up anyway," I argued.

"Maybe, maybe not."

Tara cleared her throat. "For now, let's concentrate on the ones we actually know about."

Camellia, who had been trying to break into the conversation, waved the paper in her hand. "It's a moot point, anyway," she said. "All of Harry's employees were there, except for a couple of girls who kept the shop open. One of them came to pick up the bouquets. Harry doesn't have a very big staff, and the Nickleson wedding was a huge job. He needed all hands on deck!"

Susan took the list and studied it. "Wow! So besides Harry and Chuck, that whole thing was put together by only three guys?"

100

"Well, with those three and Chuck, he had a total of five men altogether." Camellia said. "That was enough to unload everything and put the trees together."

"Where were these men when I was reorganizing my perennial border?" Susan mused.

"Hiding," I said, taking the paper from Camellia. "Like anyone with sense does when you start a yard project." I knew from experience that Susan's gardening technique involves digging up perfectly healthy plants and moving them from one spot to another until they give up and die. No true plant lover could bear to watch.

"So," I continued, "we have Bill Ellis, Jerry Lambert, and Peter Norberg." I looked over at Camellia. "Do you know them?"

Camellia nodded. "I've met each of them at one time or another. Like I said, Harry didn't have a lot of employees." She began ticking them off on her fingers. "Peter Norberg is a nice young man. He's studying art of some kind at the University of Washington, and he loves working with plants. He does a lot of the smaller arrangements, and helps with the assembly on the larger ones. He also minds the store if Harry and the girls aren't available."

"Girls?" Susan asked suspiciously. "You said there was only one other employee."

Camellia shrugged. "Well, there are a couple of girls who work doing arrangements and handling the general retail things," she said. "None of them do the really heavy work and they wouldn't have been at the wedding, so I guess I didn't count them."

"That is so sexist!" Susan complained. "I'll bet I could lift anything that stupid little punk Chuck could have."

Susan, I thought, possibly could. At about 5'9" she stands a little bit taller than I do, and has deceptively strong arms. Come to think of it I'm no weakling myself. When I'm not swamped doing paperwork for the shelter, I spend my days wrangling wildlife, lifting cages and cleaning out habitats. With a little help I could probably lift one of those trees into position, and unlike Susan I wouldn't panic if a family of raccoons fell onto my head while I was doing it!

"Well, it just so happens that *these* girls are mostly on the retail end of things," Camellia said patiently. "I'm sure Harry would hire a woman to carry trees if she wanted to do it and was strong enough. As things are, though, I don't really see the ladies as suspects since they wouldn't have been at the wedding."

"So that leaves Bill Ellis and Jerry Lambert," Tara summarized. "What do we know about them?"

"Jerry Lambert is one of Harry's oldest friends," Camellia said. "He and Harry were college roommates. Jerry was studying sculpture, and after he graduated he moved to New York. He came back to Seattle a few years ago when some of his investments went wrong, and Harry gave him a job. It turned out beautifully—with Jerry's background in sculpture, he has been able to come up with some really interesting floral arrangements. He's also helped Harry design some of the larger displays, such as the trees. Harry is seriously considering bringing him on as a partner in the business. I can't begin to see Jerry as someone who could have been involved."

"Well, you never know," murmured Susan. "Unlikely people do commit crimes. How about the last guy?"

"Bill Ellis I don't know very much about," said Camellia. "I mean, I've met him a few times and he's always seemed perfectly nice, but he and Harry aren't very close. I think he's worked at Deerborne Florist for about two years now. He's a large man, and does a lot of the heavy lifting—setting up the displays, taking delivery of big orders, that sort of thing. I've never heard any complaints about him."

"But he'd definitely be strong enough to overpower Chuck?" Susan asked.

"Oh, yes."

"But like I was telling you earlier, Susan," Tara interjected, "the killer didn't need to be stronger than Chuck if he or she had the element of surprise and knew how to use the garrote. Strength would help, of course, but it wouldn't actually be necessary. With the right technique it would have all been over pretty fast."

I shuddered, remembering Trey and Dennis' gruesome conversation at the wildlife sanctuary. I looked over at Tara. "Do you think the killer had special training, then, like being in the military?"

Tara nodded. "It's a good possibility, or else it could have been someone with martial arts training. Then again, anybody could look up the technique online and practice until they had it right."

Susan choked on her tea. "Practice? Practice on *what*?"

"It could be anything, really," Tara said, looking thoughtful. "Anything from a dummy to squashes or watermelons that were about neck-sized, or even animals."

This time I was the one who choked. "Animals?!" My hands twitched as I longed to throttle anyone who would do such a thing.

Susan shared my outrage. "Do you mean to say that some—some asshole has been going around killing animals?"

Camellia had gone dead white at the suggestion. "Oh, my god. Has there been any evidence of that?"

"No, no!" Tara hastily waved her hands to calm us. "I was just using that as an example. Don't worry, we haven't found any dead animals. It would actually make a lot more sense for the murderer to practice on inanimate objects that could be disposed of without leaving any suspicious evidence."

Although I found this statement somewhat comforting, the thought of anyone cold-bloodedly garroting vegetables as a precursor to doing it to a live human being made me shiver. I could picture the shadowy murderer as he (or even she!) came home with a big bag of squash or melons he had nonchalantly purchased at the local grocery store, lined them up on the counter, then pulled out a sinister-looking wire with handles...

"Well, just so long as no animals got hurt!" Susan said breezily. "So you're saying even poor old Mrs. Vick could have done it?"

Tara's brow wrinkled. "I really don't think so. I mean, the killer didn't actually need to be stronger than Chuck, but the murder would still have required *some* strength in the hands and wrists. Mrs. Vick is an awfully frail old thing. I just can't picture it."

"She could be insane," Susan said in an ominous voice. "In all the novels, crazy people are supposed to have super strength and Mrs. Vick had just found out that Chuck was playing the field. She could," Susan added, her voice dropping even lower, "have gone mad with jealousy, followed Chuck until he was alone by the refrigerator…"

"And strangled him with a garrote she just happened to have in her pocket?" I asked in exasperation. "One that also just happened to be made of same kind materials Harry and his workers were using? Come on!"

"Well, there you go!" Susan said defensively. "The materials were already lying around for her to use."

I rolled my eyes. "Good thing for her she used to be a Navy S.E.A.L. and knew just how to make one and use it right the first try."

Susan stuck her tongue out at me. "I'm not saying it's likely, smarty-pants. I'm just saying it's possible. It was probably that caterer girl he was flirting with, anyway."

"That's right," exclaimed Camellia. "I didn't even think of that. Tara, do you know anything about her?"

Tara sighed. "It's been hard to get information, since I'm not in on the investigation, but I think her name is Cindy something-or-other and that she works for the catering company Daniela hired."

"How could we find out for sure?" I asked.

"Daniela might be able to find out," Susan suggested. "She could ask the company for the names of the employees that were on that job. She could, I don't know, say they did such a good job that she wants to send them thank-you notes, or that one of them lost a watch or something and she wants to return it."

Camellia nodded enthusiastically. "That's not a bad idea. Companies are always happy to hear that their employees did a good job."

An idea occurred to me. "Anne would be another good person to talk to," I said. "She already knows Mrs. Vick, and she might be able to get her to talk about the murder. It's possible Mrs. Vick could give us more information about Chuck if she were approached by someone sympathetic."

"I like that," Susan said. "I still don't buy Mayor Vick's alibi. His friends would lie themselves blue in the face for him, and we can't know for sure that he didn't already know about Chuck. Mrs. Vick could have let something slip that tipped him off. Maybe Anne could find out."

Tara nodded in a businesslike manner. "So you two will talk to Anne—when?"

"Our lessons are on Tuesdays now, so we can grab her tomorrow," Susan said.

"Good. I'll give Daniela a call and ask if she can get in touch with the catering company. It seems like we might be able to get information from the other employees at Dearborn Florists, too. Camellia, can you talk to Jerry Lambert or Bill Ellis in a casual sort of way? Are you on those terms with them?"

"Yes," Camellia said. "In fact, Jerry's been calling me. He's really worried about Harry and he's offered to help post bail for him, when it's set."

"I thought he was in financial difficulties," Susan interjected.

"He says his finances have improved since he moved back and started working for Harry. I know it's still a lot for him to offer, though. I told him we should be fine, especially since Daniela has also offered to help if it's needed. For that matter, so has Tara," she added with a tender look at her young friend.

"On a police salary?" Susan asked. "You'd better make detective before you start making offers like that!"

Tara flushed. "I have some savings, and Harry's my friend," she mumbled indistinctly.

"It was a very generous offer," Camellia said softly, "but Harry actually has quite a bit of money of his own and he's refusing to even let *me* help! The best thing we can do for him right now is to get as much information as we can."

"How about if Ginger and I make a pass through Harry's neighborhood and talk to people?" Susan offered. "We could start up conversations with the part-time workers in Harry's shop while Camellia's working on the full-timers—nobody would recognize us, because only Harry and Chuck were there the day we picked up the flowers."

"And I'll try to get as much information as I can at work, no matter what Detective Smart-ass says," Tara declared. "Mark said he'll be keeping his ears open, too. He and his wife are throwing a barbecue next weekend, and I was thinking that if all of you came, it would be a great time to meet back up and compare notes!"

We agreed, and after a group hug Tara and Camellia left. I thought they looked a little more cheerful, now that everyone at least had something to do.

Susan echoed my thoughts. "Guess we've got our marching orders," she said she popped the last piece of cheese in her mouth. "It doesn't seem like a lot, but I guess it's better than not being able to do anything."

"But will it be enough?" I worried.

"Probably not. It's a beginning though, and hopefully we'll learn enough to figure out our next step. After all, we're only just getting started!"

Just getting started. If I'd known what was coming, I would have kicked her!

Chapter 12

"You want me to do *what*?"

Our regular class was over, an hour-and-a half of hip drops, fast shimmies and chest isolations. Next had come a vigorous 45-minute tahtib practice session for the student performing group, during which Susan managed to smack me twice on the same elbow with her tahtib stick. I gave her a good rap on the knuckles during our spin, though—accidentally, of course!

Now, tired and sweaty, we were trying to convince our reluctant teacher to do a little detective work.

"All we need is for you to do is talk to Mrs. Vick," Susan said persuasively. "She could know some things she wouldn't be comfortable telling the police. You already know her from her fundraising events, and you're the one who talked to her when she was so upset at the wedding. It would be completely natural for you to check up on her now!"

"You could even invite her to class," I said, struck by a sudden inspiration. "If nothing else, belly dancing would be good for her after everything she's been through."

"What a great idea!" Susan cheered. "Then all three of us could work on her."

"That's not what I meant," I retorted, glaring at her. "Mrs. Vick really has been through a rough time, you know."

Susan didn't even look abashed. "So we could make friends with her *and* see if she knows anything. We'd be killing two birds with one stone."

It was an unfortunate choice of words and both Anne and I winced.

"I am not luring that poor woman here so you two can grill her," Anne declared. "You don't realize how fragile she was at the wedding. Her whole world had been shattered."

"We know she was crying," I reminded her. "She was obviously heartbroken, even though we didn't know why then."

"We're not thinking she had anything to do with Chuck's murder," Susan said. "If nothing else, she's physically just too weak to have done it. It's possible she might know something that can help us, though."

Anne's expression softened. "I do remember how much help both of you were when Diva was killed," she said.

Less than a year before, Anne's twin sons had been among the suspects in the murder of the famous dancer known as Diva. We'd never really talked to Anne about it afterwards, but I knew that the possibility of one of her sons being guilty had terrified our instructor. She probably hadn't even realized that *she* had been on our suspect list at one point. The discovery of the true murderer had freed all three of them from suspicion, and to me that fact alone made all of the risks Susan and I had taken well worth it.

"I'll tell you what," Anne said finally, "I was planning to give Mrs. Vick a call anyway. The press has been all over her since her affair became public, and I know she needs a friend."

"I don't know why the press is bothering her, considering all of the times Mr. Mayor has been caught with his hand in the cookie jar," Susan quipped.

"It may not be fair, but that's the way it is," Anne said with a sigh.

Susan and I nodded grimly. Mrs. Vick's affair with Chuck had become almost more of a news story than Chuck's murder. Exactly who had leaked the details of the affair remained a mystery, but her involvement with the "glamorous young florist" was now common knowledge.

"Anyway," Anne continued, "I'll explain to her that Harry and Camellia are friends of mine and that I'm worried about the whole situation. It might be enough to get her to start talking about Chuck, although I really don't know what information she could have. After all, she had no idea Chuck even flirted with other women before she caught him with that girl at the wedding."

"So she says," Susan muttered in my ear, but Anne heard her.

"Look, I'm not going to go into detail about what she said to me at the wedding," Anne said. "It was a private conversation with a woman who was in a great deal of distress. All I can say is that I believed her when she said she didn't know about Chuck's other 'girlfriends.' It might have been incredibly naive of her, but up until that day she really believed Chuck loved her."

Susan called Chuck a rude but, under the circumstances, very appropriate name.

Anne gave a slight growl of agreement. "Whoever killed him," she said with more heat in her voice than we ever heard her use in class, "I think Chuck probably deserved it!"

"But Harry doesn't deserve to be blamed for it," I said.

"No," Anne agreed. "I've met him several times and I can't believe he did it either. That's why I'm willing to ask Mrs. Vick more questions than I would otherwise. Honestly, though, I don't think she'll be able to tell me anything you can use."

As it turned out, Anne was more right than we could have guessed. Mrs. Vick would have absolutely nothing to tell us. The very next morning, the local news stations switched from reporting on Mrs. Vick's infidelities to reporting the details of her murder.

Chapter 13

"Can you believe it?" Susan's voice blared from my cell phone, which I had unfortunately remembered to bring to work with me this time. The phone was now awkwardly cradled between my head and right shoulder as I swept out the young Douglas squirrels' habitat. Already annoyed by my presence in their territory, they had not been pleased by the sudden shrilling of 'Night of the Valkyries,' which was the ringtone Michael had programmed into my phone for announcing calls from Susan. I hadn't had time to switch it to something less annoying, and Susan's early morning call had jangled the nerves of everyone within earshot—namely myself and nearly a dozen juvenile squirrels.

"Did you hear me?" Susan raised her voice to an eardrum-blowing pitch and continued while I desperately pushed the tiny side button that turned down my phone's volume. "What's the matter with your phone, Ginger? All I can hear is this weird whistling."

"It's not the phone, it's all the squirrels you just terrified with this phone call," I said in exasperation, wincing as one of the youngsters used my head as a jumping-off point. A flash of its bright orange belly showed as it leapt to safety in the habitat's top branches. From there it turned to squall and whistle at me. I readjusted the phone under my chin. "What exactly are you wondering if I can believe?"

"Mrs. Vick's murder, what else?"

"Mrs. Vick's *what*?" This time it was my voice that panicked the squirrels.

An exasperated sigh came from my phone. "Seriously? You mean you don't even know about it yet? What planet do you live on, anyway, don't you listen to the news?"

My neck was beginning to spasm. "I've been a little busy this morning, Susan. Our morning person had her car break down and I'm doing everything until the interns get here. What's happened?"

"Mrs. Vick was murdered last night. Somebody broke into their house while Mr. Mayor was at some political shindig. Supposedly Mrs. Vick surprised whoever it was, and they attacked her."

I cautiously stepped out of the enclosure, being careful to make sure none of the squirrels came with me. "How awful," I said as I stripped off my gloves and gave my hands a quick wash. Then I took

114

a more comfortable hold on my phone. "What happened? Did they catch whoever did it?"

"No, and this is where it gets interesting. Whoever did it cut her throat!"

I gulped. "Oh, my god. That's horrible! Why would anyone do that to a helpless old lady?"

"Well, there are a few conspiracy theories about Mr. Vick having political enemies, but the official story is that they were just burglars and she was in the wrong place at the wrong time."

Something in her voice caught my attention. "You sound like there's more to the story," I said. "What is it?"

"Think about it, Dummy," Susan crowed. "Her throat was cut. Not quite the same thing as a garrote, but basically the same M.O.— and right after her relationship with Chuck got publicized!"

I began to understand. "So, what, are you thinking there's a connection?"

"It's a pretty big coincidence if there isn't. I mean, how many of the murders around here involve people getting their throats cut? Normal people just use guns."

"Normal people?" I was beginning to worry about my friend's definition of normal.

"Well, you know what I mean. Gangs, or estranged lovers, or people who get in fights in bars. They usually reach for a gun, or smack each other over the head with the nearest heavy object. Except for that guy last year who killed his wife for the insurance, he ran over her with his pickup and tried to make it look like an accident only that kid was there with his iPhone and got the whole thing on video—"

"Geez, Susan, you make it sound like we live in the murder capital of the world!"

Susan heaved a sigh. "My point is, going for the throat like this is kind of unusual. There's technique involved, and it wouldn't be everyone's first choice."

I walked into my tiny office and flicked on the computer. "So, the next time we get in an argument I need to keep you away from guns and heavy objects? Good to know."

"Smartass. I'll bet you a coffee that when they investigate this, they'll find similarities between this crime scene and Chuck's. Maybe enough to let Harry go! I don't think he's out on bail yet, so this could prove his innocence."

I was pretty sure Susan was setting her hopes too high, but I didn't have the heart to say so. "I hope you're right," I said, "but remember, they haven't actually caught the criminal yet."

"Oh, that shouldn't be too hard once they stop focusing on Harry," she said airily. "We'll help too, of course."

"The cops will be thrilled."

"They should be," Susan said. "The Mayor is really badmouthing the whole police department, saying they've let crime rates go through the roof and basically blaming them for everything from his wife's death to global warming."

"Lovely."

"*And* of course he's threatening that heads will roll if they don't hurry up and solve the case, and that he's going to fire everybody if he has to, and blah, blah blah…"

I had already pulled up the local news on my desktop, and was watching the Mayor deliver his harangue to the assembled reporters. "I suppose it's too much to hope for that *he's* guilty," I said, rolling my eyes. "Seeing him in prison would be a real treat."

"No such luck," Susan sighed. "Once again, he's got a butt-load of politicos vouching for his whereabouts. Rock-solid alibi. There's no way he could have done it."

I sighed. "Isn't the whole point about alibis is that anyone who has one is automatically suspicious? Innocent people don't know they're going to need one."

Susan laughed. "If you can disprove Mr. Mayor's alibi, the whole police department will thank you, starting with Tara. She wants to meet with us again tonight. The guys have another 'emergency practice' before their performance in Redvue Square next week, so we can do it without making them suspicious. Your place or mine?"

"Yours. Michael's been reorganizing his computer space, and there are cords and computer pieces all over the place."

"OK, see you at seven-ish. Don't bring any squirrels with you or Lady will eat them. She's been a little touchy lately."

I immediately felt concern for my friend's beautiful German shepherd. "Lady's not sick, is she?"

"No, she's just been having a spaz because of a new dog in the neighborhood. I'll tell you about it later. See you tonight, bye-bye!"

Susan rang off.

Chapter 14

I was greeted at Susan's door by a highly suspicious Lady. The beautiful, possibly purebred German shepherd had been found abandoned as a puppy at a truck stop several years before. A kind trucker had scooped up the underfed pup and brought her to a local shelter where Susan volunteered her services as a graphic artist. She had seen the puppy on one of her visits to the shelter, and it was love at first sight. She had refused to leave without Lady.

Usually Lady had a sweet, laid-back personality, but today she definitely seemed to be on edge. After sniffing my hand several times to make sure I was who I was supposed to be, she shoved her nose past me and glared out the door with a noise that sounded almost like a growl.

"Lady! Settle down." Susan grabbed Lady's collar to prevent her from dashing outside. To me she said, "I don't know what her deal is. Two weeks ago some new people moved into the house next door. They're really nice and they have the sweetest little dog. I was walking Lady and Upchuck and stopped for a chat, when Lady went absolutely ballistic! She was barking at their little dog, straining at the leash and baring her teeth like Cujo. The little new dog just sat there behind the fence not even twitching a whisker. It just looked at us with this disdainful look on its face like, 'Who are these barbarians I've just been forced to live next to?' I apologized all over the place and dragged Lady away, but she's been all worked up ever since. I just don't get it!"

"What did Upchuck do?" I asked curiously.

"Not much," Susan said. "At first it seemed like he wanted to go over and make friends, but when Lady started acting up he didn't want anything to do with it. Upchuck's more interested in treats than conflict."

With the front door closed, Lady seemed to have settled down a little, but her head kept twitching toward the door every time she heard a sound. Meanwhile, Susan's mongrel, a medium-sized mutt with the appropriate name of Upchuck, gave Lady a worried look and left the room.

"Weird," I said. "Are you sure the other dog didn't bark or growl first or anything?"

120

"Nope. It was perfectly well-mannered. My dogs should behave that well! Maybe there's some secret dog code that this other dog is sending out that humans can't see or hear."

"I guess it's possible" I said. "Coyotes and wolves use scent and a lot of body language along with vocalizations."

"This dog is *way* more civilized than any of your wild animals. It's this cute little terrier pug with gigantic eyes, and it's all groomed and everything. It looks like a show dog."

I laughed. "Maybe that's the problem—you know how Lady feels about groomers."

Susan shuddered. Lady's behavior on her one and only trip to a groomer's (several months ago following an unfortunate encounter with a can of paint) had become legend, and resulted in her being banned from all of the doggie boutiques in Redvue. "That's one mistake I'll never make again. It's the hose or nothing for her from now on. Maybe you're right and the new dog smells like shampoo or something!"

"It's a thought." I plopped down on Susan's comfortable sofa. "Do you really think we'll get anything more done tonight? Except for the throat motif, how much does Mrs. Vick's murder really have in common with Chuck's?"

Susan sank into a chair across from me. "I don't know," she admitted, "but that is a similarity and Tara's excited about it—I talked to her before I called you. She's going to try to get more information today, and since this case isn't officially connected to Chuck's murder she might be able to get some inside information. Anne's coming, too. She's pretty upset about the whole thing.

"I didn't realize she knew Mrs. Vick that well."

"She didn't, but I think she's feeling bad that she didn't talk to her sooner."

"Aww. She shouldn't feel bad—I mean, I doubt Mrs. Vick really knew anything useful."

"Unless," Susan said in an ominous voice, "Mrs. Vick *did* know something and that's why she was killed!"

I rolled my eyes. "Please don't suggest that to Anne if she's already feeling bad. Jeez!"

"Of course I won't," Susan promised. "Hey, could you grab Lady's collar for a second? It looks like they're here."

Lady had heard the sound of a car door and, in anticipation of getting the front door opened again, was taking up a stance nearby. Her fur bristled as she got ready to spring and get another chance at eliminating the dog next door.

"No way," I said. "You grab her collar and I'll open the door."

"Chicken."

"At least I'll be a chicken with all my fingers," I said as I headed for the door.

"A chicken with fingers?" Susan retorted, grabbing Lady's collar and taking a firm hold. "Remind me again which of us works with animals for a living."

Tara had been the first to arrive, but Anne's car pulled in as I was opening the door.

"Hi, Tara! Hi, Anne!" Susan called from the front room as she attempted to restrain Lady.

Tara eyed the German shepherd warily. "What's up with her?" she asked. Meanwhile, Susan's other dog, Upchuck, galumphed up to Tara demanding an ear rub. "Hi, sweetie!" she said as she greeted the rambunctious mixed-breed. "What's wrong with your sister? I've seen police dogs in full hunting mode that looked less ferocious."

"She's having some issues with the new neighbor dog," Susan explained as Anne entered and shut the door behind her. "Luigi Di'Ogee." She pronounced the last name as 'dog-ee.'

Anne sputtered. "Who-what?"

"You didn't tell me the dog's name," I said. "That's pretty fancy. Maybe Lady feels inferior because you didn't give her a fancy name."

Tara laughed. "I'm just glad it isn't me she's after. That neighbor dog must be terrified!"

Susan shrugged. "Mr. Luigi doesn't seem to care. He's totally ignoring both dogs. He sure is cute, though!"

Tara covered Lady's ears with her hands. "Don't listen to them, honey, you're every bit as cute and you have a nice name." Lady relaxed under Tara's touch and rolled over, inviting a tummy rub. Tara definitely had a way with dogs.

Susan carried in tall glasses of iced tea, and we all prepared to get down to business. "So," she said once everyone was settled, "let's talk murder!"

Chapter 15

Tara got us started. "Well," she said, "as you can guess, it's been a pretty tough day for everybody in the department. The Mayor's been making life miserable for the higher-ups, and that makes them cranky. The only real clue we've got is that there was an old sedan seen in the neighborhood at about the right time. It was noticed by one or two neighbors, because pretty much everybody who lives in that neighborhood is driving the latest Lexus or Mercedes. Unfortunately, the witnesses can't agree on the make or model, and the guesses for color range from grey to blue to brown. It was dark by then, and they mostly noticed that it was old and beat-up and not up to their standards."

"There weren't any clues from the crime scene itself?" Susan asked. "No footprints or anything?"

"Damn criminal didn't even leave us his business card," Tara said with a grin. "Whoever he was he's been very rude, causing us all this extra work! Of course, there's a lot of DNA evidence that needs to get processed, but as far as I know there weren't any obvious leads."

"Except for the fact that we have somebody who goes for the throat, just like whoever killed Chuck!" Susan said triumphantly.

Anne made a slight, whimpering sound.

"I'm sorry, Anne," Susan said. "I forgot you knew her. It really is awful."

"I feel so sorry for her," Anne said, her eyes clouded. "I wish I'd talked to her sooner—if nothing else to tell her how sorry I was for what she was going through. But it's even worse if she knew something that could have helped us catch Chuck's killer. If she was killed by the same person and we caught him, it could have prevented her death!"

We all quickly denied that possibility. "After all," Tara pointed out, "even if Mrs. Vick knew something definite about this killer, which is very unlikely, it would have taken time to find the suspect and get him into custody. If it was the same killer, he—"

"Or she," Susan interjected.

"Or *she* just moved too fast," Tara concluded. "What we really need to concentrate on is where we go from here."

"We're still on for interviewing people in the neighborhood of Deerborne Florist," Susan said. "We were planning to do it on Saturday morning, when everything should be open."

"And I suppose I could talk to the Mayor," Anne said, brightening a little. "I could at least offer my condolences and ask if there's anything I can do."

"That's a great idea!" Susan said. "Mr. Mayor's not my favorite person, but even he didn't deserve to have his wife killed that way. Unless he did it, of course. Ginger and I could even go with you and slip in a few questions."

I was not wild about this idea. "Why us? We didn't know Mrs. Vick from Adam! Won't it look odd for total strangers to show up asking Mayor Vick questions about his dead wife?"

"He wouldn't know we were strangers," Susan argued. "I'm sure Mayor Vick didn't take enough interest in his wife to know all her friends. Anne did know her a little, and we'd just be there as, I don't know, adjacent friends."

"I would like to have some company if I'm going to do it," Anne admitted. "Asking Mrs. Vick questions was one thing, but talking to the Mayor seems intimidating. I've only met him in person once. He didn't get involved in many of her charities."

"Not unless it helped him drum up votes," Susan guessed cynically.

"Exactly."

"And I'm keeping my eyes and ears open at the station," Tara said. "We'll know a little more after the autopsy and forensic reports are in, but there's already a lot of chitchat going on about what happened. Speaking of chitchat, don't forget about the barbeque at Dufresne's house on Sunday—I've promised to bring dancers."

"Food, beer, dancing—that combination should get people talking!" Susan grinned.

"That's the idea."

Anne perked up at the mention of dancing. "By the way, Ginger and Susan, I brought something to show you," she said. She dug inside a bag she'd brought with her and pulled out a long, sparkly dress. She stood and held it up so we could see. "What do you think?"

The dress was long and form-fitting, made out of a glittering, stretchy material with small black and red stripes. It had a scooping neckline and long bell sleeves.

"That's really pretty," Susan said. "Is it a Beledi dress?" she added, referring to the long dresses that are often used in Egyptian folkloric dances.

"Yes, and it's what you'll all be wearing for your tahtib piece. I just got these out of their storage boxes today."

"You mean we each get one?" I asked, delightedly fingering the material.

"Not to keep, but you all get one for the performance. I made ten of them for a troupe performance eight years ago, in a few different sizes. Next week we'll get everyone fitted and start practicing in them, because you'll need to get the feel of the sleeves."

My enthusiasm dimmed a little as I pictured us trying to twirl our sticks without getting them tangled up in the sleeves. Anne saw my expression and assured me that the technique wasn't hard to learn.

"You guys should come perform for us at the barbecue," Tara said.

"Oh, yeah," Susan said, "I really want to be the person who loses her grip and thwacks a police officer on the head with a huge stick! No, thanks."

As Tara and Anne prepared to leave, I gave Anne a hug. "Tell you what, Anne," I said, "Why don't we pick you up on Saturday after we're done going through the neighborhood by Harry's? We could pick up a floral arrangement to take to Mayor Vick's house, if you know where it is."

"I do," Anne replied, "Mrs. Vick held a few charity luncheons in their garden. I'm free this Saturday, so that would work."

"Looks like we're set for a big weekend of detecting," Susan said cheerily as she once again took a strong grip on Lady's collar. "I wonder what we'll find out?"

Chapter 16

As we pulled up in front of Deerborne Florist, it seemed hard to believe everything that had happened since our last visit.

"Everything looks the same," Susan commented, showing that her mind had been running along the same lines.

"Yeah," I said, hitting the lock button on my car. (I had insisted on driving this time.)

"I think that's even the same pigeon leaving a deposit on Harry's awning. If we don't save Harry, the poor flying rat won't have any place to poop."

With this dire thought in mind, we entered Harry's shop. A tall redheaded girl in her mid-twenties looked up from the front desk. "Hello," she said in a friendly voice, "how can I help you?"

I hesitated, realizing that I hadn't thought out what we were going to say.

Susan jumped right in. "We're friends of Harry's. We wanted to order some flowers to show our support."

I picked up the cue. "We're hoping his business hasn't suffered too much."

The girl's face lit up. "Oh, that's nice of you. The business hasn't been impacted too much yet, and we're hoping Harry will be cleared soon. What are you looking for?"

We perused a book of sympathy bouquets to take to the Mayor's house. The girl, whose name was Ellie, helped us pick out a mid-sized bouquet that could be made quickly. "I'll have Peter get to work on it," she said, disappearing into a back room for a few moments. "So, how do you know Harry?" she asked when she returned.

We explained a little about the wedding and how we knew Camellia.

Ellie looked at us with wide blue eyes. "So you were actually there?"

We nodded.

"How awful! I just can't believe they think Harry did it!"

This seemed promising. "So you think Harry's innocent, too?" I asked.

"Of course he is," Ellie declared, "and I'm not just saying that because he's my boss. Harry is one of the nicest human beings I know. There's no way he'd kill anybody, not even a lowlife like Chuck!"

Susan's ears pricked up. "Oh, so you weren't a big Chuck fan?"

"We only met Chuck a couple of times," I added. "We didn't know him at all."

"Chuck was a huge jerk," Ellie scowled. "He was always causing trouble, coming in late, and picking arguments. Plus, he couldn't keep his hands to himself. He was always hitting on me! And he was *married*!"

Considering how attractive Ellie was, it didn't surprise me at all that she had had trouble with Chuck!

"Did you ever complain to Harry?" Susan asked sympathetically.

"No, I'm pretty sure he would have fired Chuck, and then it would have been my fault."

"So what if Chuck got fired?" Susan asked. "It sounds like he deserved it! And it would have been his own fault, not yours—you weren't responsible for his behavior."

"I know that, but I still would have felt bad. Especially if his wife found out!"

"What's his wife like?" Susan asked. "Do you know her?"

Ellie nodded. "She's come in a few times. Chuck was never very nice to her and once in a while they got into fights while she was here. I always felt sorry for her. Chuck could get really mean and snide when he wanted to."

"I wonder why he married her in the first place?" Susan mused.

"I heard that when she moved here from Idaho she had just inherited some money from selling her family's farm. I think that's probably why Chuck married her, because it was obvious he didn't care about her at all. In fact, I think they were about to get divorced!"

"Divorced?" I said, surprised. "I never heard that!"

"Yeah, I think it had just gotten in the works before Chuck was killed. I overheard him joking with a delivery guy that it was going to be nice getting rid of the old ball and chain."

Susan shook her head. "What a lovely person."

"Has anything else been going on lately that seemed unusual?" I asked Ellie. "Was Chuck having problems with anyone?"

Ellie laughed. "Chuck had problems with just about everybody! Oh, except for Bill. Lately Chuck and Bill actually seemed to be pretty good friends."

"Bill?" Susan asked.

"Bill Ellis, one of the guys who help set up the bigger displays. They got pretty chummy the last few months, always going off for cigarette breaks together and things like that. It did seem kind of strange, because the rest of the guys didn't like Chuck at all—he didn't do his share of the work."

"Did he hit on the other girls who work here?" I asked.

"He tried, but we'd all seen him in action with the female customers, and saw how he treated his poor wife, Amy. None of us were stupid enough to get involved with him, but I think he was going out with the Marla, the girl who owns the chocolate place, for a while."

132

I was emptying a trash can in the alley behind our buildings, and I heard them out there arguing. It didn't sound like they were going to stay together."

Susan looked interested. "When was this?"

Ellie thought for a moment. "I'd say about a month ago."

"Did you catch anything they said?" I asked. "It's not just curiosity, we're trying to find out if somebody else had a reason to kill Chuck."

Ellie nodded. "I remember her saying something like, 'You're doing this way too often. We have to be careful,' and then he laughed and she got even angrier. She said, 'Well if you don't stop it you'll be out.' That's when I left—I didn't want to hear any more."

"Hmm. Sounds like she was worried about someone finding out about their relationship," said Susan. "Does she have any other boyfriends?"

"I have no idea. I run over there once and a while to get chocolates, but we've never really had heart-to-heart talks."

At this point a young man emerged from a back room carrying a sheath of white lilies surrounded by baby's breath. "Hi, Ellie," he said, "I've got them ready here. Did you want me to put them in a white box or one of our regular ones?"

Ellie looked over at us. "Some people like us to put sympathy bouquets in a white box instead of one of our standard pink and gold ones. Do you have a preference?"

Susan and I considered this and decided on a white box. After that we chose a conventional little white card with gold lettering that said, "With sympathy for your loss."

"These are friends of Harry's," Ellie told the young man while she rang up the purchase. "They were at that wedding and they're trying to find out more about what happened. This is Peter," she added, gesturing at him.

Peter was a nice-looking young man in his early 20's, tall and lanky with dark hair and brown eyes that looked shyly out from behind his glasses. He brightened when he heard we were trying to help Harry.

"Well, I know one thing that *didn't* happen, and that's Harry killing anybody. He'd never do that, not even to Chuck," Peter said.

"So you weren't a big Chuck fan either?" Susan asked.

Peter shook his head. "That guy was the worst! He had more excuses for getting out of work than anybody I've ever met, and when he did do something he messed it up about half the time. We had to redo a lot of his pieces."

"Sounds like a real jerk," Susan encouraged.

Peter looked a little guilty, perhaps remembering that his erstwhile coworker was dead. "Oh, he wasn't all bad," he said. "Chuck could be really funny when he wanted to be. I can see him being a good person to have at a party to get people laughing. He just wasn't great as a coworker."

"And his jokes weren't always in the best taste, either," Ellie commented. "Some of them went way too far."

"Yeah, and the way he joked around with some of the lady customers, I kept expecting Harry to get complaints!" Peter said.

"Did he?" I asked.

Peter shrugged. "Not that I ever heard about."

"Has anything been going on lately that seemed out of the ordinary?" I asked Peter.

"Like what?"

"Just anything unusual, or arguments that he got into, that kind of thing," I said.

Peter screwed up his face in thought. "I can't really think of anything. He'd started being on his phone a lot, but I just figured that was more work avoidance."

"Any idea who he was calling?" Susan asked.

Peter grinned. "Well, I didn't sit around listening to his conversations, if that's what you mean. I did get the general impression he was mostly talking to girls, though. No names I recognized, but once or twice I heard him call somebody Maria or Mara or something like that. I can't remember exactly."

Susan dug into her purse for her business cards. "Well, thank you both for the beautiful bouquet and for helping us try to help Harry. If you think of anything else, give us a call."

She was handing them the cards when the shop door swung open and a woman came in. Suddenly both Ellie and Peter seemed to stiffen and look uncomfortable.

"Mrs. McKenzie," Ellie said after a beat, "how can we help you?"

I looked at the woman with renewed interest. So this was Chuck's wife! I had wondered what she would be like.

Amy McKenzie was a plain-looking woman who could have been anywhere between forty and sixty. She was medium-height, with a stocky figure that was made completely shapeless by a drab housedress. She had close-cropped blond hair that was grizzled with grey, and her skin had the dull, lifeless appearance that comes from a lifetime of heavy smoking. She wore no makeup. A greater contrast to the stylish, good-looking Chuck I could not have imagined.

"I brought in Chuck's uniforms," she said in a voice that was as colorless as her appearance.

Ellie stepped forward to take a bag from Mrs. McKenzie. "Oh, there was no hurry about that," she assured her. "But since you're here, let me get you the things from his locker. Harry—" here Ellie's voice faltered a little, probably from the discomfort of bringing up the accused murderer of the poor woman's husband—"already made sure we sent you the last paycheck."

"I got it."

Ellie gestured for Mrs. McKenzie to take a seat in the lobby and hurriedly left to gather Chuck's belongings.

Susan and I glanced at each other in the awkward silence that followed. On one hand, we knew, this was an opportunity to talk to Chuck's widow and possibly get more information. On the other hand, she had just lost her husband, for crying out loud! The marriage might not have been a happy one, but the murder still must have come as a huge shock. Looking at the slumping figure in the chair, I couldn't tell if Mrs. McKenzie was suffering from grief or was simply drained of emotion. Then again, maybe she always looked like that.

Susan cleared her throat. "Excuse me, but are you Mrs. McKenzie?"

The woman sniffed. "So what if I am?" she asked gruffly.

"Um," said Susan, slightly rebuffed by the curt reply, "it's just that we knew Chuck a little bit, and we wanted to tell you how sorry we are about what happened…"

Now Mrs. McKenzie's pale blue eyes were fastened on Susan, looking her up and down, then turning to appraise me the same way. Her scrutiny made me feel very uncomfortable. "Don't go feeling sorry for me," Mrs. McKenzie said slowly. "I was divorcing that no-good bastard anyway. Somebody saved me the trouble, that's all."

Well, that was enough to shut even Susan up! We stood there uncomfortably, shuffling our feet. Fortunately for us, Peter had just finished securing our bouquet's box with ribbon and stepped up to hand it to us.

"By the way, Mrs. Barry," he said to Susan, "You handed me the wrong business card. This is one of ours." He held out the green card that Chuck had given Susan what felt like a hundred years ago.

"Oops," said Susan, "The color is almost exactly the same." She took the card from Peter and dug in her purse for more cards. "I really need to get a card case instead of just stuffing these in my wallet." She located a few more cards, then caught her sleeve on the buckle of her purse and dropped all of them.

The card from Chuck landed back side up, right by Mrs. McKenzie's feet. Susan scrambled for it, but I was sure Mrs. McKenzie's gaze had fastened on Chuck's importunate message before Susan retrieved it from the floor. Susan hastily gave Peter one of her own cards, thanked him for his help and made a beeline for the door.

"Whew!" she exclaimed once we were safely outside. "That was awkward."

Not wanting to linger within sight of the shop, we hurried over to Chocolate Noir.

"Ahhh," Susan sighed as the soothing smell of chocolate wafted over us. "After that little exchange, I *need* some chocolate!"

Marla was once again behind the counter. As before, she helpfully guided us through the staggering wealth of treats and helped us make our selections.

By the time our purchases were being rung up, Susan had recovered enough to get back into gossip mode. "It sure is a shame, what's going on next door," she said, nodding towards Deerborne Florist. "Do you know them well?"

Did I imagine it, or did Marla's face suddenly look guarded? "Oh, the florist?" she said. "Yeah, I heard that some bad things were happening over there. It sounded like the owner had killed one of his workers or something? I don't know the whole story."

Considering what Ellie had overheard, I figured that Marla was probably following the whole story pretty closely. Even if she and Chuck had broken up and she didn't care about him at all anymore, it simply wasn't human nature to be that incurious about the murder of a former boyfriend! Why, then, was Marla pretending not to know what was going on? After all, it wouldn't seem at all strange for her to know what was going on—as an adjacent business owner, it would be perfectly natural to know the details.

"So you don't stay in touch with the other business owners on this street?" I asked, sounding as casual as I could.

Marla looked even more uncomfortable. "Not really," she said. "We don't have meetings or anything like that. I see employees from the other businesses once in a while, and of course we often have the same customers—people who buy flowers sometimes want chocolates to go with them—but I'm not on a first-name basis with most of them."

I could tell from Susan's narrowed eyes that she wasn't buying Marla's story either, but she decided to try another tack. "Have you noticed anything unusual going on lately?" she asked.

Now Marla just looked confused. "Like what? Drug deals on the sidewalk or something?"

"Well, that would certainly count," Susan said hopefully.

"Of course not," Marla said, looking slightly offended. "This is a nice neighborhood! Why are you asking, anyway?"

"We're actually friends with the owner of Deerborne Florist," I said hastily. "We just don't think he could have committed the crime, and we're trying to find out what happened."

Marla was definitely looking frosty now. "You should probably let the police handle that," she said. "But no, I haven't noticed anything strange. Here are your chocolates." She thrust the bag at us. "Have a nice day."

Susan doggedly handed her a business card. "Well, thank you for your time, and if you do think of anything, please give us a call. We'd really appreciate it." She gave Marla one of her nicest smiles. "We're just trying to help a friend."

Once again we found ourselves leaving a shop feeling like idiots. "Talk about getting the bum's rush," Susan complained as we got back into the car. "I feel very unpopular right now. Plus, we didn't learn diddly-squat!"

"That's not true," I argued. "We know that Chuck had trouble with his coworkers. We found out that Chuck was in some kind of relationship with Marla the chocolate lady, and that they had an argument. We also know his wife didn't like him at all and that she was divorcing him."

Susan looked thoughtful. "The divorce thing sure was a surprise. Do you think she did it?"

I waited to answer her until I'd gotten the car safely past a semi-truck that was taking up all of its lane and part of ours. "That would be a great solution," I said, exhaling in relief as the giant truck got farther away in the rearview mirror, "but it just doesn't seem likely. As she said herself, all the murder did for her was save her the trouble of getting a divorce. Why file for divorce if you're going to murder your husband anyway?"

"Oh, I don't know," Susan said, "divorces can get nasty. Maybe Chuck said or did something that pushed her over the edge."

"But she wasn't even at the wedding."

"She could have snuck in, pretending to be a guest. It's not like they were checking people for ID as they came in."

I agreed reluctantly. "Ok, so she might not be the most likely person, but it wouldn't have been impossible for her to do it. Now what about the girlfriend? Marla definitely wasn't telling us everything she knew."

"That's for sure. She didn't want us to know she even *knew* Chuck, let alone that she was in a relationship with him. Maybe the breakup was really bad and she had it in for him."

I shrugged. "Of course, it would seem kind of weird to have two complete strangers just walk into your store and start asking you a bunch of questions. Maybe she just didn't see any reason to talk to us. She might have already told the police about their affair."

"Hey, that's something we can ask at the barbeque," Susan said, sounding more enthusiastic. "They might be less closed-mouthed around us than they would be around Tara, if she's being specifically kept off the case."

I wasn't as sure as Susan seemed to be that police officers would talk about their current cases with civilians, but I didn't want to spoil her good mood. "Maybe," I said as I pulled onto I-90, "but for right now, the next stop is Anne's house, and then the Mayor's."

"Oh, yeah." Susan rubbed her hands together in anticipation. "Time to see what Mr. Mayor has to say for himself!"

Chapter 17

Anne lived in a pretty little house on Mercer Island, a tree-lined island city on south Lake Washington. When we got there she invited us in for a few minutes, explaining that she wasn't ready to leave just yet because her sons—here she bestowed a motherly glare upon her twin teenage boys Justin and Jason—had just been sent home from a special summer course for showing disrespect to a teacher.

"It wasn't our fault," argued Jason, or possibly Justin.

"You had to be there," his brother agreed.

"Both of you worked so hard to get that scholarship to Redvue Prep," Anne said sternly, "and the summer classes are part of that. I know you don't like Mr. Andrew, but you still have to do the work and behave yourselves."

One or the other of them looked at us with innocent blue eyes under a mop of dark hair. "We did all the work," he declared. We just didn't do it with enough—," here he choked for a moment, "*gravitas*." Both of them dissolved into snorts of laughter.

"Gravitas?" asked Susan.

"We were doing our presentation on 'Macbeth'," said one of them,

"Using *only* the finest of Scottish accents, of course," said the other.

"*And* in kilts,"

"…complete with sporrans,"

"…when out of nowhere Mr. Andrew stopped us and said were weren't 'approaching the material with enough gravitas'," whooped the first.

"…and so Justin," here Jason, apparently, pointed a finger at his gasping brother, "said that was impossible, because whenever we order tacos we *always* ask for extra gravitas!" They both doubled up again in laughter.

"They got sent home for that?" Susan asked sympathetically.

Anne rolled her eyes. "Mr. Andrew takes Shakespeare very seriously," she said, "and he doesn't have much sense of humor."

"Try *any*," said one of the laughing twins.

"Alright both of you," Anne commanded, "while I'm gone, you are going to clean out all of Those Boxes in the Garage

The laughter ceased instantly. "Also," Anne continued, "you are going to apologize to Mr. Andrew first thing in the morning. In person."

The gloom deepened as their sentence was pronounced, but neither twin argued. They left the room sadly. Whether it was the threat of having to apologize or of cleaning out Those Boxes, their spirits seemed to have been dampened somewhat. Not entirely, however, because as they disappeared I thought I heard a whispered "gravitas!" followed by snickers.

Discipline restored, Anne gathered her things and joined us. She admired the bouquet and accepted a chocolate, and then Susan and I brought her up to date as I headed back onto I-90.

"They were really getting a divorce?" she asked.

We nodded, and the three of us debated whether Marla or Amy McKenzie seemed more likely to be the murderer until we reached Redvue. Then Anne had to start giving me directions to the Mayor's part of town.

"Check out these houses," Susan commented as we drove through the Mayor's neighborhood. "These people must be millionaires, at least. It's almost like Beverly Hills!"

Considering housing prices in the Seattle area, I figured that anyone owning one of the mansions we passed must be a millionaire many times over. Even the Nicklesons' house looked small in comparison. There was something self-consciously pretentious about the sweeping driveways, excessively decorated marble fountains and 6-car garages. The houses were set on large lots, but not nearly large enough for the ostentatiousness of the buildings. Each one looked like it should have been set atop a 50-acre estate!

Anne grimaced. "Everyone here has a lot more money than taste, that's for sure! Margaret was a nice woman, but John Vick is an incredibly crude, arrogant man." A brief smile flickered across her face and mischief crept into her voice. "Wait until you see what's in their front yard."

I took a left turn as directed and slowly pulled up in front of an enormous white monstrosity of a house. In the middle of the front lawn was a white marble fountain topped by—

"Good grief, is that supposed to be a statue of Mayor Vick?" I gasped.

"Oh my god!" Susan sputtered, "and without his pants!"

Sure enough, a larger-than-life image of the Mayor rose up majestically out of the water. In the best European tradition, he was entirely sans clothing. I won't describe where the water was spouting from.

I choked. "Haven't the neighbors complained?"

In the seat behind me Susan shook and sputtered with laughter. Anne sighed.

"Just two months ago, I was working with Margaret on a fundraiser for the Humane Society while that was being built. She was absolutely mortified, but he wouldn't listen to anything she said. And yes, some of the neighbors have complained, and even gotten a petition going to have it taken down. It hasn't been going on long enough to gain momentum yet, though."

"Trust our Mayor to make it come down to a big free-speech thing and use his own bare butt to win votes," Susan said, still laughing, "and his butt's not even the worst part. Couldn't he have at least pointed his front *away* from the street?"

"It's too embarrassing to even look at," I agreed. "Poor Mrs. Vick!"

For a few moments we continued to gape at the unappetizing lawn ornament.

Well, let's get this over with," Susan said finally, opening her door. "Although it's going to be pretty uncomfortable trying to question somebody who's got a big nude peeing statue of himself in the front yard. What was he thinking!?"

Carrying our sheaf of flowers, Anne led the way up a grand marble staircase to an enormous front door.

"Do you think a butler's going to answer?" Susan whispered to me as Anne pressed the buzzer.

Actually it was a plump grey-haired lady in a denim shirtdress who answered the door. Her name, as it turned out, was Annie Pierson, and she was a sort of combined secretary and housekeeper. At previous fundraising events, the accident of having similar names had helped our teacher get to know the woman better than if she had just been another member of the public.

"Why hello, Anne, dear," the housekeeper said with a wink.

"Hello Annie," said our Anne, smiling. She introduced us and explained that we had come to offer our condolences.

146

"Well, he isn't seeing everyone, but I know you and Margaret were friends. I'll see if he's available."

"How have you been, Annie?" Anne asked sympathetically. "This must have been a terrible time for you, too."

The older woman heaved a sigh. "It certainly has been," she said. "I was out of the house when it happened, and I feel bad about that. If poor Margaret hadn't been alone—"

"Now Annie, you can't think like that," Anne said firmly. "You could have been murdered too. You know Margaret wouldn't have wanted that."

Annie shivered. "It doesn't feel the same in here since it happened. I find myself looking over my shoulder a lot."

"That's understandable," Susan said. "They haven't even caught the guy who did it!"

I dug my elbow into Susan's ribs—a woman who worked in the house where a murder had just been committed was probably already scared enough!

Annie was nodding. "I wouldn't even be here still if there weren't so many details that need to be taken care of for Margaret's charities. She has—had—several events coming up for organizations she really cared about. There is still so much paperwork to do for them and other things to be arranged. I couldn't just leave everything in a mess."

It occurred to me that Annie might be a very good source of information. "Couldn't the Mayor have taken care of some of those things?" I asked, hoping to keep her talking.

Annie snorted. "Him?" He never cared about any of her charities! He only put up with her 'throwing money away', as he put it, because being associated with the things she did gave his public image a boost. Oh, he'd show up every once in a while to give a speech and have his picture taken, but it was all just for publicity."

Susan had caught onto my strategy. "Maybe he'll continue her work now, as a way to deal with his grief."

Annie shook her head. "If you ask me, he isn't grieving much. He'll put on a show to get sympathy from the public, though. This will probably win the next election for him. In reality," she continued, her voice scathing, "having Margaret gone will just give him a freer hand to play around with all of his sweet young things. No, I don't think he'll miss her much."

She was leading us down a hall toward an impressive-looking set of double doors. I guessed that it was where Mayor Vick had his study, so I decided it was time to take the bull by the horns. "Margaret must have been very lonely, with a husband like that," I said. "Do you think that's why she started seeing Chuck McKenzie?"

Annie froze. *Uh-oh*, I thought, *maybe I went too far!*

But apparently Annie needed to talk. "Chuck McKenzie," she said in a frosty tone, "was an absolutely worthless human being. He saw that poor Margaret was lonely and neglected, and he used that to take advantage of her. I tried over and over to tell her that he was only after her money, but she insisted they were in love. And he was thirty years younger than she was!"

"Men marry women that much younger than themselves all the time," Susan pointed out.

"Yes, and ten to one those young women are after the exact same thing—money."

"Do you think Mayor Vick knew anything about it?" I asked.

"I don't think so," Annie replied. "He never paid enough attention to Margaret to notice anything she did. Although," she said, her eyes becoming thoughtful, "Margaret did mention that she would have to tell John soon, because Chuck wanted to marry her."

"Marry her?" Susan exclaimed. "He was already married!"

"I think Margaret's idea was that they would both get divorces from their spouses and then get married. I don't for a moment believe that Chuck meant to go through with it—he was trying to get more money out of her at the time. He said he'd lost some money on an investment and was hard up."

"When was this?" I asked.

"Let me think. It would have been about two weeks before Chuck McKenzie was killed. Of course, I tried to talk her out of telling John anything—he had plenty of affairs, but he wouldn't have taken kindly to having his wife do the same thing!"

By now we had reached the double doors and were speaking in hushed tones.

"Do you think Mayor Vick might have gotten violent if he found out?" Susan nearly whispered.

Annie hesitated. "I doubt it," she finally whispered, "although he can have a bad temper sometimes. If one of his staff members makes him angry he'll shout and swear, and usually fire them immediately. I've never seen him get physically violent, though. Of course, if he found out his wife was having an affair...I guess we'll never know."

With that, she knocked on the door of the Mayor's study. Upon hearing an annoyed-sounding "Come in," she opened the doors and ushered us inside.

Mayor Vick stood beside his desk, looking out through a window at a carefully-landscaped back yard. At about 6', he could have been a football player in his high school or college days, but he had definitely run to fat since then. As he turned to greet us, I recognized the well-known face that had once been handsome and boyish, but now was red and puffy, with sagging jowls. His thinning blond hair was making an unsuccessful attempt at a comb-over. All in all, he looked a little like a pig. His statue was much better-looking. I winced. *That statue!*

Annie introduced us. "These ladies were friends of Margaret's," she said in an appropriately hushed tone.

Mayor Vick nodded somberly, his expression changing from faint irritation to one of solemn regret. I had seen him assume the exact same expression on the news many times, whenever he needed to address some piece of bad news. Accidents, crimes, floods and other tragedies always got that same look.

Anne stepped forward and held out the sheaf of flowers. "We just wanted to say how sorry we are about what happened. Margaret was such a wonderful woman."

The Mayor continued to nod and look solemn. "That's very kind of you," he said in his characteristically deep voice. "Margaret was a generous woman with a great heart. She will be deeply missed."

"Speech, speech," Susan hissed in my ear. I gave her a subtle elbow jab.

"Her charity work was appreciated," Anne continued, "And she made a real difference in people's lives."

"She always did everything she could for the community," rumbled the Mayor, "Sometimes too much, she wore herself out."

Tired of the conventional conversation, Susan stepped up from behind me. "Mr. Mayor, have there been any developments in the investigation? Are they any closer to catching the person who did it?"

Mayor Vick's head snapped around and he seemed to notice Susan and me at the same time. For a second his pale blue eyes glinted at us as he appraised who and what we were.

"Are you reporters?" he finally asked, looking like he was trying to decide whether to be annoyed or play up to us.

Anne hastily assured him that we were just civilians who had known his wife. This was stretching the truth a bit, but we had met her, however briefly.

"We're just worried that the killer is still out there," Susan said, trying her best to sound womanly and frightened. Not easy for somebody who once chased off a burglar with a plumber's wrench! "After all, this is the second time it's happened in a couple of weeks!"

The Mayor's eyebrows rose. "Second?"

"Didn't you know?" Susan pressed. "A man was killed in practically the same way at a wedding recently."

Mayor Vick knitted his eyebrows in thought. "Oh, do you mean the Nickleson wedding? Of course it was a terrible thing to happen to my friends, the Nicklesons—" here he puffed out his chest a little as he mentioned the famously wealthy family—"but it was hardly the same type of crime. Just a dispute between a florist and one of his employees, if I understood correctly. And they caught the man who did it. There's no possibility of a connection."

"Unless they didn't get the right person," I said, trying to work up some courage. I found the Mayor's attitude so irritating that I forgot to think about him standing there naked like his statue. "The people who know Harry, the florist, don't think he could have done it. If there was a mistake, then there is still a very dangerous person on the loose and it could be the same one who killed Margaret."

Anne spoke up then. "It does seem like an unusual way to kill someone. Could there have been a mistake when they arrested the florist?"

The Mayor winced and turned toward the window, his back to us. "If you don't mind, I would rather not dwell on the way my poor wife died." He took a handkerchief from his pocket and dabbed at what I suspected were perfectly dry eyes. "It's up to the police to catch this criminal, although they haven't done a very good job of it so far. I have a city to run. My personal tragedy must not keep me from doing my duty." He turned partially back to us, his handkerchief still obscuring most of his face. "Annie, would you please show our guests out? I have some papers to sign."

"Yes sir," Annie said tonelessly. She led us out of the study and back down the hallway. I could see how stiff her back was from behind, and when she turned to let us out her lips were pressed in a thin hard line.

"He doesn't care at all," she said as she opened the door for us. "He's barely even bothering to pretend. Poor Margaret, she at least deserves to have someone grieve for her!"

"She has you," Anne said sympathetically, laying a hand on the woman's shoulder. "Do you really have to stay here, though? It must be terrible to have to deal with him every day now."

"I'm only staying long enough to clear up some of the details with the charities and the funeral," Annie assured her. "As soon as that's done I'll be taking another job in Seattle. There's no way I'm going to act as that man's secretary—I only worked for Margaret."

We drove away in a depressed silence. Even the sight of the ridiculous statue didn't cheer us up much.

"What an awful person," Anne said finally, shaking her head. "I've only met him a few times and he seemed like a stuffed shirt then, but I never dreamed he could care that little about his wife!"

Susan looked thoughtful. "Could that be an act in itself, though?" We looked at her in surprise. "I mean," she continued, "suppose he found out about her affair and killed her himself, or arranged it somehow. Wouldn't it seem less suspicious if he pretended not to care at all than if he looked overwhelmed with emotion? A jealous man would probably be more emotional than he seems to be. Maybe the way he's acting is a kind of double-bluff."

"That seems pretty complicated," I said doubtfully.

"Here." Susan passed around a box of chocolates from Chocolate Noir. "I think we all deserve a chocolate break after that experience."

We agreed, and our spirits rose as we relished the treats. Soon I heard Anne giggle beside me."

"What's up?" I asked.

"That statue," she said. "That *awful* statue!" she burst out laughing.

Susan snorted so hard she inhaled part of a chocolate and spent the next few minutes choking. We were all in a much better mood by the time we dropped Anne off at her house.

"So, what's next on the agenda?" Susan asked as we headed back to Redvue.

"The barbecue. I saw an email from Tara this morning giving us directions. She says we don't have to bring anything, but I think it would be nice to whip up a salad or something to take along."

Susan shook her head. "Rabbit food? For cops? No way. I'm bringing beer, and lots of it. We need to get those guys talking!"

Chapter 18

I parked behind Susan's BMW and pulled out the veggie plate (complete with garlic dip) that I'd bought at a supermarket on the way to the barbeque. Susan was already dragging a case of beer out of her trunk.

"So, I wonder which house it is," she said with a grin.

It was pretty obvious which house was holding the festivities. The modest split-level overflowed with laughing people, and cars were parked all the way down the block. Four sandy-haired boys of varying ages and several adults were tossing a football around on the front lawn while a cloud of smoke billowed from behind the house. The smell was absolutely mouthwatering.

"I smell barbeque," Susan said as we carried our offerings to the front door. "Yum!"

We were greeted by an attractive woman in her late thirties. Her sandy blond hair and bright blue eyes declared her to be the mother of the four young football players.

"Hi, I'm Celia DuFresne—Mark's wife," she said as she led us to the kitchen. "You must be those friends of Tara's I've heard so much about."

Susan held up her hand. "Hey, they can't prove anything!"

Celia laughed. "Don't worry, I've only heard good things. Now where are we going to put this plate?" She took the veggie plate from me and tried to wedge it into a spot on a counter that was already overloaded with chips, containers of dip, salads, cookies, and cakes. A round kitchen table held hot dog and hamburger buns along with every topping imaginable, while another counter offered a huge array of drinks ranging from fine wines to a viciously bright grape soda.

"Wow, and I thought belly dancers threw good spreads," I said, impressed.

"Cops must take their food seriously," Susan agreed while she tried to find a spot for the beer.

Celia rolled her eyes. "Between a house full of police officers and my four boys, there will hardly be a crumb left by tonight. You would not believe how much they can eat!"

"Incoming!" A large, handsome man with light brown hair careened around the corner carrying a huge plate full of freshly-barbequed hot dogs and hamburgers. His entrance startled a white cat that had been sleeping on top of the refrigerator. The white cat leapt down, fixed the man with an outraged stare, hissed and stalked out of the room. "Sorry, Miss Hiss," the man called after it.

A sudden rumble of footsteps behind him announced that he was being closely followed by a hungry crowd.

Celia whipped out two plates and handed them to us. "Get yours now—they'll be gone in about 30 seconds," she laughed.

Mark DuFresne, the man with the plate, set it down and handed me a pair of tongs. "She's right," he said, nodding at the growing crowd in the kitchen, "these won't last long." He planted a kiss on Celia's cheek. "Good luck with the hordes, honey! I'd better get back to the grill."

Susan and I Susan eyed the plate full of grilled goodies. Along with the hot dogs and hamburgers, there were also skewers of different types of meat, seafood and vegetables. I selected a hot dog and a skewer of shrimp and pineapple. Susan chose two cooked-to-perfection hamburgers. We quickly loaded up with toppings while a crowd of men and women swarmed over the barbeque plate. To add to the confusion, the four boys arrived smeared with dirt and grass and apparently dying of starvation. I guessed they ranged in age from 8 to about 13.

"Mom! Bobby took the last hot dog," complained one of the younger ones.

"There are more coming, Daniel," Celia assured him.

A burly African-American man adroitly dipped a hot dog off of his plate onto Daniel's. "Here you go, kid," he said with a grin, messing up Daniel's hair. "Wouldn't want you to die of hunger."

"Thanks, Greg," Celia said. "Here, take another hamburger. King Tut, no!" This last was directed at another cat, an enormous tabby that had appeared out of nowhere to raid the plateful of meat. It gave her an 'I don't know what you're talking about' look out of its huge tawny eyes before disappearing out the back door with an entire hamburger patty in its jaws.

"I think you guys just got cat-burgled," Susan commented, provoking groans from the people still in the kitchen. Most of the crowd had moved outdoors after grabbing their food.

"I'll be happy if he throws up outside after he finishes that," Celia said, brushing her hair out of her face. "He always gets sick after eating human food, but it never stops him."

"That's cats for you," Susan said cheerfully. I could have pointed out the reason that one of her own dogs had ended up with the name 'Upchuck,' but decided that the people in the kitchen didn't need the graphic details.

Once we had our plates loaded, we joined the crowd outside. I spotted Tara in a cluster of people relaxing on the lawn upwind of an impressively large barbeque grill.

Tara saw me at the same time and waved us over. She introduced us to several large men who worked in her department. It struck me that although she was significantly smaller than many of her colleagues, I would back her in any fight. Her slim figure was

158

whipcord-strong, and the confident tilt of her chin indicated that she fully believed in her ability to handle trouble.

It wasn't a guy's-only party, though. There were quite a number of women sprinkled around the back yard. In the midst of Tara's group of friends stood an attractive woman of about 50. In spite of the informal surroundings, she was dressed very nicely in a dark pants suit and heels—which didn't disguise the fact that she had a beautifully curvy figure and probably stood no higher than 5'2"! With her blonde hair piled in an elegant bun on top of her head and her open, friendly face, nobody would ever have guessed she was a cop. Tara introduced us to her first.

"Guys, I want you to meet Detective Dorothy Beresford," she said. "She heads up the identity theft task force in Redvue."

"Call me Dot," the woman said with a friendly grin, putting down her plate to shake hands with us. "I hear that one of you recently had a credit card skimmed?"

Susan stopped munching her burger long enough to nod mournfully.

Dot sighed sympathetically. "It's always a terrible experience for people," she said, looking at Susan. "Tara's been telling me about your experience, and it fits with some of the data we've collected. A number of people living on the Eastside have been victimized, but they don't live or do business anywhere near each other. We've been looking for a common thread—a place all or many of them shopped, got gas, or used ATMs, but they're so spread out it seemed like they didn't move around in the same areas at all."

That made sense. The 'Eastside' of the Seattle area includes a huge swath of country east of Lake Washington, ranging from quickly-growing downtown areas close to the lake to rural areas stretching north, south and east. The rapid growth of technology in the area has created monstrous traffic pretty much everywhere, and people tend to stay in their local areas unless they have to commute. I had recently taken a class in Everett, a city north of us, and had been astounded by how much had changed since the last time I'd been there. Technically it wasn't that far away, but fighting through the traffic to get there was such a pain that I hadn't visited for over a year!

"Could the thieves be moving their skimming equipment around the region, targeting different machines so they're harder to pinpoint?" Susan asked.

Detective Beresford swallowed a bite of salad. "Yes, that's one of the ways they avoid getting caught," she said after a quick drink of water, "but we do expect to see, for instance, a 'hot spot' of activity for a little while. If we can tell that X number of victims used the same ATM within the same time period, it tells us to keep a watch on that location."

"Our best hope is when the criminals get lazy or greedy," Tara interjected. "They leave their skimmers in the same place for too long, or cash in on the stolen numbers immediately after skimming them. Then we can get a really good idea of when and where the thefts are occurring."

160

"That's right," Dot said, "but in this case, we weren't seeing that happen. What we did see was that many of the people whose cards were used illegally all went to the same general area in Downtown Seattle. They either worked there or had recently visited businesses there."

My ears pricked up and I felt a slight chill down my spine. Suddenly I had a feeling I knew what area of Seattle she was talking about. Sure enough, Dot pulled out her cellphone and brought up a map of downtown Seattle. Then she zeroed in on one section and held up the phone so Susan could see the screen. "This is the general area," she said, pointing. "Had you visited any businesses around there within, say, a month before you found out your card had been compromised?"

Susan stared at the screen. It took her a few seconds before she replied. "Yes," she said finally. "I certainly did."

Almost directly in the center of the area on the screen was the street that contained Deerborne Florist.

Chapter 19

We stared at the screen for a few seconds more. Then Susan and I both darted questioning looks at Tara. A slight shake of her head indicated that she didn't want us to point out the coincidence, at least not yet.

Susan turned to Dot. "I used my card in a couple of places on this street, a week before the hold was put on it," she said, pointing to the street on the camera. "Do you think that's where the number got skimmed?"

"Yes, if you used your card in that area at that time it fits in very well, but to find out your card has been skimmed within a week is actually pretty fast. It's not like stealing the physical card, which

162

alerts the victim to cancel it as soon as they realize it's gone. A skimmed number can be used anytime, without the owner being any the wiser. Smart crooks wait a while before using your number, just to confuse the issue. Still," she flashed a big grin, "they do get greedy, and that's when we get them! I'd like to get a complete list of all the places you used your card, if you don't mind."

Susan growled. "Mind?! I'll give you every bit of information I can if it will help your catch those creeps. I had to go without my credit card for over a *week*!"

I snickered. For my friend, a week without credit cards would have been unendurable.

Dot laughed. "It's irritating, I know, but at least we have some laws in place now that protect you from being liable, at least for credit card fraud. Debit cards are much less safe. Of course, the card companies themselves are always coming up with new ways to make the cards secure, but those measures get hacked pretty fast."

"Who does this kind of thing?" I asked, curious. "Is it gangs, or just individual people who have the right technology?"

"The answer to that is yes and yes," Dot said, rolling her eyes. "It's a complicated issue, because nowadays the card skimmers are easy to get. Organized crime does get involved, but so do smaller groups and even individuals. Just last month we broke up a ring in Tacoma—there were six people involved, and together they had stolen several hundred thousand dollars' worth of cash and items purchased online. They completely cleaned out one elderly woman's savings account using her debit card and PIN, which they got from mounting a camera and a skimmer on the ATM she used. I'm happy to say we'll be able to get most of that money back to her, but a lot of victims aren't as lucky."

"Good for you," Susan cheered. "You're like a superhero!"

Dot laughed. "It always feels good when we can help people get their money back or help restore their credit. It doesn't happen nearly enough, though. Even though we cooperate with all the other police departments and the prosecutor's office, we just never have enough people to analyze and track the data."

"Sounds tough," Susan said.

Dot's eyes twinkled. "It keeps us busy," she agreed. "Bradley here is one of my chief analysts," she added nodding at one of the men in the group. "He spends most of his time looking at reports and crunching numbers. He's the one who identified the area where we think your ring might be centered."

"Don't call them *my* ring," Susan protested. She fixed Bradley with a stare. "I want you to get those guys!"

Bradley threw her a mock salute. "Yes, Ma'am!"

Dot drew out a small card case and handed us each a business card. "Here's my phone number and e-mail, if either of you can think of anything else that might be helpful," she said. "We're always happy to get information from the public. By the way, Ginger," she said to me, "I absolutely love your name—I have a huge orange cat that we call 'Big Ginge!'"

Susan eyed me and burst out laughing. "I'm calling you that from now on," she teased.

164

"Try it," I said.

At this point our conversation was interrupted by a screech of microphone feedback. Mark Dufresne had abandoned the grill and picked up a microphone, and the earsplitting sound it made sent a yard full of brave officers diving for cover.

"Sorry everybody, just some technical difficulties," Mark said. This was greeted by a number of hoots and several rude remarks.

"I know you've all been waiting for this," he continued as the hubbub died down, "so without further ado, here we are—Dufresne and the Blue Lines!"

A number of other officers had joined him on the deck. One went to a keyboard, another carried a guitar, and a third took a seat at a drum set. Celia had appeared and was pushing buttons on a sound control panel. For the first time I noticed two large speakers on the deck.

"Hoo, boy, what are we in for?" Susan murmured to Tara.

"They're actually pretty good," Tara whispered back, "but they're *loud,* too. I came prepared." She surreptitiously pulled a small baggie containing several pairs of earplugs from her pants pocket. "You might want some of these."

Susan and I each took a pair, but waited to see how loud the music would be before inserting them.

Tara had been right on both counts. The blues band played well, but like so many bands, they had their amplifiers cranked up way too loud. Fortunately, Celia noticed this and tweaked something on the soundboard. The music settled into a slightly more tolerable range. I slipped the earplugs into my pocket, just in case.

Mark Dufresne had a pretty good voice, and he and the band had apparently written their own songs, too. The crowd laughed as they sang 'On the Beat Blues,' complete with a harmonica solo played by Mark. "You Can't Use Your Siren for That' and 'Hell Yeah, I Have a Badge' were also well-received, but the crowd's favorite seemed to be a blues ballad called 'The Pissed-off Possum in Parker's Patrol Car."

"Where do they get this stuff?" Susan shouted to Tara, tears streaming down her face. She was laughing so hard I thought she would choke.

"Real life!" Tara yelled back. "Last year this *huge* possum got into Officer Parker's patrol car—nobody's sure how, but he blames his partner who was 'sick' that day. Anyway, it didn't want to leave. Even the police dogs were terrified of it. It ripped that car to shreds before they were able to lure it out with some donuts."

"Police with donuts? Imagine that."

"Funnn-ny!" Tara finger-flicked Susan on the back of her head.

"Ow, police brutality," Susan complained, trying to flick her back.

The party was soon in full swing. The band had an infectious rhythm, and soon a few brave people got up and started dancing. Not to be outdone, the three of us who were belly dancers got up, too. Soon Tara, Susan and I were leading the dancing crowd in hip and shoulder shimmies.

166

The only awkward moment came when Detective Harris arrived and accidentally stumbled into Tara as he tried to avoid a collision with a lady carrying four cups of soda. Their eyes met, and Tara's expression immediately turned icy cold. Without a word she turned and walked away. Detective Harris stared after her, looking somewhat bewildered. I felt a little bit sorry for him.

Susan had noticed the exchange as well. She nudged me and gave me a knowing look. "He liiiikes her," she sang into my ear.

"Shhhh!" I said, giving her a return dig with my elbow. "He might hear you."

We spent the rest of the afternoon watching Tara and Detective Harris avoid each other. It was like a watching a pair of magnets repel each other. If one of them went to the grill, the other moved away to the far side of the lawn. If one of them sat down to watch the band, the other gravitated toward the kitchen.

Susan ground her teeth in frustration. "Oh my god, it's like we're in junior high again! Why can't they just admit they like each other and talk like regular adults?"

"It's none of our business," I said. "They'll just have to work things out on their own."

In spite of my words, I found their behavior irritating as well. For one thing, Tara was trying so hard not to be anyplace Detective Harris might be that she wasn't helping us gain more information about Harry's case. Without Tara, we didn't have anyone to introduce us to the other cops, or to tell us who might be a valuable source of information.

Even so, I nixed Susan's idea of walking up to Detective Harris and telling him 'to stop being a jackass and go ask Tara out.' I pointed out that Tara was still so mad about being kept off Harry's case that any suggestion of romance from Detective Harris would result in an impressive explosion. I did *not* want to be responsible for that. Shoot, I didn't want to be anywhere near when it happened!

Susan shrugged grumpily and munched on a huge oatmeal raisin cookie in a rebellious silence.

Finally, we decided that we'd both had enough. We managed to corner Tara to tell her we were leaving. She seemed too distracted to care. Then we found our hostess, thanked her for the party and the wonderful food, and headed for our cars.

Susan was still gloomy.

"Chin up," I said, "we actually did find out something important. There's an identity theft ring operating in the same neighborhood as Deerborne Florist! If nothing else, it's a pretty big coincidence. Who knows, there might be a connection between that and Chuck's death."

A thoughtful look started to spread across Susan's face. "You know, a couple of things those two kids at Deerborne's said could tie in. Remember how Ellie said Chuck had suddenly become best friends with Bill Ellis? And, oh, what was his name—Peter?—said that Chuck was on his phone more than normal, and we thought it might have been with Marla?

I nodded slowly. "And what was it that Ellie said she overheard between Chuck and Marla? Something about 'doing something too often' and needing to be careful? What if she wasn't talking about his flirting? What he was skimming too many cards from the same location?"

"Like *my* card!" Susan fumed, getting the idea. "I'll bet the little turd skimmed my card when I paid for the wishing tree! It would have been the perfect opportunity."

"It's certainly possible," I said. "Dot did say that getting greedy was what gets a lot of identity thieves caught. Chuck could have been getting greedy—and just plain lazy—by using the skimmer right where he worked, and cashing in on the numbers too soon."

I was starting to feel excited. "You know, this is actually starting to make sense! If Chuck, Marla, and maybe Bill Ellis were part of a theft ring, and Chuck was putting them in danger, that would be a whole new motive for Chuck's murder."

"It's certainly a better motive than Harry's," Susan said, "and Bill Ellis was actually there at the wedding."

I had been about to unlock my car, but now I put the keys back in my pocket. "We should go back to the barbeque," I said. "Dot and her team need to know what we've figured out. Detective Harris, too."

Susan held up her hand. "No. We don't have any proof of anything, just a few ideas about what might have happened. If we go to Dot or Detective Harris, it'll come out that Tara is still looking into Chuck's death. She could get fired, and they probably wouldn't take our suspicions seriously anyway."

"Well, have you got a better idea, Sherlock?"

A slow, sneaky smile spread across Susan's face. I knew that look, and it filled me with suspicion. "As a matter of fact, I have," Susan said, "but it's going to take some work before we're ready."

That didn't sound good. "Ready for what, exactly?" I demanded.

But Susan just gave me a little wave, got into her car, and drove away.

Chapter 20

I didn't have much time to worry about Susan and her dubious plans that night. When I got home, I found Michael in a life-or-death struggle with Banshee over the kitchen sink. Soap suds and water were everywhere.

"What on earth is on her fur?" I wailed. Banshee's fur dripped with a strange, iridescent black substance. Michael was splattered all over with the same substance. Banshee's eyes were shooting sparks of fury and Michael's forearms dripped with freshly-drawn blood.

"Just grab her scruff and hold on," Michael said grimly.

The next few minutes were unprintable. We scrubbed Banshee numerous times with cat shampoo, then thoroughly rinsed her and got her bundled into a succession of towels. By the time it was over all three of us were using language that would have gotten us kicked out of a sailor convention.

When Banshee was finally ensconced deep into a dry towel—our last—and emitting only muffled growls and faint threats of what she was going to do to us later, I turned on Michael.

"What—the hell—happened!?" I panted.

Michael cradled Banshee in one arm as he gingerly sucked blood out of his other wrist. "It was an accident," he began feebly.

"I guessed that," I said, rinsing my own scratched arms under the sink.

"Well, I was in the garage working on some stuff, and I had an open oil can on the bench…"

"She isn't supposed to *be* in the garage!" I pointed out.

Michael rolled his eyes at me. "You know that doesn't stop her," he said.

I knew. We did our best to keep Banshee inside, but despite our best efforts she occasionally slipped past us. The previous owners of our house had installed a cat door in the garage, and although we had nailed it shut, Banshee somehow knew that freedom lay beyond it. Every time we went in or out of the kitchen door that opened into the garage, Banshee was there trying to dodge past us.

"I came inside to get a drink of water, and when I opened the door to get back in the garage, she ran between my feet and tripped me."

Looking at him more closely now, I saw that he had a large bruise blossoming on one of his temples, and another one on the hand that

172

had sustained the worst of the scratches. "Are you OK?" I asked, concerned.

Hu shrugged it off. "It's just a couple of bumps. Luckily I caught hold of the broom by the door and it broke my fall a little. Anyway, by the time I got back up she'd already knocked over the oil can, panicked, and was tearing around the garage. I finally pinned her down behind the work bench, but by then she was pretty much covered with oil. I knew I couldn't let her lick any of it off, so she went straight into the sink. That's about when you walked in."

"Thank goodness you caught her before she ingested any," I said. "She could have been poisoned!" I cautiously scratched an ear that was sticking out of the towel. The growling from the towel became more distinct.

"Yeah, you might not want to do that just yet," Michael said, giving the bundle in his arms the same kind of look actors do in movies when they realize they're holding a live grenade. "I don't think she's quite ready to socialize. Unless," he paused, his expression looking even less happy, "you think we should blow-dry her or something. Could she catch a cold? You're the animal expert."

I shuddered. "Nobody needs that," I said quickly. Let's just towel-dry her as much as we can, and turn up the heat a little so she won't get cold."

Michael thrust the wrapped-up cat into my arms. "*You* towel-dry her! I need a shower."

"Coward." Banshee was recovering her wits now, squirming and kicking against the towel. The growl became more pronounced and ominous.

"You got that right!" Michael disappeared up the stairs and into the bathroom.

Later that night, when things had settled down and Banshee, now mostly dry, had been mollified with her favorite canned food, Michael and I relaxed into our couch and ate a pizza I had discovered in the freezer. We were both sporting bandages, and neither of us felt up to cooking.

"Did you have fun at your friend's barbeque?" Michael asked, lazily surfing through programs with the remote. I had invited him to come along that morning, knowing he would refuse. Even the promise of barbeque wasn't enough to lure him into what he expected to be a gathering of dancers. I hadn't mentioned the fact that most of the attendees would be cops.

"Yeah, we had a good time," I replied vaguely. "A live band and lots of dancing." Which was perfectly true, after all.

"Sorry I missed it," he said.

"Liar," I laughed. "I know a day of dancing isn't really your idea of a good time." A new thought occurred to me. "What were you working on, anyway? You hardly ever use the workbench—garages are more Jim's territory."

"Oh, I tinker every once in a while," Michael said, huffing up indignantly. "I don't *just* work on computers. What, you don't think I'm enough of a he-man?"

"I don't know," I said, getting up from the couch. "We could go upstairs and find out." I threw him an inviting glance as I left the room.

It was only later that night that I realized he hadn't answered my question.

Chapter 21

Monday marked the day that Buster was moved into his new enclosure, so it was all hands on deck. He had to be lured from his smaller enclosure into a cage, which was not something he wanted to do. We used various baits and waited patiently, but the young cougar refused to move.

Finally, tired of waiting, Trey removed an object from his pocket, tossed it between the bars and yelled, "Go get it, Buster!" To everyone's astonishment, Buster immediately sprang into the cage after the object. Bang went the trapdoor, and Buster was locked up and ready to change habitats.

"Catnip mouse," Trey explained as we stared at him.

"Good idea," said George, "but I'll bet it's not going to last very long."

Next the cage was covered by a thick blanket, to minimize stress on the cat as he was carried to the brand new Green Room. Once everyone was clear, the trapdoor was lifted and Buster trotted out, the catnip mouse still in his jaws. He still limped a little, but Nancy had assured us that exercise in the larger space would help strengthen his leg. All of the workers applauded as Buster made his first round of the space, and George's face beamed with happiness.

By the time things settled down I had worked up an appetite, and realized I'd forgotten to bring my lunch. "Hey, guys," I said, sticking my head into the room where Trey and Dennis were giving baby birds their noontime feeding, "I'm heading over to the sandwich place, do either of you want anything?"

Trey decided on a roast beef hoagie, and Dennis requested a batch of jalapeno fries. I headed out the door and walked down the road to Ernie's Snack Shack, a little deli that specialized in gourmet sandwiches and fresh-cut fries. I tried not to go there too often, since their sandwiches tended to be on the high-calorie side, but I enjoyed indulging every once in a while.

I was waiting for my order when a familiar figure walked in. "Detective Harris?" I asked in surprise. "I've never seen you here before."

He smiled. "I happened to be in in this part of town for a meeting, so I thought I'd drop in. They have good sandwiches here."

"I know," I said ruefully, "almost too good!"

177

Detective Harris laughed, and joined me at the table where I was waiting. He was a good-looking man, I thought, and from everything I had seen of him, a nice one. It was too bad Tara was so angry at him.

I was just wondering if I should bring up the subject when Detective Harris broke the silence. "Listen, I'm glad I ran into you," he said, sounding a little awkward. "Would you mind if I asked you about something?"

"Isn't asking people things your job, more or less?" I asked cautiously. Was he wanting to talk about the case or Tara?

We were interrupted by a waitress handing me a huge bag of food. "Yours is coming right up, sir," she told Detective Harris.

"Why don't we go talk in my office at Wild in Redvue?" I suggested. "Two of these orders are for my workers." He agreed, and when his order came he gave me a lift in his car.

As we pulled up in front of the sanctuary, a large Jeep pulled up beside us. The doors immediately flew open and two of our wildlife rehabilitators scrambled out. They were both gasping for air, and the minute I stepped out of the car I knew why.

"Davis! Ryan! What on earth—?" I stopped, choking myself. I noticed that Detective Harris had taken several steps backward.

"You know that lady who called this morning because she heard weird noises in her shed?" Davis Myer said.

"Let me guess," I said. "A skunk?"

"Not *a* skunk," Ryan Fowling said proudly. "Six skunks! Babies." He opened the back of his vehicle and pulled out a carrier covered by a heavy blanket. Growling and squealing sounds came from inside, along with a very distinctive smell.

The smell wasn't contained by the carrier, though. "Oh, no," I groaned, "did you guys get sprayed?"

"Not me," Ryan said, pointing to his partner. "Him. And was it ever not fun to be in the same car with him."

At this point Trey came outside. "Got some new visitors for us? Whoa! Somebody here does *not* smell good!"

"Him," Ryan said, pointing again.

Trey coughed and laughed at the same time. "Oh, man, you must have gotten hosed!"

Davis nodded glumly. Then he brightened. "We got all six of them, though. They're pretty thin, so something must have happened to the mom. It's a good thing that lady called us when she did."

I took charge. "Davis, go do the hydrogen peroxide and baking soda thing, shower and get into new overalls. Put yours in the wash *with bleach*! Trey, take the babies in to Nancy and have Pete help her get them weighed and measured. After that, I've got your lunch. I'll leave it in the break room."

Trey grimaced. "I'm not all that hungry now," he said sadly. I didn't worry, knowing that few things were capable of destroying Trey's appetite for long.

In the break room I handed Dennis his fries and left the bag containing Trey's food. Then I led Detective Harris to my office.

"Busy day?" he asked sympathetically. I was amused to see that his eyes were watering badly. I handed him a box of tissues, and took one for myself. Even as babies, skunks can produce some intensely noxious fumes!

"It's not the first time," I said with a sigh.

"I always thought tomato juice was the thing for skunk spray."

"Tomato juice doesn't do much more than mask the smell. Skunk spray has oils that are really hard to get off. Our usual recipe is about a quart of hydrogen peroxide with a quarter cup of baking soda and a few drops of dish soap. After that, it's lather, rinse, repeat."

Detective Harris laughed. "Well, it certainly sounds like you're prepared—you actually have a shower here?"

"Oh, yeah. And extra overalls in all sizes. Most of us also keep a change of clothes in our lockers, just in case."

By now we were settled into my office, with Detective Harris sitting across from me and our lunches spread on my desk. It seemed like a good time to find out what was on his mind.

"So, Detective Harris," I began.

"Call me John, please," he said.

"Thanks," I said, "and call me Ginger. What would you like to talk about?"

Detective Harris swallowed a bite of sandwich, but didn't continue immediately. He looked uncomfortable and—was I imagining it? He even looked like he was blushing slightly. I decided to help him out.

"Was it," I said, trying to choose my words delicately, "something about Tara?"

Now he was definitely blushing. I felt the corners of my mouth beginning to twitch. Susan had been right all along. But then, she was unusually skillful in sniffing out budding romances.

"Yes," he said, clearing his throat. "I understand that you and Mrs. Barry are close friends of hers, and I was wondering if, well, if you might know..." his voice faltered.

Oh my god, I thought, *it really is just like being in Junior High again.* This was a full-grown man, a police detective, trained both in combat and the art of detection. Presumably he had encountered many tough characters and situations in his life, but nothing had prepared him for the simple problem of finding out whether or not a girl liked him. I picked up my sandwich and took a bite to hide the fact that I was seconds away from cracking up.

"You see," he said in a rush, "Ms. Ericson and I have always seemed to be on good terms, but lately she's been acting as though I've done something wrong. She won't talk to me."

I sighed. "Have you considered the possibility that she's upset because you got her blocked from doing any work on the Chuck McKenzie murder case? She's a very good friend of the man accused of doing it."

"Which is exactly why she can't be on that case!" Detective Harris—or John—exclaimed.

"Do you think she'd suppress evidence against him if she found it? She was the one who told you about the argument Harry had with Chuck, remember."

181

"Of course I don't think she would," he said indignantly. "Ms. Ericson is one of the best officers we have on the force. She would never compromise an investigation, no matter what her personal feelings were."

"Then why not let her at least help?" I suggested.

He suddenly looked miserable, and again I felt sorry for him. "What if she found concrete evidence that Harry Deerborne is guilty?" he asked, running a hand over his close-cropped hair. "Of course she would turn it in, there's no question about it, but can you imagine how she'd feel? That's why it is standard procedure not to have officers work on cases that involve their friends and family. I had to make sure the Chief knew the situation."

I smiled. "You care about her."

"Well, yes," he admitted. "I have a—very high regard for her, and I would hate to see her get hurt."

At this point, what could have become a serious conversation was interrupted by a crash and shouts from outside my door. Detective Harris rose out of his seat, sensing trouble, but I just rolled my eyes and used the opportunity to take a bite of my sandwich.

"Trey!" This time it was Nancy King shouting. "Come and get your damn raccoon!"

This was followed by the all-too-familiar sounds of chittering, pursuit, laughter and swearing. Seeing that I was unconcerned, Detective Harris resumed his seat. I, on the other hand, swallowed my bite, sighed, and went to open my office door to look out.

Right on cue, Trey trotted up to my office with a wriggling, chattering Houdini in his arms. Detective Harris' eyebrows rose.

"Hey, Ginger," Trey greeted me cheerfully. "Everything's under control." He nodded at Houdini, who had started to growl and bite at Trey's thick safety gloves in a friendly way.

"That's wonderful, Trey," I said. "Now get him out of here before he poops all over everything."

But Trey had spotted Detective Harris sitting in my office. "Oh, wow, you're that policeman who was on TV!" Trey's eyes were wide with admiration. "So, you're like, a *real* detective, aren't you? With a badge and everything?"

"Yes," Detective Harris said cautiously.

"Trey," I started to say.

"So you're the guy in charge of all the murders. Solving them, I mean, not doing them. Wow. And you catch all the bad guys."

A smile twitched at the corners of Detective Harris' mouth. "We try," he said. "Looks like you've caught a criminal there yourself." Houdini, startled by the new voice, looked at the detective and bared his teeth. "A pretty tough one," Detective Harris added.

"Awww, no, he's really a sweetie," Trey said, giving Houdini a little squeeze. "He just likes to break in every now and then." Houdini chittered back at him and then went back to trying to bite through his gloves.

Trey continued to stare at Detective Harris in awe. "So, Detective...,"

"Harris," he supplied.

183

"So Detective Harris, do you have any criminals that you catch over and over again, but if they didn't keep doing stuff and getting arrested you'd kind of miss them?" He affectionately scratched Houdini on the top of the head. Houdini snapped at his hand.

Detective Harris shook his head. "I can't think of anyone, offhand," he said.

"*Trey*," I said, louder this time.

"I know, I know," he said, taking a firmer hand on Houdini's scruff. "Get him out of here before he poops—whoops, too late on that one!"

Sure enough, a couple of dark objects plopped down Trey's front and landed on the floor. The room filled with an unpleasant odor. "Sorry, Ginger," Trey said. "I'll take him out and get that cleaned up." He flashed Detective Harris a friendly grin. "Not to worry, officer, this is why God gave us overalls!" Whistling, he turned and headed outside with his captive.

A funk-filled silence followed. At last Detective Harris said, "You have an—interesting job."

"Why don't we go to the break room while that gets cleaned up?" I suggested.

We both gingerly stepped over the raccoon scat and left the room.

"Actually, I need to get going," Detective Harris said. "I really appreciate you taking the time to talk to me." Despite the comedy relief we'd just had, he still looked glum.

"Listen," I said as we paused in the hallway, "the truth is that Tara hasn't spoken to us about you very much, except that she is upset

184

about being kicked out of the investigation. Maybe you just need to talk to her about your reasons. If she realizes that you do respect her abilities, she won't feel so insulted and maybe you can get back to being friends." I smiled at him. "If it makes you feel any better, Susan believes that Tara really does like you, and that's the reason she's taking this so hard. Susan's hardly ever wrong about things like that. Maybe you and Tara just need to clear the air."

"I hope you're right," he said, looking a little brighter.

We shook hands, and Detective Harris headed for his car. Trey, coming back from the area where he usually deposited Houdini, waved at him as he left.

"What a day," I said to myself.

Chapter 22

At our Tuesday night bellydance class, I filled Susan in on my strange conversation with Detective Harris.

"Whoop!" Susan cheered. "Was I right or was I right? Now all we have to do is get ahold of Tara and—"

"No," I said firmly. "We have to stay out of this, it's none of our business."

"Says the person handing out *luuuv* advice to our handsome detective. Besides, when has that ever stopped us before?"

"It's never stopped you, anyway," I said, "but in this case I think we need to let them work this out on their own. They're adults."

"They certainly aren't acting like it," Susan grumbled. "OK, fine, we'll give them a couple of days to get their act together. Besides," she added with a grin, "I don't know if I could keep a straight face around Tara right now. I've got the best plan to get more information and she wouldn't let us do it if she knew! If I go around her looking guilty she might get suspicious and figure it out."

A feeling of impending doom crept over me. "What exactly are these plans of yours?" I demanded.

At this point Anne clapped her hands to get our attention and start the class.

"Tell you later," Susan whispered gleefully.

"Gather around everybody," Anne said, "I've got the costumes here and I want to get everyone fitted so we can start practicing in them. The sleeves will make a big difference in the way you can swing your sticks and I want you to start getting used to it now."

Everyone ooh'd and ahh'd as Anne pulled the glittering Beledi dresses from their box. The dresses were stretchy enough to accommodate different figure types, and Anne had done some preliminary sorting by length so she had an idea of which costumes would fit which dancers. Even so, Susan's turned out to be a little short.

"My ankles show," Susan complained. "Nobody else's ankles show! It looks weird."

Anne sighed. "I had a feeling it would be too short, but it's the longest one I have. When I made these, there wasn't anyone in the troupe as tall as you." She examined the hem with a practiced eye. "I can take it down by about half an inch, but that's all."

"My ankles will still show," Susan said with a worried look in the mirror. "I have boney-looking ankles, too."

"Everybody has bones in their ankles, Dummy," I said unsympathetically. I've always wanted to be a little bit taller. "We couldn't stand on them if we didn't."

Susan just made a face at me and continued frowning at her feet.

"It isn't that bad," Anne said. "I'll take it home and add some trim to the bottom once I let out the hem. It will work for practice tonight, though."

A few other dancers were going to need slight adjustments on their dresses as well, and Anne quickly marked the trouble spots with safety pins before having us line up for practice. I could tell some of the shorter ones were regarding Susan's height with envy, while she was slumping to try to be shorter.

"You know what?" I said quietly, slipping an arm around Susan's shoulders, "We're all being stupid. Everybody in here is different, and everybody in here is beautiful. I think you have nice ankles. In fact, you have fantastic legs—even Michael thinks so."

Susan, who had been looking a bit more cheerful when I began my pep talk, gave me a sudden frown. "Is that so?" she asked suspiciously. "It's nice of you to say so, but why would *your* husband be making comments about *my* legs?"

"He didn't," I said hastily. "I mentioned it once and he agreed with me, that's all." I decided not to add that he had very quickly

188

stated that my legs were ten times nicer—perhaps worrying that he had been unwise in offering any opinion on the subject of Susan's legs, even if it had been to agree with me.

Susan gave me a look. "So you're talking to Michael about my legs? That's kind of weird, you know."

Feeling that if I heard one more mention of ankles or legs or any other appendage I was going to scream, I picked up my tahtib stick and threatened to smack her with it. She grabbed her own, and Anne used this as an opportunity to get the class back in order.

"Everybody pick up your sticks like Ginger and Susan, and I'll show you how to hold your sleeves so they aren't in the way."

We soon learned why Anne wanted us to start practicing in costume. If we held our right sleeves correctly (pinned securely to the body with the left hand) the sticks didn't catch on them. If we forgot, or if the stick came too close to the left sleeve, the stick would catch a sleeve and go flying. Even if we did have the sleeves under control, we weren't used to dancing in floor-length dresses. A few of the students, myself included, snagged the ends of our skirts with our sticks. Susan and I were concentrating on sleeve-wrangling so hard that when it came time to grab the stick with both hands, spin and hit our sticks together, we did it wrong and banged our fists together instead.

"Dang! I thought we had this move," Susan said as she sucked her knuckles.

"Me, too," I said as I vigorously shook out my hand, trying to confuse the pain signals. "Looks like we can only concentrate on one thing at a time."

"It will get easier," Anne promised as the class prepared to head home. "Don't forget, for the next three weeks I want everyone who can make it to come here at noon on Sunday. We'll be doing extra rehearsals to get ready for the festival. It's only a few weeks away, ladies!"

"If we live that long," Susan moaned, looking at her bruised knuckles.

I laughed. "If nothing else, our reflexes are getting a good workout. We'll be real martial artists by the time we're done here."

"And our hands will be as tough as leather from all the times we smack them with each other's sticks. Move over, Bruce Lee!"

Once we had left the studio and were about to get into our cars, I decided it was time to find out what Susan's "plans" were. "OK, what's this big secret idea you've had and why wouldn't Tara like it?" I demanded.

A smile I knew well and had learned to dread crossed my friend's face. "So, the guys have this big extra practice on Thursday night, right?"

"Yes," I said cautiously.

"Turns out, that's the perfect time to go do some sleuthing. There's a big art gallery show happening downtown, and Chocolate Noir will be one of the caterers. I found out about it through one of my artist friends. It should be a big deal for such a little shop, so you can bet Marla's going to be there. That means we can go have a snoop in the store and the apartment above it!"

"What?!" I gasped.

"Hear me out," Susan said, holding out a hand. "I did some checking and found out that Marla actually lives right above the shop. We can search both places at once. If she is involved with the identity theft ring, there might be evidence in one or both places."

By this time, I had managed to catch my breath. "Let me get this straight, Susan," I said. "Your big plan is to break in to a business and a residence to find evidence that we couldn't even tell the police about because we did something completely illegal to get? Next plan, please."

"Well, when you put it that way it sounds bad, sure, but we could phone in an anonymous tip if we found something. Then the police would go in and find it themselves."

"No," I said firmly. I had a vision of alarms going off and both of us being hauled away in handcuffs. I described it to Susan.

"I don't know about the apartment, but the shop doesn't look like it has an alarm. I noticed it the last time we were there. Maybe Marla feels confident enough not to have one because it's a nice part of town and she lives right there in case anything happens."

"No," I repeated.

"Oh, come on," Susan said persuasively. "There's no way we could get caught—Marla will be gone, and the shop will be closed. None of the other businesses around there are open at night either, so there'll be nobody to see us. We won't be stealing anything, so there won't be anything to show Marla we've been there. We won't be breaking in, either—I can get us in, easy!"

I already knew this from a previous adventure. Susan's career as a graphic artist brought her into contact with people from a wide number of industries. She had once done a series of ads for a locksmith, who had taught her a few tricks of the trade for fun, surely never expecting her to actually use the expertise. The time she had used it, things had not gone well.

"The last time I let you break into someplace we almost got killed," I reminded her.

"But we didn't, and we caught the criminal," she insisted. "plus this time we actually know where the criminal will be so she can't catch us! Anyway, I'm just going to pick a few locks. It's not breaking in if you don't break anything."

"I think Tara would disagree."

"That's why she can't know. Come on, you don't want Harry to go to jail, do you?"

"No," I said, feeling my will weaken.

"Then we're all set. We won't be hurting anybody or damaging anything, and if we don't find anything suspicious we can cross Marla off the suspect list. She'd want us to do that, wouldn't she? If she's innocent we'd be doing her a huge favor."

The way Susan's mind works never ceases to astound me. Logic has a whole different meaning to her than it does to ordinary people. I opened my mouth to lodge a feeble protest, but Susan interrupted my thoughts.

"Do you get it? Great! Remember, there's no risk to us, and we might end up doing a lot of good—it's a win-win. I'll pick you up at 7:30 on Thursday!"

And before I had a chance to say anything else, Susan jumped into her car and peeled out of the parking lot.

Chapter 23

Wednesday passed by in a blur as I dealt with a number of crises at the wildlife shelter. June is when a lot of spring babies start venturing out and getting themselves into trouble. We had two juvenile crows, a mink, and a young bobcat come in within the space of two hours, and between getting the youngsters settled (happily none of them were seriously injured) and coping with the everyday tasks of the shelter, I didn't have a chance to formulate a good argument against Susan's plan.

Thursday brought much of the same, and at 7 p.m. I found myself saying goodbye to Michael without having had a chance to talk to Susan. I had called her cell phone once, but there had been no answer.

Probably she was avoiding me until zero hour to prevent me from chickening out.

"Don't wait up for us," Michael was saying cheerfully as he hitched his bagpipe bag over his shoulder. "We're working on something special and it might go late. Do you and Susan have anything fun planned for tonight?"

I managed a faint grin. "Um, you know Susan," I said, giving him a quick kiss. "Just full of ideas."

Michael rolled his eyes. "Don't I know it. Don't get into too much trouble. See you." He went out the door.

I spent the next half hour worrying. Susan pulled up at 7:30 sharp and entered with a springy step. "Are you all ready to go?" She looked at me and added, "For Pete's sake, is that what you're wearing?"

"What's wrong with it?" I asked. I had put on a fresh pair of cargo pants and a T-shirt, my standard uniform at the shelter.

"Wrong with it?" Susan demanded. "What part of being stealthy don't you understand? Your pants are practically white, and so is all of that skin you're showing! You're going to glow in the dark."

By this time, I had noticed that Susan was pretty much dressed as a ninja. She wore a black hoodie, black yoga pants, black gloves and black tennis shoes. Even her hair was pulled back with a black scrunchy. She needed only a balaclava to complete the look.

"My pants aren't white, they're khaki," I argued, "and at least I look like a normal person. Your outfit screams 'I'm going to burgle somebody tonight!'"

"Everything you have on will reflect light," Susan declared, ignoring my comment. "Change."

Black tends to make me look washed out, so I don't have a lot of black things in my wardrobe. Susan was finally satisfied with a dark pair of jeans, a long-sleeved brown shirt and a deep green scarf over my bright hair. She also insisted that I put on a pair of dark gloves. I hoped we weren't going to stop anywhere coming or going.

"That'll have to do," she said finally. "Let's go."

My stomach felt queasy as we headed west. I hoped against hope that we would find the little shop open and the street teeming with people when we got there, forcing Susan to abandon her hair-brained scheme. No such luck. Exactly as she had predicted, Chocolate Noir and the apartment above it were dark, as were all of the businesses on the deserted street. There wasn't even a coffee shop in the immediate vicinity. Odd for Seattle.

"Perfect!" Susan crowed as we made a slow pass down the street. "This'll be a piece of cake." She pulled into the alleyway behind Chocolate Noir and Deerborne Florist and drove a block or two down it. "We don't want to park too close," she said.

"Why not? We might want to make a quick getaway."

"There's absolutely no reason why we might need to 'make a getaway' as you put it," Susan said firmly, "but if somebody happens to drive by and notices our car it would be better if it weren't right outside Chocolate Noir or Harry's."

This didn't make any sense to me. If we weren't actually stealing or breaking anything, it shouldn't matter if somebody noticed our car—it wouldn't be connected to any crime. Susan was adamant, however, and we compromised on parking just one block away.

"OK, this is it," she said, pulling her hoodie over her head and tightening the drawstrings around her face until only the tip of her nose was visible. "Now pull your scarf over your face."

"What? How am I supposed to see?"

"It's sheer enough to see through a little. Stop whining."

If we hadn't looked suspicious before, we definitely did by the time we exited the car. Faces shrouded and heads down, we ducked into the shadows and skulked our way up the block to the corner occupied by Chocolate Noir. Susan was tiptoeing like a cartoon character. I would have laughed at her, but I noticed that I was doing the same thing. It seemed like forever before we finally stood at the back entrance.

Susan fumbled with a key ring to which various lock picking tools had been attached. In that deserted street, they sounded louder than a set of finger cymbals going full blast. I mentally cursed the client who had taught Susan the fine art of lock-picking.

"Geez, Susan, do you think you could make a little more noise with those things?" I hissed.

"Would you be quiet, I'm trying to focus here." One after the other, she tried inserting her tools into the lock. The minutes ticked by as she jiggled them around, swore, reinserted them, jiggled them some more and pulled on the door handle.

"We should go," I urged. "Half of Seattle could have seen us by now!"

"Shhh, I've just about got it," she insisted.

I was about to disagree and demand that we leave when we both heard a faint click.

"Oh, yeah!" Susan cheered. I quickly shushed her. She turned the handle, opened the door and we tiptoed inside.

"Wow, it's really dark in here," whispered Susan as she quietly pulled the door shut behind us.

I had already discovered this, having stubbed my toe against a trash can that stood by the door. I pulled a small LED flashlight from my purse and set it to red light, which I thought would be less visible from the outside. We looked around.

We were in a small hallway with a staircase on the left and a bathroom on the right. Straight ahead was a doorway that, to judge from the smells that came from it, led to the kitchen and shop. We went there first.

The gourmet kitchen had a few dim emergency lights in the ceiling, so we were able to see without our flashlights. The area was spotlessly clean, with gleaming stainless steel counters, trays, vats and refrigerators. Whisks and other mysterious tools of the chocolatier's trade hung from hooks. The intoxicating smell of chocolate permeated every nook and cranny.

"Check this out," Susan whispered, "I think I want to live here!"

I sternly turned my mind from the tempting aroma. "Focus, Susan—we need to look for evidence and then get out of here as fast as we can."

A brief search of the kitchen yielded nothing suspicious, and we proceeded into the shop itself. This made us both nervous, because there were emergency lights here as well, and if somebody passed by they might notice us inside. I had visions of us getting hauled away by the police, and wondered how I was going to explain it to Michael.

"I don't think we need to look at anything but the cash register and stuff behind the counter," Susan said quickly. "There wouldn't be anything in the part of the shop customers use."

I agreed, and we both ducked behind the counter. The first logical place to look seemed to be the cash register. It was locked, of course, but the credit card swiper next to it got my attention. For extra light, I beamed my little light on it and we both leaned in to study it.

"It looks OK," I said. "There isn't anything strange attached to it."

Susan jiggled the slot where the card would be swiped. "There isn't a card skimmer over the slot, anyway. Of course, they probably wouldn't just leave it on all the time."

"Especially not if Marla was already worried that Chuck was swiping too many numbers at the same location," I agreed. "That sounds like she wouldn't be using it at all in her store from now on."

Susan nodded in the dim light. "In which case she wouldn't be keeping a skimmer down here at all. An employee might find it."

This made sense, so we decided to take the investigation upstairs. The buildings in this part of Seattle were old, and the narrow, creaky staircase made entirely too much noise for my comfort. Here there were no emergency lights, and it was pitch dark. Susan brought out a larger flashlight than mine and forged ahead.

199

"Shhh," I urged as Susan clomped past me.

"Shhh, yourself. You're the one making all the noise."

At last we reached the top and found ourselves looking at another locked door—Marla was taking extra precautions against intruders entering her living space. Susan went to work on the lock. This time we weren't actually exposed to the public eye so I felt a little better about the amount of time it took, but as Susan scraped and jiggled at the lock I made a mental note to never go burgling with her again. Not unless she practiced a lot more.

After about an hour the lock clicked and we tip-toed through the door. "Good thing that bolt wasn't thrown," I said, noticing a sturdy deadbolt on the inside of the door.

"That could only be closed from the inside," Susan pointed out, "for a bit of extra security once Marla's inside, I guess."

I liked the sound of that. "Then let's close it now."

Susan argued that we might want to make a fast getaway, and in the end we decided to leave the door unbolted. Then we cautiously looked around by the light of my flashlight.

The small apartment featured a tiny kitchen, a bathroom, a bedroom and what we figured was a combination living room and office. In spite of the cramped space the rooms had a certain old-fashioned charm, with high ceilings and pretty if worn crown moldings.

Since Marla's shop occupied the corner of the last building on her block, she had windows on three sides—draped mostly with lace curtains, so we didn't dare turn on the lights. Still, I felt confident enough that we wouldn't be seen by a casual passer-by that I allowed Susan to use her flashlight, which was a lot more powerful than mine. She aimed it at the floor and cupped her hand over the top of it to keep the beam from bobbing around and attracting attention.

A quick snoop through the kitchen yielded nothing, other than discovering a secondary staircase off of a small pantry. I aimed my flashlight through the small window in its center, but couldn't see more than a few steps. It seemed to lead down to the side of the building that faced the alleyway's cross street. It too had a large deadbolt in place to ensure that no intruders could sneak in. As we turned away from this staircase, Susan tripped over a pan on the floor and went skidding across the kitchen. By the time she came to rest she had pulled a number of other baking pans and assorted cups off of a counter. The crash sounded like dynamite in the quiet room.

"Geez, Susan!" I exclaimed.

"Well excuse me, but it's not my fault Marla left her baking pans on the floor for people to step on."

I frowned down at the offending pan. "That's weird," I said, "Marla seems to keep her kitchens tidy. I wonder what that was doing down there." I looked up to where similar pans were hanging neatly from a rack. On the counter below it, a glass salt shaker had broken, and salt and glass covered the surface and dotted the floor.

Susan stood up, rubbing her behind.

"Susan, did you break that salt shaker?" I asked, pointing.

Susan shrugged. "I have no idea. I think I grabbed at a counter, but I don't remember a salt shaker being there."

"Well, at least you didn't cut yourself on the glass," I said, taking off her gloves and inspecting her hands.

"Let's just get this done," Susan said, pulling the gloves back on. "There's nothing else to find in the kitchen."

Next we turned our attention to the bedroom. Here there were heavier curtains, so we decided it would be safe to turn on a small bedside lamp to aid our search.

"Hey, this is some nice lingerie," Susan said in approval as she rootled through Marla's dresser. "She really likes Victoria's Secret." Susan grinned and held up a lacy, red, heavily-padded bra. "Guess she doesn't feel like she's got enough going on up there. This beauty would add at least two cup sizes."

"Susan!" I exclaimed in horror. "Put that down. We're here to look for evidence, not to go through Marla's underwear." I was beginning to feel horribly guilty.

"I'm just saying, there's nothing wrong with getting a little boost if you need it," Susan snickered, eyeing my chest. She is always trying to get me to wear a push-up.

I didn't dignify this comment with a reply. "We're done in here," I said coldly. "Let's check out the living room." I switched off the light as we left.

Marla had furnished her apartment mostly with 'shabby chic' antiques, and her computer sat on a beautiful old roll-top desk, alongside a mug filled with pens and a pile of unopened mail. Susan switched on the computer, but it was locked with a password and we couldn't get past the first screen. Susan tried typing in 'Password,' 'Marla' and 'Chocolate,' and then gave up.

"We could spend forever trying to get the right password," she complained.

Personally I was happy we couldn't hack into the computer. What we were doing felt like a huge invasion of privacy, especially after going through Marla's underwear. Even if we did suspect Marla of killing Chuck, it didn't seem right.

With some difficulty, I managed to keep Susan from opening the mail on Marla's desk. "That's a felony, I said."

"Whatever. It mostly looks like advertisements, anyway, except for that green envelope. That looks more like somebody sent a greeting card." Then she pointed to a telephone on the desk. "Hey, the message light's blinking. Let's see what it says." She pushed the flashing red button before I could stop her.

"Hey, Marla?" came a harassed-sounding young woman's voice. "Where are you, you were supposed to be here with the truffles half an hour ago. We're having trouble with the fondue pot, too. Could you give us a call if you're going to be any later? Without the truffles we're not sure how to arrange the rest of the display."

"That's strange," I said. "As the owner, you'd think she would be the first person there."

"Maybe her car broke down, or she got stuck in good old Seattle traffic," Susan mused. "She isn't *here*, that's the main thing."

I was getting nervous. "Let's just go through these drawers and then leave," I urged. "We don't know if Marla might be coming back for something."

Susan agreed that we shouldn't spend any more time than we had to. We started opening desk drawers.

"Man, these antiques sure had a lot of little drawers and slots and things," Susan said. "Give me a straightforward file cabinet any day."

"Speaking of which," I said as I picked up an envelope with Marla's name on it, "there's a file cabinet next to the window over there. Why don't you look at that while I finish up here—and be careful with that flashlight while you're over there. We don't want it to be seen out the window."

"You sure worry a lot," Susan commented, but she did angle her light downwards as she crossed the room.

The smaller drawers on the roll top held only typical office supplies, and the slots held bills—one side of the desk seemed to be used for her private papers, and the other side for the chocolate business. I found an invoice for what seemed to be one of the vats we had noticed in the gourmet kitchen, and my eyebrows rose. Being a chocolatier certainly didn't come cheap!

Next I opened the larger drawers that went down the sides of the desk. I found plain and letterhead paper, envelopes, business cards, and—my breath caught in my throat.

In the last two drawers were credit card skimmers of various shapes and sizes, obviously designed to fit over a number of different legitimate card swipers. One was only the size of a quarter, while the biggest one looked like it would fit on a standard ATM. There were also what I decided might be miniature cameras, for capturing unlucky ATM users' PINs. A nearly-empty box of blank credit cards in the bottom drawer sat on top of a small machine that, I guessed, could stamp them with stolen numbers and names.

I gave a low whistle. "Susan, get over here," I said as quietly as I could in my excitement. "I think I found something."

Susan quickly came over to my side of the room. "Holy cow, we hit pay dirt," she said gleefully. She put down her flashlight and started digging through her oversized purse. "All we need to do now is document it."

I'll admit that I hadn't even thought about what we were going to do if we found evidence. It had seemed like such a long shot. Now I realized just how sticky our situation was—we couldn't exactly go to the police with evidence we'd found by breaking into somebody's home!

I was about to bring this up when Susan pulled out her new camera. I winced. "I hope you found a way to turn off the noise that thing makes," I said.

"There isn't anyone around to hear it except for us," she pointed out. "Anyway, I went through the manual today and it so happens that I figured out how to turn all of the noises off. So there." She started pressing buttons on the back of the camera. "Just need to turn the flash on and the noise off..." she muttered to herself.

At that moment I heard a sound that froze my blood. It was the slamming of the back door that led to the alleyway. Someone had entered the building.

"Oh geez, oh geez, oh geez!" Susan whimpered.

"We have to get out of here," I urged as footsteps began to ascend the stairs. "We can take the staircase by the kitchen and nobody will even know we were here."

"We came for evidence, and I'm getting evidence!" In spite of my tugging at her sleeve, she raised her camera and aimed it at the desk drawer.

'CLICK-WHIRRRR-CLICK!' went the camera, along with a blinding flash.

A man's voice called up the stairs, "Hey, Marla? Are you still there? I thought you were going to be away at—"

Startled by the voice, I jumped and my elbow sent the mug full of pens crashing to the floor. The mug shattered and pens went flying. Susan leapt backwards, knocking over a small table that was topped by an exquisite crystal vase. The vase also shattered.

"What the—Marla? Marla!" Footsteps began to thump up the stairs.

"Time to go," said Susan, pushing me ahead of her into the kitchen and toward the other set of stairs. I hastily drew back the bolt and began to charge down the pitch-black stairs. And tripped over something soft.

Behind me, Susan tripped as well and fell heavily against me. Together we rolled end-over-end down the stairs. I dropped my flashlight, but it landed with a ping beside my head and I grabbed at it. Shaking, I aimed it back up the stairway even though I was already pretty sure what I was going to see.

Sprawled halfway down the staircase, Marla lay with unseeing eyes starting out from a horribly congested face. A nasty length of wire was buried in her neck. Caught in the beam of light, blood trickled down the stairs. Marla would not be delivering any more truffles.

Chapter 24

For a second, Susan and I both froze in horror. Then Marla's body, no doubt disturbed by both of us falling over it, slid down toward us by one step. Her head made a dull, thumping sound as it struck.

Susan and I levitated off the floor and blasted out the back door. How we made it to the car I'm not sure—I think we flew. Susan cranked the engine and we sped away with a screech of tires.

I was panting almost too hard to talk. "I think…I'm going to be sick." I said faintly.

"Not in my car, you're not," Susan declared. She handed me a bottle of water from a case she usually kept on the backseat. "Sip some of that, take deep breaths and stick your head out the window if you're still going to hurl."

I felt a little better after following her orders (the sipping and breathing part. No way was I going to stick my head out the window at the speed we were going.)

Once I was sure my interior wasn't going to do anything unpleasant to Susan's, I pulled out my cell phone out of my purse and switched it on.

Susan glanced at me sharply. "What are you doing?"

"What do you think? I'm calling the police."

"With your cell phone, are you kidding me? They'll trace it right to us."

"I was planning on giving my name anyway. Susan, we just left the scene of another murder! We have to report it."

"Oh, right," Susan said. Holding an imaginary phone up to her head she went on. "Hello, police? My friend and I just broke into this girl's apartment and went through all of her stuff, and then we made a huge mess tripping over things and knocking stuff over, and then we found this person's dead body, and we fell all over that, too. We didn't kill her, though. Must have been somebody else. Okay, thanks, 'bye!"

Susan scowled. "We'd be in prison before the guys are even back from band practice."

She had a point—it seemed probable that our activities would strike a police officer as being a wee bit suspicious.

"We still have to report it, though," I said dismally. "It's our duty."

"Duty, schmooty!" Susan said. "I never said were weren't going to report it. I just think there are ways to do it without us landing in the hoosegow! Now let me see…" I noticed that she had slowed down and was scanning the stores we passed. I was about to ask what she was looking for when she gave a triumphant cheer.

"Here we go," She said, pulling up into the parking lot of a convenience store. Oddly, she selected the parking space furthest from the entrance.

"You've decided that we need nasty convenience-store coffee?" I asked. "Like we haven't suffered enough tonight."

But Susan's eyes were fixed on a pay phone outside of the store. "Keep your scarf around your face," she instructed, adjusting her own, "I just hope we aren't close enough to the security cameras for them to pick up my license plates."

"What?" I asked, but she was already out the door. She hurriedly fed coins into the pay phone and spoke for about 60 seconds. Then she sprinted back to the car and gunned the engine. Once again we sped off in a cloud of tire smoke.

"Anonymous tip," she explained once we were safely back on the freeway. "I just said that they'd better check out that address because there had been a crime. The operator didn't even know I was a woman because I *talked like thiiis*." Here she lowered her voice into a masculine growl.

"Excellent," I said, rolling my eyes. "You sound like somebody out of a slasher film. Now they're going to think it was just a prank."

"They'll still have to check out the apartment."

I wasn't so sure, but it was too late to do anything about it now. Instead I started worrying about any traces we might have left at the crime scene. "Susan, what are we going to do if they find evidence that we were there?"

"Like what kind of evidence? We didn't exactly leave our business cards."

"Any evidence! Like DNA or hairs, or, I don't know, anything."

Susan laughed. "You've been watching too much CSI. We both had gloves and scarves on, so we didn't leave fingerprints and probably didn't leave hairs. As far as I know we didn't spit on the floor or blow our noses on the curtains. Even if one of your carrot hairs does turn up, we have an explanation—we've been there twice, you know. Legally."

Not in the apartment, I thought. Still, we had at least taken some basic precautions and I was glad Susan had made me were the gloves and scarf.

A new thought occurred to me as we sped back across Lake Washington. "Susan, who do you think that man was?"

Susan whipped around a slower-moving car, making me whimper and squeeze my eyes shut. "What man? And stop squeaking while I drive, it makes me nervous."

"The man who came in from the alleyway," I said patiently. "You know, the one we almost broke our necks running away from?"

"Hmm," Susan mused, "that's right. You know, I almost forgot about him in all the excitement. Gosh, maybe he was the killer! We got out of there just in time."

"He couldn't have been the killer," I argued. "When he heard us making a racket, he called up to Marla. That means he didn't know she was dead."

"Good point. Maybe it was her boyfriend, or somebody else in the identity theft ring. Somebody with a key, anyway. I'm pretty sure the back door locked behind us when we came in."

I closed my eyes and tried to remember everything that had happened in the chaotic moments just before finding Marla's body. I had a vague feeling that I was missing something. Something familiar. That voice had reminded me of someone, but who?

Susan broke in on my thoughts. "You'd think somebody who knew her well enough to have a key would also know that she wouldn't be there that evening. Or at least wasn't supposed to be there."

"I think he did. Didn't he say something about thinking she was going to be away? I frowned, trying to remember. Oddly, I still had a feeling that the voice had been familiar. I couldn't place it, though.

"So why was she there?" I asked finally. "I mean, why was she there at all when she should have been at the party?"

Susan shrugged. "Maybe she was getting ready to go when she was killed."

"What happened to all the chocolates, then?" I asked. "We didn't see any of the chocolates she was supposed to be bringing."

"I'll bet she had already loaded them in her vehicle. I think I remember seeing a van with her logo on it parked near the shop when we drove away."

"I guess so," I said. I tried to picture the scene. "So everything's ready, the kitchen is cleaned, and one or more employees loads most of the chocolates into a company van and goes on ahead. Marla goes upstairs, maybe to tidy herself up or put on a party dress, intending to follow them with the truffles."

Susan picked up the story line. "But somebody's waiting for her there, or slips in behind her, kills her and gets away before we arrive."

I shivered. "I wonder how close we came to meeting the killer?"

"Probably pretty close." Susan sounded as uneasy as I felt. "Whoever it was left through the alleyway door, though, and we didn't meet anyone in the alley."

I frowned "What makes you think the killer used that door?"

"Think about it. The kitchen staircase, where we found Marla, was bolted from the inside. It was a manual bolt, not one with a key, so it couldn't have been locked from the outside of the door. Now, the alleyway door to her apartment had one of those bolts on it, too. Marla probably bolted both doors at night for extra safety but she didn't bolt that one while she was changing because she meant to go right back out. The killer couldn't bolt it either, because he or she had to leave that way to get back downstairs."

It made sense, but there was one thing I didn't understand. "Why bolt the door to the second staircase at all, then?"

"I don't know, maybe to delay anyone from finding the body. Probably only Marla would have used that staircase, so under normal conditions it could have been quite a while before anybody else went there."

"Good point. Eventually her employees would get worried enough about her to check her room, but even then they probably wouldn't think to open a bolted door to a staircase that never got used."

Susan nodded. "So by the time somebody found her, probably because of the smell, it would be almost impossible to tell exactly when she was killed."

My stomach turned at Susan's inelegant description, but it at least made sense of the locked door. As for the rest of it... I shook my head. "But who is *doing* this? It's insane! On one hand, we have an identity theft gang. OK, so they might have a disagreement that turned violent. That doesn't account for Mrs. Vick getting killed, though. Then again, if we go with the theory that some woman hated Chuck and killed him for the way he treated her, that explains Chuck's murder but not the other two."

"And if Mrs. Vick was killed for some reason that involves the Mayor, how does that connect with Chuck and Marla?" Susan added. "I can almost see Mayor Vick being involved with a theft scheme, but not his wife. She sounds like too nice a person—and it's not like either of them needed money!" she sighed.

By now we had reached my house. It seemed as though ten years had elapsed since we'd left on our little adventure, but it had really only been a couple of hours. Michael wasn't home yet.

"So," Susan said as she pulled into the driveway, "what do we do now?"

I stared at her. "You don't think we've done enough for one night?"

"I meant in general. We don't seem any closer to a solution than we were before."

"Why don't we watch the news and see what happens," I suggested. "After all, when the police find Marla's body, they'll also find the evidence from the identity theft ring. Maybe something will point them in the right direction and *they'll* solve it." *Not to mention that it would keep us from getting into even more trouble*, I thought but didn't say aloud.

Susan followed me up the pathway to my front door and we went inside. "I don't know about that," she said gloomily, "they haven't been doing such a great job so far." She flicked on the TV and turned to the news.

So far there weren't any stories about bodies being found in Seattle, and I began to worry again that Susan's call to the police had been written off as a practical joke. "Maybe we should call them again, and this time not use silly voices," I said.

"Give it time," Susan said. "They're probably just starting their investigation now. It wouldn't have had time to make the news yet. If we don't hear anything about it by tomorrow, we can call again but *not*," she insisted, "from our cell or home phones."

I agreed completely. Despite my sense of duty, I had no wish to explain our activities to the police.

215

It became a moot point when breaking news interrupted a story of underfunded transportation projects. The police had discovered Marla's body after all.

Chapter 25

Susan and I watched in rapt attention as a woman with shellacked blond hair reported on the discovery. "Tonight an anonymous tip led to a grisly discovery in downtown Seattle, where police discovered the strangled body of a young woman. The body has not yet been officially identified, but is believed to be that of Marla Birch, the owner of an upscale chocolate shop by the name of Chocolate Noir. Police are asking anyone with information about this crime to contact them at—"

The screen flicked off. I was about to demand that Susan, who still had the remote, turn the TV back on when I realized that I had also heard the sound that had alerted her—the slamming door of Michael's car.

Susan raised a finger to her lips. "Not a word," she said. *As if I planned to tell Michael what we'd been up to!*

"You'd better take off the gloves and headscarf, too," she said, pulling off her own and stuffing them into her purse. My purse wasn't big enough so I stuffed them under the couch. A paw reached out and scratched my hand—apparently Banshee had heard Susan's voice and taken refuge when we arrived.

Michael entered the front door whistling and swinging the huge duffel bag that carried his bagpipes and related paraphernalia. "Hey, Ginger, Susan," he said, nodding to us both. "Did you have a good evening?"

Susan was faster off the mark that I was. "Oh, sure," she said airily, "it's always a good evening when nobody gets arrested."

Or killed, I thought. Then I gulped, remembering that Marla actually had been killed. Even though Susan and I hadn't had anything to do with it (besides tripping over Marla's body) I still felt guilty.

Michael noticed the look on my face. "What's wrong, honey?" he asked.

In answer, I held up my hand with the telltale claw marks. "I got too close to somebody's hidey-hole," I said. Which wasn't too far from the truth!

"Banshee," Michael scolded as the perpetrator grudgingly came out from under the couch to greet him. He scooped her up and tickled her under the chin. "Bad kitty. You should be ashamed of yourself."

"That would imply that cats have a conscience," said Susan. "Or souls, for that matter."

Michael snuggled his face into Banshee's ruff. "Did you hear that, Sweetie? You should have scratched nasty old Aunt Susan instead of poor Ginger."

Susan blew a raspberry at both Michael and the cat. "Well, I guess I'll get going if I'm going to be insulted here," she said, getting up from the couch. She gave me a meaningful look. "We can talk about that thing tomorrow," she said.

"Yeah," I said, "that thing."

Michael set Banshee, who was starting to wriggle and look annoyed, down on the couch. "More dancer drama?"

Susan grinned. "You have no idea." She waggled her fingers by her ear to signal 'Call me' as she left.

I forestalled any further questions from Michael by asking about his bagpipe practice. "So, what's with all the extra rehearsals? Are you getting ready for a big show?"

"We do have a performance coming up," he said. "Our leader is coming up on his retirement and we're planning a party and a big surprise for him after the show."

I considered this. On one hand, the term "big surprise" would usually sound kind of ominous coming from a member of a bagpipe band. On the other hand, if this guy led their practice sessions, he was presumably immune to their playing—he might even be deaf.

"That's nice of you," I said.

"Hey, your cop friends probably know him. He's something pretty high up in the Puyallup police department, but he's about to retire—Detective Dave McGirk? I don't know what he does exactly, but he's been a cop practically forever."

"Hmm, I'll have to ask Tara next time I see her," I said, hoping to make it sound like we only met occasionally. *Partially deaf and a lifetime of being a cop*, I thought. This guy could probably survive a big bagpipe surprise. Maybe.

I didn't want to think about cops. I chewed my bottom lip, wondering how many laws Susan and I had broken that evening. Breaking and entering, certainly. Burglary? Was it burglary if we didn't take anything? I didn't think so, but we had definitely gone through Marla's possessions without her permission. There had to be a law against that. Finally, of course, we had disturbed a crime scene. Granted, that had been an accident, but I felt sure that Detective Harris, for example, would not approve. Last but not least, we had fled the crime scene. Was there a law against that, like in a hit-and-run? I chewed my lip harder.

"Are your lips chapped?" Michael enquired solicitously. "I've got some lip balm somewhere." He dug through his pockets and handed it to me.

"Thanks," I said feebly. Explaining everything to Michael would be even more complicated than explaining to the police. Hopefully neither would be necessary. Hopefully the police, given the new evidence, would now be able to solve this whole mess without any more "help" from us. Hopefully…

That night I dreamt that Susan and I were back in Marla's apartment, searching her bedroom. We heard the sound of a bolt being slid back and the creaking of the kitchen door. Slow, stumbling footsteps came across the kitchen and living room. Then Marla stood in the doorway, her face congested and blue. The horrible cord was still embedded in her neck, which was crusted with dried blood. As I watched in horror, Marla raised an accusing finger toward us and rasped through her swollen lips, "What are you doing with my underwear?"

Susan turned around and cheerfully held up the lacey bra. "Oh, hey, Marla. Do you mind if Ginger keeps this?"

I woke in a cold sweat. Damn Susan! She couldn't even behave in my dreams.

Chapter 26

Friday morning at the shelter had the usual number of emergencies, but I still had enough time to check on the news every once and a while. The story hadn't changed much. Marla's body had been discovered, but there was no mention of the fact that she had apparently been involved with an identity theft ring. It seemed strange that this detail had been omitted, and I wondered if that detail had been left out because the police didn't want it to hamper their investigation.

The one new detail was a note the police had found in a pile of mail that appeared to be a death threat. It simply stated, "Your time is up. People like you don't deserve to live." There had been no signature. I wondered if there had been a falling out among thieves, but if so it seemed odd that no mention had been made of Marla being involved in something criminal.

At 3 o'clock, my cell phone went off. I had made sure to stuff it in my purse that morning, just in case there was more news.

Sure enough, the call was from Susan and she launched into speech without any preamble. "Ginger! Thank god you actually have your phone today."

"Why," I asked suspiciously, "is there someplace we need to break into tonight?"

"Geez, Ginger, not on a cell phone! Don't you ever watch spy movies?"

I let this one pass, but I did shut my office door to prevent anyone in the sanctuary from overhearing. "What's going on? I've been pretty busy today, is there more news?"

"It's what isn't in the news that's bothering me. Why haven't they said anything about the desk full of identity theft stuff? Or the guy that was there?"

I pointed out that the news hadn't said anything about us being there, either. "That man probably left before the police arrived," I said, "just like we did."

"Maybe. But that still doesn't explain why they aren't saying anything about the theft ring."

I sighed. "That does seem strange, but they might be keeping quiet about it for a reason."

"Like what?" Susan demanded.

"I don't know," I admitted. "The only thing I can think of is that they might be trying to figure out who else was in the ring, and they don't want to tip them off."

Susan snorted. "If the bad guys know Marla's body was discovered along with all of their equipment, I think they're already tipped off. Unless they're complete idiots, they *have* to know the police will be looking for them."

An idea suddenly occurred to me—one we hadn't thought of yet. "You know," I said slowly, "there might be one perfectly good reason why nobody's mentioned the credit card swipers and things. What if the equipment wasn't there when the police arrived?"

"So what, like, we imagined the whole thing? Those sure looked like credit card swipers to me."

"Listen," I said patiently, "we weren't the last people in that apartment before the police got there, remember? The man we heard coming up the stairs was. We know he wasn't the murderer, but what if he was a member of the identity theft ring? He obviously knew she wasn't going to be there tonight, but he didn't seem to be worried about getting caught by her if she had been—otherwise he wouldn't have called out to her when we made all that noise. So it's not like he was sneaking in. Like you said, he probably even had a key. Maybe, as a member of her gang, he was coming by to pick something up or drop something off for her."

"Like what?"

"I don't know, maybe some more of those blank credit cards. She was almost out of those, remember. Anyway, once he heard us and ran run up the stairs, he'd have seen the open kitchen door and found Marla's body, just like we did. Then he probably freaked out—"

"—just like we did," said Susan. "I think I see where you're going with this."

"Once he saw Marla, he realized he'd stumbled right into the middle of a murder scene. He would have wanted to get out of there as quickly as possible, but he had a big problem: he couldn't leave all of that evidence behind. There might have been something that would have pointed to him once the police started looking for the theft ring."

"So before he left, he grabbed all of the swipers and dummy cards and took them with him," Susan ended for me. "Bye-bye, evidence."

Gloom settled over me. "Dang," I said. "That means we're the only ones who know what Marla and her friends were up to. Susan, we have to go to the police now. We're in way over our heads."

There was a brief, moody silence on Susan's end of the phone, during which I became vaguely aware of scuffling noises outside my office door. They seemed to be getting louder.

"Got it!" Susan practically shouted in my ear, making me jump and knock over my coffee. "We don't have to go to the cops at all. I just remembered that we have—"

Someone rapped loudly on my door and then cracked it open. "Hey Ginger, are you awake in there?" Trey asked, sounding out of breath. "I don't want to bug you, but there's been a big problem with the baby skunk cage." With the door partially open I could hear the all-too-familiar sound of a chase in progress.

"Susan, I have to go," I said hastily. "There's a situation here."

225

"You and your freaking animals! Never mind, I'll take care of everything. Just leave it to me and *don't* go saying anything to the cops yet. Call you later." With that, she rang off.

Ordinarily this statement would have filled me with dread, but I was too busy trying to remember how many baby skunks we currently had in stock. Too many, I thought grimly, and from the sound of it every single one of them was making a break for freedom. I hastily threw some tissues on my desk to soak up the coffee, then grabbed the safety gloves, safety glasses and an old overcoat I kept on a hook by my desk, and left the office.

Chapter 27

"Pewweeeee! Honey, you know I love you but WOW, you smell bad!"

I was in too bad a mood to even bother replying. I gave Michael a look and stomped up the stairs toward the bathroom.

He followed and sympathetically got an armful of fresh towels out of the linen closet and handed them to me. "Skunks up to their old tricks?" he said. It wasn't the first time I had come home smelling of mustelid.

I made an inarticulate sound of frustration as I took the towels. "It was our juveniles this time," I growled. "They're so tiny but they're so fast, and they bite and they spray everything. And I mean *everything*! We're going to have to get a new keyboard for the computer at the intake counter. Probably a new monitor, too."

Michael nodded gravely. "You can't exactly hose those down, that's for sure. Don't worry about it—I can probably fix you up with a new set from my collection. I'll go in with you tomorrow."

I felt a smile starting to break through my scowl. "It won't smell good," I warned. "We gave everything a pretty thorough scrub-down, but it's still going to be awhile before the smell really goes away. Poor Jane even got it in her hair!"

Michael shuddered. "As long as you keep Jane at least ten feet away from me, I should be able to hold my nose long enough to get you up and running again."

"You're a sweetie," I said, moving forward to hug him.

Michael backed away. "Whoa! That's close enough, woman. Go make with the suds already."

Fortunately, I hadn't been sprayed too badly thanks to my protective clothing. Unlike the unfortunate volunteer Jane, I had had the presence of mind to grab one of the disposable plastic hair covers we kept on hand for such emergencies. No one had escaped unscathed, though, and I had received a direct hit up my coat sleeve as I grabbed one of the little rascals. The spray had somehow managed to soak my shirt and arm, under the coat! The shirt I had simply thrown away and replaced with one of the spares I kept at work. Now, as I scrubbed the affected area over and over with hydrogen peroxide and baking soda paste, I made a mental note to tuck my coat sleeves into my gloves next time.

To further prove his sweetness, Michael ordered a pizza for delivery and combed his "collection" (a graveyard of electronics that resided in the basement) for a keyboard and monitor that might work as replacements at the shelter. By the time I was more or less deodorized and my hair was dry, dinner was waiting and several keyboards and monitors were stacked by the front door, along with an enormous bag of cords. According to Michael, you can never have enough cords when you're working on computers, and the one you end up needing is always the one you didn't bring.

The rest of the evening passed so peacefully and I was so tired, it wasn't until Saturday morning that I remembered Susan's ominous promise to "fix" everything with the police. As Michael and I headed for the shelter with a trunk full of computer parts, I began to worry about what she had planned.

"Holy begeebers, this place smells," Michael observed as we entered the front office.

"You should have been here yesterday," I said.

"No thank you." He immediately declared both the keyboard and monitor to be beyond help, and they were unceremoniously dumped into a thick plastic bag and hauled out to our recycling bin. Then, with the windows and doors open and a fan put in place to speed ventilation along, he got to work.

I wasn't scheduled for duty that day, so after a quick check to make sure everything was running smoothly I found a quiet spot and called Susan.

"Didn't I tell you not to worry?" she replied to my first barrage of questions. "I told you I had everything under control. The police know all about the identity theft ring now."

My stomach did a flip-flop. "Susan, what did you do?" I demanded.

"Wouldn't you like to know," she replied. I could just tell she had an enormous smile on her face. "Come on, I'll bet you can't even guess!"

I ground my teeth, a habit my dentist has been making comments about for a number of years. "Susan, I don't have much time for a private conversation. I'm at the shelter and somebody could come around the corner any minute. Would you just tell me what you did, please?!"

"Geez, you're grumpy," Susan commented. "Fine, here goes. Remember that picture I took of the drawer full of skimmers and stuff?"

I hadn't remembered. In all of the panic and chaos of the moment, I had completely forgotten about Susan's ill-timed camera shot. "I remember that the racket almost got us caught," I said. "but did the picture actually come out?"

"It was perfect!" Susan crowed. "Not only did I get a shot of the desk and the drawer with all the skimmers, but there were a couple of letters to Marla on top of the desk. It's obviously her desk in her apartment, and she just as obviously had that identity theft equipment in her desk. It's air-tight evidence!".

What do you think we should do now, call Tara?"

230

"Are you out of your mind? If we tell Tara anything about it, we'd make her an accomplice to our break-in. That's why we didn't take her with us in the first place."

"And here I thought it was because it was a stupid idea and she wouldn't have let us do it to begin with," I muttered.

"What's that?"

"Nothing. Anyway, what do you want to do with the photo?"

"Oh, I already did it," she replied airily, "I sent a copy of it to Dot."

I was confused. "Who is Dot?"

"Dorothy Beresford," Susan said, "the detective who's in charge of the identity theft task force, remember? She gave us her business cards?"

A dull pain was beginning to form above my left eye. "Susan, how is telling Detective Beresford about what we did any better than telling Tara?"

"Hey, you were the one who was all, like, 'We have to go to the police!' yesterday," Susan said defensively, "but anyhow my idea was way better than that. I didn't tell anybody anything—I just sent the picture to her anonymously. How's that for good thinking?"

I frowned. "Anonymously? How did you do that?"

"I copied the picture onto a flash drive and mailed it to the Redvue City Police Department, care of Detective Beresford," Susan proudly informed me. "Plus, I put a little sticky note on it that said she might want to look up the details of the Marla Birch murder case. I thought it would save them some time."

I rubbed the sore spot above my eye. It sounded crazy but there was, just barely, a possibility that it would work. On the other hand, it could get us into more trouble than we would have been in otherwise.

"Well, what do you think?" Susan asked.

"I don't know," I said. "You're sure there's no way to trace it back to us?"

"I don't see how it could."

I could think of a lot of ways: fingerprints, hair fibers, whether or not Susan had put a return address on the package...

"Susan," I said anxiously, "you didn't put your return address on the envelope, did you?"

"Of course not. I used my neighbors' address."

I groaned.

"What?" she demanded. "We had to get the pictures to the police one way or another, and an envelope with no return address would have been suspicious. They probably would have just had the bomb squad blow it up, just in case. This way it looked like legitimate mail. Stop worrying, I covered our tracks. I used a different zip code so my neighbors wouldn't get in trouble."

I started grinding my teeth again. It was possible that the police wouldn't investigate the return address, but if they did—how long would it take them to spot the fake zip code and realize who lived in close proximity to the genuine street address? If by 'covering our tracks' she meant practically giving away our exact location, she couldn't have done a better job, I thought bitterly. But there was no point in going into that now.

"So, who do you think is doing all of this?" I said.

"I have no idea. The guy who came into the shop after us wasn't the murderer, or he would have already known Marla was dead. We've been over that. If he was a member of the identity theft ring, it makes me think that whoever killed her *wasn't* in on the thefts—I mean, how many more people could have been in the ring? But who else could it be?"

I didn't know either, and from the sound of footsteps coming down the hall there wasn't time to discuss it now. "Susan I have to go. We can talk after the rehearsal tomorrow."

"Dang, I forgot about that! We need the extra practice, though."

"That's for sure," I said with a laugh. "Talk to you tomorrow."

As I put my phone back in my purse, Michael came around the corner. "Hi, Ginger, I got everything hooked up. Your front desk is up and running again."

"Thank you so much," I said, giving him a kiss.

"Eww, Mommy and Daddy are kissing," said Trey, popping around the corner.

"Very funny," I said. "How is the new skunk cage holding up?"

"The little buggers are doing their best to break out again, but George is working on it. So far his new hardware is keeping the stripy ones behind bars."

Michael grinned. "Trey's been introducing me to your fragrant friends. How can something that cute smell that bad?"

"When they're biting you from one end and spraying you from the other, the cuteness wears thin pretty fast," I assured him.

"My eyes sure started watering when I walked into that office," he agreed. "Whew!"

Once Michael had packed up all of his gear, we headed to Ernie's Snack Shack for lunch. As I munched on a French dip sandwich, I thought about my strange meeting there with Detective Harris only a few days ago. I wondered if he'd plucked up the courage to talk to Tara. I hoped she hadn't shot him down if he had!

Chapter 28

At the studio the next day, Anne re-distributed our costumes. She had attached several inches of trim to Susan's dress, effectively hiding her feet. My dress had been taken up an inch or two, and I was happy to find I was no longer tripping over the hem. I wondered how on earth Anne found the time to raise twins, teach, and alter countless costumes at the same time.

Practice went a little more smoothly now that everybody's costume had been altered for them. By the end, I wasn't getting my stick caught in my sleeve nearly as often. Susan and I even did the spin-around-and-hit-our-sticks-together move without hitting our knuckles.

Susan then ruined it by dancing around in a circle singing, "We did it, we did it," and smacking her stick on the floor. The stick bounced right back up and hit her in the eye.

While Susan sat in the corner rubbing her injured eyeball, the rest of us scrambled in our purses to find remedies. These included: one half-used packet of Kleenex; one Band-Aid with a children's cartoon character leering from the package; one pair of tweezers; a safety pin ("What exactly are you planning to do with that?" Susan demanded); several different types of aspirin and ibuprofen; a bottle of water; an energy bar; and finally a bag filled with ice (complements of Anne from the studio's breakroom.)

Susan accepted the makeshift icepack and told the rest of us to leave her alone and keep practicing.

Once rehearsal was over, the whole class hauled Susan over to the mirror to examine her wounds. Fortunately, the stick had only grazed her cheekbone, not the eye itself. The damage was minimal—a small red welt. "And here I thought I was going to get my first black eye," Susan said, poking at the welt with a touch of regret. "I was going to tell everybody I'd been in a bar fight."

"Sorry," Anne said, laughing, "the most that bump is going to turn into is a slight bruise. Take it from somebody with two boys. When they were eight, Justin dared Jason to do a double jump off of a diving board. Jason started his jump from too far back, landed face-down on the board instead of in the pool, and broke his nose. He had two black eyes for ages!"

"The poor thing," we all chorused.

"Oh, *he* didn't mind very much once the pain had died down. He had two beautiful shiners to show off to all of his friends at school. *I* was terrified that his father and I were going to get a call from Child Services."

"I'll bet Jason told everybody he was in a bar fight," Susan grumbled.

Anne nodded. "Among other things."

Once everyone in class was assured that Susan would not be losing her eyeballs any time soon, they began to trickle out. Anne waggled her eyebrows at us as we were getting ready to go, so we stayed behind to talk to her.

"I ran into Camellia yesterday," she began once we had found seats on the cushions that lined one wall of the studio. "She wanted me to pass this along to you because she's had to make an emergency trip to Montana. Her goddaughter is having a baby, and it's coming a couple of weeks earlier than expected."

"Oh, no," Susan said.

"Is everything OK?" I asked.

"Camellia said everything seems to be fine and they're not expecting any serious complications, but she wanted to be there and that means leaving earlier than she planned."

"Of course," I said.

"Has she had a chance to talk to Harry's employees?" Susan asked.

"Yes, but she didn't think she learned very much. It would have been convenient if Jerry Lambert and Bill Ellis had worked together the whole time, but once they were finished with the big aisle trees they were off working on different displays."

"So they can't alibi each other," I said.

"Exactly. But there also didn't seem to be any reason for them to have killed Chuck. They didn't like him, but Camellia said she didn't get the feeling that they hated him, either. They were mainly annoyed that he wasn't pulling his weight on the setup."

"That sounds like our Chuck," said Susan.

"It also sounds like a dead end," I said despondently. "Camellia didn't learn anything else from them?"

"Just that they wished Harry well, and said they'd do everything they could to help."

"Everybody loves Harry," Susan said, giving her stick a vicious swing, "except for whoever is framing him for murder! Why can't we get just one good clue?"

Anne shrugged sympathetically. "It doesn't seem like we're getting anywhere," she admitted.

I could have pointed out that we actually had discovered quite a few clues in the last couple of days—just not ones we ought to mention in front of Anne. Instead I eyed Susan's wildly waving stick and said, "Would you watch it with that thing? You've already cause one injury today!"

"Well, at least the dance is coming along," Anne said with a smile. "You two are doing really well."

Anne stayed behind to work on a new choreography, but Susan and I gathered our things to leave. "Do you suppose she really meant that," Susan asked as we walked down the hallway toward the exit.

I shifted my dance bag and my purse so I could get a better grip on my tahtib, reflecting that the more dance you studied, the more gear you ended up carrying around. "Meant what?" I asked absently.

"That we're getting better at this stick dancing thing. It seems to me that we're dropping our sticks and whacking each other just as much as ever, and the performance is practically tomorrow!"

"Oh, it's not that bad," I argued. "We still have a couple of weeks. We actually did the spin right this time—in fact, we were doing just fine until you broke out your little victory dance."

"Hmph."

My hands were too full to use the door handle, so I turned to bump the studio door open with my rear end. I noticed that behind me, Susan had a very anxious look on her face. "It'll be fine," I insisted, wondering why she was getting so worked up. Then I turned around and saw what she was looking at.

A police car was parked sideways behind our two cars. Leaning against it with her arms crossed and a grim expression stood Tara. "Guess what, ladies," she said in an even tone, "we're going to go have coffee. Now."

Chapter 29

Tara practically frog-marched us into a coffee shop across the street. Once we had our coffees, she ushered us into a secluded back booth.

"I think this is kidnapping," Susan muttered in my ear.

I gulped. We were clearly in trouble.

Tara took a sip of her coffee, then planted both elbows on the table. Resting her chin on the tips of her fingers, she began. "Some interesting things have been happening over the last couple of days," she said, somehow managing to stare at both of us at once. "The public has suddenly become very helpful. First of all, we got an anonymous tip to check out Chocolate Noir, the chocolate shop next to Harry's. When a patrol arrived, they found the owner, Marla Birch, dead."

"That's awful," I said, at the same time that Susan said, "I think I saw that on the news." We did our best to look innocent.

Tara ignored this. "They also found," she said pointedly, "a 'bigger mess than a herd of elephants could have made if they'd been trying to tap dance,' to quote the responding officers. Even the body appeared to have been stumbled over, by someone who had first crushed a pen with their shoe and then stepped in broken glass—there were ink blots tracked partway down the staircase where the body was found, along with glass fragments."

Damn. I had a feeling that the whole looking innocent ploy had just flown out the window as Susan and I desperately tried to remember if we'd stepped on one of the pens on our way out, or in one of the many piles of glass. One or both of us must have. Where were our shoes, and should we dispose of them somehow?

Tara's eyes were steely grey as she observed our reaction. "And it gets even better," she said. "The next day our Redmond station got *another* bit of anonymous help, this time a flash drive with a photo of a drawer filled with identity theft devices along with a purple sticky note advising us to reference the Marla Birch murder. The envelope was addressed specifically to Detective Beresford. When investigators compared the photo to a desk drawer in Marla's apartment, they decided that it was the same desk, but that the equipment had been removed. Marla Birch had apparently been involved in identity theft."

241

Now," she said, tapping her fingers together, "Who do I know that a) suspected someone in that neighborhood of being involved in ID theft and/or murder; b) knows how to pick locks (here she fixed Susan with an icy stare); c) knew that Detective Beresford specifically would be the person to contact with any evidence involving ID theft, instead of just sending it to the Seattle Police Department, and d) already has a history of getting themselves into dangerous situations and contaminating crime scenes?!"

I gulped. It was true that I had stepped in blood and thrown up the first time Susan and I had discovered a body, but it wasn't like I'd done it on purpose.

Susan drew in a breath to speak, but Tara stopped her by slamming her hands on the table. "Don't. Say. Anything." she said through gritted teeth. "I know I asked you for help in clearing Harry, but this is not what I meant. There is a big difference between talking to people and breaking and entering and destroying a crime scene. Whoever—and I mean *whoever*," here she fixed us with a meaningful gaze, "entered that apartment after Marla was killed, did it illegally and, if they'd met the murderer, could have been killed themselves. If they had been caught there by the police, they would have been arrested as suspects." She paused for a moment before adding significantly, "It's a good thing nobody knows for sure whose footprints those were."

Tara took another sip of her coffee, then leaned back in her seat with her arms crossed. "As of now," she said quietly, "you two are off the case. I don't want you poking around, I don't want you talking to

242

anybody who's involved, in fact I don't even want the two of you leaving your homes until this is over! I'd put you under house arrest if I could. I appreciate that you want to help Harry, but remember that if the same person really is responsible for these crimes, then that person has already killed three times. I don't want the next corpses to be yours."

With that, she got up to leave. She couldn't resist a parting shot, though. "And by the way," she said over her shoulder, "most digital photos can be matched with the camera that took them through a number of things in the metadata. Also, the correct way to anonymously report crimes is through the Crime Stopper hotline or website, not by directly mailing things to the person in charge or calling the general police number and using a fake voice. I mean, geez!" She stalked out of the coffee shop.

It was a minute or two before either of us spoke. Then Susan broke the silence. "It's not like we knew Marla was in there dead and deliberately messed up the crime scene," she said resentfully. "How are we supposed to know when and where killers are going to go leaving their stupid bodies all over the place? They don't exactly give us their schedules."

I swallowed hard. Tara had been speaking quietly enough to not be overheard by other people in the shop, but I still felt like I'd spent the last half hour being yelled at by a drill sergeant. I finally managed to say, "Can they really trace that photo back to your camera?"

The uneasy look on Susan's face did not qualm my fears. "Um," she said, "I'm not sure. I didn't think about all the tags that

243

automatically get recorded on digital pictures. Maybe I should have checked."

"Isn't that the kind of thing you do for a living?" I asked hotly. "'Maybe I should have checked.' You think?"

"I'm not a photographer," she argued. "When clients want pictures in their ads, I have a professional photographer take them and give me the photos to work into the design. It's a totally different thing. Now that I think about it though," she added, looking even less happy, "I have heard that some cameras include both the camera's information and the GPS info along with the picture. I don't know if mine does or not."

I buried my face in my hands. Why, oh why, hadn't I simply refused to go along with Susan's plan?

"And I never even thought about the stuff we got on our shoes," Susan continued glumly. "Maybe we should get rid of them—and the camera. We could donate them to a thrift store or something."

"I don't think that would help," I said, feeling too dispirited to point out that this was all her fault. "We probably tracked glass and ink into your car and onto our carpets. We'd never be able to get rid of all the traces."

Susan chewed absentmindedly on a stray lock of her hair. "Dang," she said, "being a criminal is *hard*."

"We're not criminals!" I said. "I mean, not exactly. We didn't steal anything, or kill anyone."

"Keep your voice down," Susan reminded me, looking around nervously. Fortunately, the coffee shop wasn't busy and we had the corner to ourselves.

I lowered my voice. "Look," I said, "The most we are guilty of is breaking and entering. If worse comes to worst, we'll just come clean about what we did. Maybe we'll only get a couple of years in jail."

"Wow, you're such an optimist."

I stood up and stretched my tense back and neck muscles. "Well," I said, "at least it doesn't sound like Tara's going to turn us in—not unless she has to because we confess or she gets absolute proof we were there."

"She knows, though."

"She suspects, but that's not the same. As long as she doesn't know for sure it was us, she doesn't have to say anything."

As we left the coffee shop and headed back to the dance studio's parking lot, I couldn't help nervously looking around for Tara's patrol car. Thankfully, it was gone.

Susan fished around in her purse for the keys, but hesitated before getting into her car. Instead she turned to face me. "So," she said, "what do we do now?"

"What do you mean?" I asked.

"I mean where do we look next? We talked to the Mayor already, we talked to the employees at Harrys, and we talked to Marla—although I guess being killed herself kind of wipes her off the suspect list. Who's left?"

I nearly choked. "Are you out of your mind?" I exclaimed. "We broke the law. We came within minutes of running into a killer, and now we could get arrested because we left trace evidence at a crime scene! I think we've done enough."

"Hey," Susan said defensively, "We didn't know it was a crime scene when we broke into Marla's place."

"That's going to sound great in court."

"A few minutes ago you were the one assuring me that Tara wasn't going to rat us out," Susan said. "Nobody else could even begin to guess we were in Marla's apartment, so I think you're right, we're OK there. What we need to do now is to figure out who was in that apartment before us, and who that guy was that came in after us." She wrinkled her eyebrows. "Boy, Marla's place sure was busy that night!"

"We don't need to figure anything out," I declared. "We got lucky this time, and maybe we were able to give the police some evidence they wouldn't have had otherwise. Now, like Tara said, we're off the case. The police can take it from here."

Susan shook her head. "They won't, though," she insisted. "Even if they do make the connection that Marla and Chuck were working together and were killed by the same person, they'll probably still assume it was Harry. He's been out on bail, you know."

My stomach sank. I hadn't thought of that. Harry *had* been out of jail during Marla's murder. I wasn't sure about Mrs. Vick's.

Susan continued persuasively. "The police are probably going to think that Harry was in on the identity thefts, too. He could even have been the ringleader, using the floral business as a home base. Then he lost his temper and killed Chuck because Chuck's shenanigans were going to get them caught—when you think about it, that's an even better motive than the one the cops had before."

I groaned. It made a crazy kind of sense. Had our efforts actually put Harry in more danger? "But what can we do?" I asked hopelessly. "We're out of leads. Like you said, we've talked to everyone already."

Susan gave a deep sigh. "Sure seems like it. We can't give up now, though. Even Tara thinks we still might be able to help."

I stared at her. "How do you figure that? She was ripping us a new one less than ten minutes ago!"

"*But* she also told us where to send anonymous tips," Susan reminded me. "That must mean she thinks we either still have some information or that we're capable of digging up more clues—she just can't be a part of it anymore or she risks losing her job."

"That's not the impression I got," I said, unlocking my trunk and dumping all of my dance gear inside. "I'm pretty sure she told us that just to underline how unbelievably stupid we were. Did you actually call the police department instead of 911?"

"Yeah, I thought 911 would be tracing the call, but the police department probably wouldn't. I looked up the nearest station on my phone and called that number from the payphone."

This logic escaped me, but it did explain how Tara knew that the anonymous caller had used such a bad fake voice—by now it was probably a huge joke in all of the local police stations. I was just imagining a bunch of police officers doing Susan imitations when Susan broke into my train of thought.

"I wish we did have more information for them. We could free Harry and maybe even get a reward!"

"Maybe they wouldn't throw us in jail," I said. "That would be more than enough reward for me. Anyway, we don't have more information, so it's a moot point."

"Yeah."

In the end we drove away without coming up with a plan, which made me feel relieved and guilty at the same time. I didn't want to let Harry and Camellia down, but we were facing a dead end.

The rest of the weekend went quietly. It wasn't until I was brushing my teeth before bed on Sunday night that I realized we *did* still have a piece of information for the police. A big one. Not only had we failed to tell them about the person who entered the building after us, but all of a sudden I knew why that man's voice had seemed familiar.

The voice had belonged to Bill Ellis.

Chapter 30

"Bill Ellis? Are you sure?" Susan goggled at me over her hamburger. On Monday morning I had called for an emergency get-together over lunch. We had opted for fast food drive-through so we could talk in the privacy of a car. My car, of course—Susan had gotten hers detailed in the hopes of removing any evidence, and she refused to let its squeaky-clean interior be sullied by dripping sauce or spilled fries.

"Yes," I said. "Remember when he and Harry were trying to get that limb back onto the tree before the wedding? Bill Ellis did a lot of talking."

"He did a lot of cussing," Susan remembered, "but then, so did Harry." She screwed up her face in an effort to remember. "I suppose the guy at Marla's might have been him, but I couldn't swear to it in court. I was too busy freaking out to notice his voice."

"I'm positive it was him," I said. "His voice has a kind of raspy sound. I noticed it at the wedding and I thought, 'that guy sounds like a smoker!'"

Susan nodded. "And we know he smokes, because those kids at Harry's said Bill had started taking a lot of smoke breaks with Chuck recently." Her eyes lit with excitement. "So Bill Ellis was involved with the theft ring, Chuck was making trouble, and Bill was right there at the wedding! He must be the one who killed Chuck."

"Hang on," I said, "if we're thinking the same person did all three murders, it can't be Bill Ellis. He could have killed Chuck, but we know he didn't kill Marla, and I can't think of any reason at all for him to have killed Mrs. Vick."

"Yeah," Susan said with a groan. "That's the one that just doesn't fit, however you look at it. There's no way she would have been involved with the identity theft ring. I wouldn't put it past the Mayor to be up to something illegal, but Marla's operation seems kind of small-scale for him. Why would he bother?"

I agreed. "He definitely seems more like a widespread-corruption kind of guy."

"What if there is more than one ring," Susan hazarded. "Maybe he was in charge of a bunch of different groups?"

I mulled this over. "I don't know. I suppose it could be, but it still seems more likely that he'd be involved in something politically dishonest than in actual petty crime."

"Petty?" Susan's exclamation splattered the dashboard with partially chewed hamburger. "You get *your* credit hard swiped and see how petty you think it is!"

"I know, I know," I said hastily. "The important thing is, what do we do now?"

Susan frowned. "I'm not sure. I guess we could give the Crime Stopper thing a try."

"Another anonymous tip? Tara would go up in smoke!"

"She already has," Susan pointed out, "and I don't think she'll be any madder if we give them one more piece of information."

I wasn't so sure about this. Besides, another thought had just struck me. "If we turn Bill Ellis in right now, and they find evidence that he was there, he could become the prime suspect in Marla's murder."

"Works for me."

I stared at her. "But we know he didn't do it! All we'd accomplish would be trading one innocent person for another—and that's if the police make the connection between Marla's death and Chuck's. If they don't, we'll be trying to clear two innocent people instead of one."

"Innocent my backside," said Susan. "If you're right about Bill Ellis being the guy who came in after us, he's the only person who could have taken away that equipment in Marla's desk. He had to be in on the theft ring."

"Exactly," I said. "Bill Ellis is guilty of theft, not murder. I know you're mad about your credit account, but getting him charged with murder is going too far."

"A few days in jail wouldn't hurt him," she grumbled, "but you're right. He didn't kill Marla. And you know, as satisfying as it might have been to give Marla a punch in the face or something, I do feel bad about what happened to her. She didn't deserve that."

We both shuddered, remembering the ghastly sight of Marla's body sliding down the stairs.

"Yeah," I said. We were both silent for a moment.

"So anyway," Susan said finally, "what do *you* think we should do? You're the one with the super ears."

I heaved a sigh. "I don't know. On one hand we can't just sit on this information, but on the other—"

Susan interrupted. "I have an idea."

"And?" I said nervously.

"We make one more anonymous call, but not to the police. We call Bill."

"Huh?" This made absolutely no sense to me.

Susan grinned. "Listen, it's brilliant! We call Bill and tell him we know he's been part of an identity theft ring. We'll say we also know he was in Marla's apartment. So we tell him that unless he turns himself in as part of the theft ring, *we'll* tell the police where he was that night and he'll be in a lot more trouble! He'll turn himself in, and

252

maybe rat on anybody else who was in the gang. There might be someone we don't know about yet, and that person could be the killer."

I rolled my eyes. "Do you really think that a hardened criminal is going to turn himself in to the police because a couple of idiots call him up and say 'We know what you did?' That's insane."

"Would you rather tell him in person? Just because he hasn't killed anybody yet doesn't mean he won't. I'd rather not let him know who's threatening him."

"Either way we wouldn't be threatening him, we'd be warning him." I said patiently. "What he'd probably do is get rid of all the equipment, so that if we did call the police there would be nothing for them to find."

"So you're saying we should tell the police instead."

"Yes," I said. "No. I don't know!" I thumped my head on the steering wheel in frustration.

Susan glanced at her watch. "Well, I have a new client meeting in half an hour, and you need to get back to your critters. Let's just think about this, and if either of us comes up with a brilliant idea we can call each other. We could try to have some kind of strategy by class time tomorrow."

I drove us back to the wildlife center and Susan hopped into her car. As she waved goodbye, I leaned against the building and blew out an exasperated sigh.

"Something wrong?" asked Trey, coming through the doorway.

"No, I'm just trying to think."

Trey shook his head. "Bad idea," he said gravely. "The more you try to think, the less your brain works. I like to just sit back and let the ideas come when they're ready."

It seemed like good advice, so I dug into a pile of paperwork and tried to put the insanity of thefts and murders out of my mind. It worked for a while, and when a man rushed into the center with a juvenile blue heron tangled up in fishing line, I managed to completely forget about crime for an entire hour.

Once the struggling bird was freed, Nancy King examined it closely. "Fortunately, there was no hook on the line and he didn't injure his wings or legs thrashing around," she said. "I think we'll just give him some fluids and keep him overnight to make sure nothing else is happening. Then we can release him back into the same spot—after we check it for more fishing line." She wiped a strand of hair out of her eyes. "I wish people would be more responsible with their fishing gear, it's one of the worst hazards to wildlife in the water!"

I nodded. Fishing line and fish hooks accounted for many of the marine animal and bird injuries we encountered.

I headed home in a better mood, satisfied that most of my animal charges were doing well. My animal at home was not so happy. Even before I opened the front door I could hear bagpipes. And a yowling Siamese.

I scrabbled in my purse and found the earplugs that I keep for just such occasions. Stuffing them in my ears, I fumbled with the lock and let myself in. "Michael?" I yelled, even though I knew it was pointless. My voice is no match for bagpipes.

Two sets of bagpipes, as it turned out. Michael and Jim were both in the basement wailing away. I thumped down the steps. As soon as they saw me, they stopped playing and blessed silence filled the air.

"Why are both of you here?" I demanded. "Poor Banshee is upstairs having a fit!"

They looked slightly abashed. "Susan's home working on a new project, and she'd kill me if I practiced there," Jim explained.

"And we thought if we practiced down here with the door closed it wouldn't bother Banshee that much," Michael added.

I stared at them. Did they really have no idea how loud they are? Even in the basement with the door closed, the whole neighborhood could hear them!

"We have to practice extra for the show we're doing for Dave," Michael said. "I told you about that, didn't I?"

"Hey, we're actually going to be at the same shindig as you and Susan," Jim said enthusiastically.

I was confused. "Shindig?"

"The Strawberry Festival," Michael explained. "We're performing there, and that's where Dave's surprise party is going to be."

"Plus, we have a surprise for him of our own," Jim said, looking proud.

Michael dug an elbow into Jim's side and gave him a sharp glance. Jim shut up. They were clearly up to something, but whatever it was I didn't have time for it—my phone had started to buzz inside of my purse.

"Well, I hope you're done practicing because Banshee is about to have a nervous breakdown," I said, retreating up the stairs. "And I'll bet the neighbors might be calling the cops."

"We were pretty much done," Jim assured me, starting to pack up his things.

Out of sight of the guys, I dug out my phone. To my surprise, the caller was Anne, not Susan.

"Hi, Anne," I said, "what's up?"

"Ginger, the weirdest thing just happened," Anne said. "I just got a call from Annie Pierson. She's been going through Mrs. Vick's correspondence—it got backed up because they were busy planning a fundraiser. Mrs. Vick had a lot of unread mail. Most of the mail was advertising, but there was one letter in a bright green envelope and it caught her eye. She opened it up and it turned out to be a threat!"

My ears pricked up. "A threat? What did it say?"

"I don't know if I've got it word-for-word, but it basically said that women like her didn't deserve to live and wouldn't be tolerated anymore."

"A death threat, then."

"Yes, but one she never saw. It's so sad, because if she'd known someone was after her, she might have taken more precautions."

"Like not staying home alone," I said thoughtfully. "I hope Annie has given it to the police."

"Oh, she has. Now they're going through all of her papers and her computer, to see if there was anything else."

I was silent, thinking. It didn't seem likely that Mrs. Vick had received an earlier warning, because of course she would have called the police. I didn't think the search would find anything, but you never knew. What really struck me was the similarity between the warning Mrs. Vick had gotten and the one found in Marla's apartment. More evidence, if it were needed, that the two deaths were connected.

"Ginger? Are you there?"

"Yes, sorry. Thanks for letting me know. I'll tell Susan. We should all get together soon to compare notes again."

"I think so too."

We rang off. Then I wondered what Susan and I would tell everyone if we did get together—without Tara, obviously. Should we fess up and tell the rest of the group what we had done and the evidence we'd found? On one hand it would feel good to get some outside advice. On the other, telling them would put them in the same position that we were in.

I was just about to call Susan when I heard Jim and Michael thumping up the stairs with all their gear. Jim was carrying an enormous duffle bag as well as his bagpipe case, and it crossed my mind that they seemed to be having the same problem with ever-expanding bags of stuff that Susan and I had as dancers.

"What's in the bag?" I asked.

Jim shrugged. "Oh, you know, just music, tools, and other bagpipe stuff. Hey, are you and Susan going to come see our performance at the festival?"

"I hope so, if our performances aren't scheduled at the same time." It wasn't really a lie. I liked to support the two goofballs in their musical hobby—they had certainly sat through more than their fair share of less-than-stellar belly dancing! We could always sneak earplugs into our ears if necessary.

"So, are you up for another practice tomorrow afternoon?" Michael asked as he opened the door for Jim, who didn't have any free hands.

"Yep," Jim answered. "In the Grange this time," he told me hastily, adding that the community's meeting hall hadn't been available for practice today.

"We're having extra practices too," I said. "We need all the rehearsal we can get!"

"The Strawberry Festival's sure coming up fast," Jim said ruefully.

"You'll be fine." I assured him.

Once Jim had gone, Banshee crept out of hiding. She fixed Michael with a blue-eyed glare and hissed.

Michael looked so guilty I couldn't help laughing.

"Give her some of the new tuna treat," I suggested, "she's crazy about it. You might end up with less retaliation."

Michael scooped some of the treat into a bowl and set it down. Banshee stalked by him, threw him another dirty look and buried her face in the treat, growling slightly and bristling her tail.

"Progress," Michael said hopefully.

"For now. Let's just hope she doesn't spray your shoes or something."

"That smell does *not* come out," he agreed. Then he looked thoughtful. "You know, I think I'll just go shut the door on the shoe closet right now."

"I think that's a good idea."

Unfortunately for Michael, he neglected to shut the door on his bedroom closet. Banshee quickly discovered this lapse and took full advantage of it. The rest of the evening was spent doing laundry while Banshee sat on the couch looking unbelievably smug.

I didn't get a chance to call Susan that night, but when I finally tumbled into bed, I made a mental note to call her in the morning. We had some serious decisions to make.

Chapter 31

Susan called me first. I was just getting into the car when my phone buzzed.

"Ginger, have you heard the latest?" she asked.

"If the latest is that both Mrs. Vick and Marla got death threats before they were killed, then yes."

"You *have* heard." She sounded disappointed.

"Anne called me last night," I explained. "Did she get ahold of you too? We had a Banshee event so I never got to call you."

"Oh, no, is the little couch shredder OK?"

Despite her flippant words, I heard the real concern in Susan's voice. I quickly explained.

Susan dissolved into laughter. "Banshee sprayed the whole closet?" she choked. "How? She's such a tiny little thing."

"She has an impressive range," I said darkly, "especially when she's mad. Apparently she disapproves of bagpipes in the basement."

"You can't blame her for that," Susan said, still laughing.

I tried to get us back on track. "So, how did you hear about the letters?"

"It's on the news—don't you ever try to keep up with current events?"

"Not early in the morning, when I'm trying to get to work," I said. "What are they saying about it?"

"People are finally making the connection between the two deaths," Susan said with triumph in her voice. "The police will know for sure once their handwriting expert compares the two notes."

I thought for a moment. "Do you think Chuck got one too?"

"You'd think he would have gone to the police if he had, unless he didn't take it seriously."

"Or he didn't want the police sniffing around and maybe finding evidence of the identity theft ring." I added.

"Good point."

Remembering the thoughts I'd had after my conversation with Anne, I asked Susan what she thought of calling a meeting with our fellow conspirators and telling them about our adventure at Marla's.

I heard Susan breathing on the other end while she considered this. "I just don't know," she said finally. "We'd be putting them in a tight spot if we're not planning to confess our sins to Tara, and if we do that she for sure is going to have to report us."

"I wonder how many years you get for burglary," I said glumly.

"If we didn't steal anything, we aren't burglars."

"Trespassing, then. Whatever they figure out we're guilty of."

"Hmm. Let's not jump the gun," Susan said hastily. "The guys are going out to practice tomorrow afternoon. Why don't we get together at my place and hash out all of our ideas and the evidence we've found? Then we can at least get our facts organized if we do decide to go to the police."

This seemed like a good idea. If nothing else, it postponed having to make a decision. "Why don't we write down everything we can think of beforehand, and then compare notes?" I suggested. "Then we can pool our ideas tomorrow. I'll be getting off my shift at about four. See you at 4:30-ish?"

"Sounds good," Susan agreed, and rang off.

I slipped the phone back in my pocket and headed for the sanctuary, wondering if we would come up with anything new tomorrow. To be honest, it didn't seem likely.

Chapter 32

The next day, things ended up being too chaotic at the sanctuary for me to write down much. When I got to Susan's, I found that she was in the same boat.

"I hope you've had some big ideas," she said as she restrained Lady's attempt to charge past me. "I've been working on my new client's ad campaign. Let's just say I've been learning way more than I ever wanted to know about chickens. Lady, *no!*" This last was directed to Lady, who had started barking hysterically and lunging at the now-closed front door.

I watched, interested. "She's still doing that?"

Susan rolled her eyes. "More than ever," she said. "I just can't figure out why she's so determined to get at the neighbor's dog. All he ever does is sit and stare at her with his big goggly eyes."

"Maybe that's the problem," I said. "He's refusing to respond to her aggression."

"I think he's insulting her telepathically," Susan said.

"Could be that, too."

Absently patting Lady on the head, Susan headed for the living room and plopped down on the couch. Upchuck jumped up and put his head in her lap, apparently jealous of the attention Lady was getting.

"Dogs," Susan sighed, rubbing Upchuck's floppy ears.

"At least they aren't spraying your closet," I said.

"Anyway," said Susan, coming around to business, "where are we in this so-called investigation?"

I sank into a recliner opposite the couch. "Pretty much nowhere. For a while Marla seemed like our best suspect, but I guess getting killed exonerates her."

"And it's not Bill Ellis," said Susan, sticking her feet on the coffee table. "Who's left?"

"Well, I guess it could be the Mayor," I said, "but like we've said before, why on earth would he have killed Marla—unless he was in on the identity scheme, which isn't likely, and Marla was somehow a danger? And if he killed both Marla and Chuck because of the ring, how does killing his wife make sense?"

Susan sighed heavily. "She found out about it and was going to turn him in?" she hazarded.

"What about the death threats? 'Women like you don't deserve to live' sounds more like a jealous lover than a person who's killing off people who were involved in a crime."

"OK, forget the Mayor for now," Susan suggested. "How about the other employees at Harry's?" She produced a small notebook and consulted it. "There's Jerry Lambert," she said. "Camellia is sure that he and Harry were friends, but Lambert could have a reason for wanting to get Harry in trouble."

I raised my eyebrows. "By killing three people? I could see it if Jerry Lambert was in on the ring, but that still wouldn't explain Mrs. Vick."

"Gahhh!" Susan pulled on her hair in frustration. "If the identity theft ring is the reason for the killings, it doesn't explain Mrs. Vick. If somebody was jealous about Chuck's affairs, it doesn't explain Marla. None of it makes sense."

"Could it have been one of the other employees?" I asked.

Susan looked at her notebook. "Peter Norberg or Ellie Meyers? I hope not, I liked them both. Besides, why would they? All of the problems with Jerry Lambert being the killer would apply to them, too."

"Maybe there's a reason we haven't thought of yet," I said.

Susan shook her head and stood up. "You know what? We're not getting anywhere. We need caffeine. I'll make some coffee."

I agreed, and trailed after her into the kitchen. Lady and Upchuck followed us, sensing that food preparation of some sort was about to happen.

Susan measured out the coffee while I leaned against the counter and scratched Upchuck's ears. Lady planted herself by Susan's feet.

With my free hand, I idly flipped through a pile of mail that had been shoved off to the side. "Is there a bill you're trying to avoid?" I quipped. "You've got at least a week's worth of mail here."

Susan blew a strand of hair out of her face. "It's my chicken guy," she said. "I've been spending all my time trying to come up with a new way to sell humanely-raised organic free-range eggs. Who's got time for mail? Anyway, nobody gets bills by mail anymore. It's probably just all ads."

I was about to comment on the irony of Susan avoiding ads while she was trying to come up with new ones when my eye fell on a bright green envelope addressed to her. Something about it bothered me. I had seen the same thing before, recently. A green envelope in a pile of unopened mail, sitting on what? Not a kitchen counter. A desk. An antique roll-top desk.

Marla's desk.

A chill crept down my neck and swept down to my toes. Disjointed memories suddenly came together as I stared at the envelope. Green envelopes. Green business cards, one of them Chuck's and one of them Susan's. Money. Money taken from a lonely old woman. Money from the sale of a farm. Money from theft. An unscrupulous man who used his good looks to take advantage of women. Chuck laughing to his coworkers about his divorce.

I had stopped rubbing Upchuck's ears, and with a whine he turned and left the kitchen. Suddenly pricking up her ears, Lady followed. Susan flicked the coffee pot on and reached into a cupboard for a box of cookies.

"Susan?" My throat had gone so dry it came out like a squeak.

Susan turned around. "What's wrong with you?" she asked, "and where did the dogs go? They always hang around when I bring out the cookies."

"Susan," I said again, a little more firmly. "Do you still have Tara on speed dial?"

"Yes, but why—"

"Call her," I interrupted. "Call her *now!*"

Susan looked at me as if I had gone crazy, but something in my face made her dig the phone out of her pocket and flip it on. "Now would you please tell me what the hell—hey! What's Lady doing outside?"

Lady was indeed outside. Her wild barking was beginning to register on my ears. Through the kitchen window we could see her racing back and forth in front of the fence, trying to get at the neighbor's dog. Luigi Di'Ogee haughtily sat and stared at Lady, not even bothering to respond. Upchuck had followed Lady out and was chewing on a piece of rawhide while he watched the action.

"I must not have latched the door all the way when you came in," Susan grumbled. She set the phone down on the counter. "Hang on, I'll go get her."

She turned and took a step toward the living room but suddenly stopped dead. I also turned around, and froze.

Amy McKenzie stood in the doorway between the living room and the kitchen. She looked just as drab as she had at Harry's, but somehow there was a difference. Her pale blue eyes still showed no emotion, but their very deadness was more menacing than any show of anger or hate could be.

Susan had been struck dumb with surprise for a moment, but she now found her tongue. "What—who are you? What are you doing in my house?" She took another look and knitted her eyebrows, puzzled. "I've seen you somewhere before, though…Oh! At Harry's?"

"Hello, Mrs. McKenzie," I said. "I'm guessing this is from you?" I held up the green envelope. I didn't have to open it to know what was inside.

A slow smile appeared on Mrs. McKenzie's face, but it didn't brighten her face any. "Oh good," she said. "You're together." She nodded at me. "Now I won't have to hunt you down when I'm done with this whore."

"I'm sorry, this *what*?" Susan had been putting two and two together while Mrs. McKenzie and I talked. "Wait, do you think I was having an affair with Chuck? Or that Ginger was? That's crazy!"

"That's why she's been killing all of these people," I said. I looked Mrs. McKenzie straight in the eye. Susan's phone was still on

268

the counter, but she hadn't hit the button to speed-dial Tara. Maybe if we distracted Mrs. McKenzie I could unobtrusively hit it now. "Am I right?" I asked.

Mrs. McKenzie only grunted in reply.

"Hang on," Susan broke in, "Mrs. Vick might have been having an affair with Chuck, but Marla wasn't. Neither were we. Anyway," she added to Mrs. McKenzie, "why would it even matter to you? You said yourself you were divorcing him."

I sidled a little bit closer to the phone. On one hand, there were two of us and one of her. Surely if it came down to a fight we would win. Then again, we didn't know if she was armed, and even if she only had a knife she could do a lot of damage to one or both of us.

"She claimed that she was divorcing Chuck," I said, making a guess, "but that wasn't actually true, was it? Chuck was divorcing you. He'd gone through all of your money, so he was leaving. It was the last straw."

Then anger leapt into those eyes. Mrs. McKenzie uttered a string of curse words that would have been impressive on a pirate ship. "That bastard thought he could do anything he wanted," she said. "Spend my money, sleep with anyone he liked, insult me to my face, anything! And then, after all of that, to think he could divorce me. Think he could just walk away." She smiled again, and I felt a shudder deep inside. Mrs. McKenzie wasn't just angry. She was insane.

Chapter 33

"So how did you do it?" Susan asked. "Kill Chuck, I mean. You weren't even at the wedding."

The creepy smile held. "Oh yes, I was. Chuck had a number of overalls from that florist place. He expected me to wash them. I washed them, alright, and nobody looked at me twice when I was walking around at the wedding. All I had to do was avoid the other employees and wait until I caught Chuck alone."

With Susan holding Mrs. McKenzie's attention, I managed to slip my hand over the phone. Holding my breath, I tapped the 'send call' button on the screen. To cover up any sound the phone might make, including Tara's voice, I continued the conversation.

"It was a pretty good idea to use materials from Deerborne's to strangle Chuck," I said. "Did you intend to put the blame on Harry?"

"I didn't care who got blamed, I just wanted to give the cops a link to the florist shop to put them off the scent."

"What about the death threats?" I asked. "Why send those?"

"I wanted all of you to know what was coming," she said, her smile becoming even more eerie.

"You should try e-mail next time," I suggested, stepping away from the phone and trying to hold her attention. "Nobody opens regular mail anymore. Mrs. Vick and Marla never even saw your notes." I waggled the green envelope in my hand. "Neither has Susan—and I'm guessing I've either got one coming or buried in my own mail pile as well?"

"Is that what that card is?" Susan asked. "I thought it might be a thank-you card from Kalina and Harun."

I handed Susan the card. She opened it and read the contents. "Wow, that's pretty rude," she commented.

Over the top of the note, Susan threw me a glance, imperceptibly tilting her head toward the door that went from the kitchen to the garage. I understood—if we made a break for it through the living room, we'd have to get past Mrs. McKenzie. The kitchen door was on the other side of the room. The garage door itself was closed, but there was also a back door in the garage that led to the yard. It wouldn't slow us down as much as waiting for the garage door to open. I gave Susan a quick nod.

"How did you even know how to kill somebody like that?" I asked, hoping Mrs. McKenzie hadn't noticed the exchange.

"My parents were real wackos," she said. "When the farm stopped paying, they thought the government was behind it, and started a militia group. I grew up knowing how to use guns, knives and of course—" here she broke off and pulled out a lethal-looking piece of wire and lovingly took a good grip on both ends. "Everything they believed was stupid, but I learned some useful things. Like how to get rid of my no-good husband and his whores."

"He wasn't having an affair with Marla," Susan pointed out. "They were involved in an identity theft ring, but they weren't lovers. Neither were we," she added, indicating the two of us.

"And I suppose you just happened to have Chuck's card with his number on it?" Mrs. McKenzie sneered. Then anger flared in her eyes again. She started to shout. "Don't lie to me! I know what you two are, I know what that chocolate maker was, and I know what that little red-headed bitch at the florist is. I'm tired of all of you! None of you deserve to live!" She lunged forward.

"Time to go," yelled Susan. To my amazement, she grabbed a broom that had been leaning up against the counter and twirled it, tahtib-style, at Mrs. McKenzie. The broom end altered the balance of the makeshift weapon, however, and instead of hitting Susan's opponent, the broom handle swiped the nearly-full coffee pot. The pot and its contents flew across the kitchen and landed on Mrs. McKenzie.

We ran for the door as Mrs. McKenzie shrieked, whether from fury or being spattered with hot coffee I didn't know. I yanked the door open, ran into the garage and headed for the back door. Susan was right behind me. Unfortunately, Mrs. McKenzie was right behind her. The coffee barely slowed her down.

I was sprinting across the lawn when I heard an "Oof!" behind me. Turning to look, I saw that Susan had tripped over one of the dog toys scattered around the yard and sprawled face first into the grass. Mrs. McKenzie was on top of her before I could race back. I saw a glint of sunlight reflecting off of the garrote as Mrs. McKenzie tried to whip it around Susan's throat. I ran back, but I knew I wouldn't be in time.

Suddenly there was a flash of black and tan fur as Lady charged straight into Mrs. McKenzie. It had finally dawned on the German shepherd that her owner was in trouble. Mrs. McKenzie was knocked off of Susan and the garrote went flying. Lady went after her and latched onto her jacket. For a few seconds they rolled on the ground.

Then Mrs. McKenzie whipped out a huge hunting knife and lunged toward the dog. Righting herself, Susan desperately started to scramble over to them on her hands and knees. I had reached them by this time, and tried to drag Mrs. McKenzie back. She gave me a kick that sent me reeling backward and knocked the breath out of me. Lady, growling and snarling, renewed her grip on the jacket. Mrs. McKenzie raised the knife over Lady's head.

"No!" Susan screamed. Gasping for breath, I could only watch in horror, sure that the brave animal Susan loved so much was about to die.

But the blow never fell. There was another flash of fur, this time brown, black and white, as Luigi Di'Ogee vaulted the fence and in one swift motion pinned Mrs. McKenzie's arm to the ground. Lady took advantage of this to jump on Mrs. McKenzie's chest, further pinning her down and snarling into her face. Mrs. McKenzie began to shriek a stream of curse words as both Susan and I rushed forward to make sure no harm came to either dog. I grabbed the knife and the garrote while Susan threw herself on Mrs. McKenzie's legs and held tight. Upchuck bounced around us, barking hysterically and trying to find out what fun new game everybody was playing.

I suddenly realized that the sound of police sirens had been getting closer for the last minute or so. There was a screech of brakes in Susan's driveway, and the sound of footsteps running on gravel. Tara and Detective Harris burst around the corner of the house. They reached us at the same time.

"It was her," Susan yelled, not giving up her hold on Mrs. McKenzie. "This bitch tried to kill my dog! *She tried to kill my dog!*"

Tara pried Susan off Mrs. McKenzie as Detective Harris did the same with the two canines. He quickly handed the dogs over to me, then flipped Mrs. McKenzie face down on the ground and slapped handcuffs on her as he read her her rights.

"She's been behind all the murders—she told us," I panted. "She came here to kill Susan. Then she was going to kill me."

"We know," Tara said grimly. "We heard the whole thing on the phone."

Other units had been pulling up as well, and a number of officers showed up. Detective Harris handed Mrs. McKenzie off to them and they half dragged, half carried the her into a police car as she screamed obscenities.

Susan sat on the grass and hugged Lady, despite the dog's clear wish to follow the officers and tear Mrs. McKenzie to bits. "You saved my life," she sobbed into Lady's thick fur. "You saved my life. Don't you ever, *ever* do that again!"

Upchuck whined and licked Susan's face, apparently wondering why Susan would be so upset after such a fun game. "You goofball," Susan said, scratching Upchuck's ears. Upchuck settled happily down on his haunches, relieved that everything seemed to be OK.

I also collapsed on the grass. The adrenaline was wearing off and I could feel my limbs starting to shake.

"Are you two OK?" demanded Tara. She sounded pretty shaky herself. "What the *hell* did you think you were doing, facing off with a killer like that?"

This gross miscarriage of justice shook Susan out of her emotional turmoil. "We didn't do anything," she protested, outraged. "Mrs. McKenzie followed *us*! She broke into my house—we had nothing to do with it, except that that lunatic thought we were sleeping with her skeezy husband. How in the world is this our fault?"

"It isn't," Detective Harris said, gingerly trying restore calm. "Listening to that phone call on the way here was just a little…unnerving. Especially for a friend who cares about you as much as Tara does."

This got my attention. He had used Tara's first name!

Susan was also eyeing the pair with an air of speculation. "You guys got here at the same time," she mused. "Like you were in the same car, or something."

"We were having coffee at Georgio's when my phone went off," Tara said hastily. "I just thought we'd get here faster if we both took my patrol car." Was I imagining it, or did her face look a little flushed?

I eyed Detective Harris. He also seemed a bit embarrassed. He noticed my look. "I took your advice and asked Officer Ericson if we could have a talk," he said.

"Her advice?" Tara asked sharply. "What advice?"

Susan gave a rich, significant chuckle. "It looks like that must have been some talk, whoever's advice it was," she grinned. Then she pointed. "Hey, look at that!"

We followed her pointing finger. Lady had escaped Susan's grip and wandered up to Luigi Di'Ogee, who had been sitting politely by the side as the humans talked. From Lady's lowered head and general attitude, I had a feeling she was apologizing for her previous rude behavior. After all, Luigi Di'Ogee had saved her life and helped protect her owner. Luigi Di'Ogee answered with a soft bark. Upchuck trotted up to the pair and cheerfully deposited a badly-chewed piece of rawhide at their feet.

"Looks like everybody's making new friends today," I said.

I might have imagined it, but I think Detective Harris winked at me.

Chapter 34

The day of the Strawberry Festival dawned warm and clear, despite a mixed weather forecast that had warned of possible showers. In our beledi dresses, we nervously adjusted our grips on our tahtib sticks as we waited for our time to perform. Then Kalina and Harun took the stage.

They had returned from their honeymoon two weeks before, and were now performing their first duet as a married couple. We whooped and hollered like anything as Harun adjusted the harness that held his tabla (Egyptian drum) so he could stand and move around with Kalina.

He started to play a fast-moving rhythm called a *malfouf,* and Kalina circled the stage doing a *choo choo* shimmy—an energetic shimmy done up on the balls of the feet. It takes incredibly strong calves and I couldn't even keep one going for ten seconds, but Kalina kept it up all around the stage. Then she shimmied up to Harun. He started to play complicated improvised rhythms and she interpreted them visually with her graceful movements. We watched in awe as the music and dance blended seamlessly, performed by two accomplished artists who were also in perfect communication.

By the time they came to the amazing finish, with Kalina jumping into the air and landing in a full layback on the stage floor in perfect time to Harun's last drum strike, we were cheering too wildly to remember that we were nervous. Harun and Kalina, radiant and smiling from ear to ear, joined hands and bowed. Then they kissed, and the applause went through the roof.

"How are we going to follow that?" Susan hissed in my ear when the clapping and cheering finally began to subside.

"By getting up on stage," I said resolutely. "What's the worst that could happen?"

Susan shot me a look. "What's the matter with you? You can't ask a question like that right before a performance!"

This sent a wave of nervous snickering through the rest of the group.

"At least you can't lose your bra this time," Susan grinned. I glared at her—true, my bra top had come loose during my very first

279

public performance, but this wasn't exactly the time to bring it up. Then I started laughing, too.

At that point our music started, and the whole troupe had to struggle against attacks of the giggles as we took our positions on stage. Even so, I was surprised by how well we did. All of that practicing had finally paid off—Susan and I whirled our sticks without getting them tangled in our sleeves. When we did the final spin we both remembered to raise the right side of our sticks, and our sticks crossed with a satisfying thwack. No fingers or other body parts got whacked in the process! A quick sideways glance at our fellow troupe members confirmed that everybody else had gotten it right too. Not a single yelp of pain or the clatter of a stick hitting the ground. With a feeling of having achieved the impossible, we took our bows. The audience cheered and we left the stage.

Anne rushed up to us first. "You were amazing!" she said, hugging us. "And you thought you'd never get the hang of tahtib!"

Tara and John—I was finally starting to get used to calling the detective by his first name—came up to congratulate us.

"Those sticks should be classified as weapons," John laughed. "You ladies looked pretty fierce up there."

"They are weapons," Tara clarified. "Tahtib is a real martial art as well as a dance!"

"I believe it."

Susan and I exchanged glances. Neither of them had actually said anything to us, but it certainly seemed as though Tara and John had patched up their differences and at least become friends again. If they

280

ended up becoming more than that, well, there might be some hurdles with HR and police regulations, but they could handle it.

Camellia made her way through the crowd, followed by Harry. Harry carried a load of bouquets, which he thrust into our arms. "I know you both worked hard to get me proven innocent," he said, looking a little misty-eyed. "Thank you. And that was a lovely performance."

"Harry!" Tara ran up to him and gave him a hug. He handed her a bouquet.

"And thank you, too, Tara," Harry said with a wink, "although I know you 'weren't supposed' to be working on the case." He grinned at her and they both laughed.

Another voice came up from behind us. "Speaking of cases," said Detective Dot Beresford, "there has been an unexpected break in that identity theft case we talked about a few weeks ago."

We turned to see Detective Beresford, looking extra smart in a beautifully-cut suit in a deep navy blue that flattered her complexion. Her blond hair was up in an elegant French twist. Her skirt ended just below her knees, accentuating her curvy calves and well-shaped feet in their high-heeled navy pumps.

I looked at her in envy—no amount of designer clothing or expensive hair stylists could ever make me look as put-together as this woman did, and she seemed to be able to do it without effort. In that French twist, my hair would frizz instantly. My nylons would run in those shoes, the navy suit would be covered in cat hair, and I would, for sure, slosh coffee all over that crisp white blouse. The woman was an artist.

"What kind of break?" Susan was asking.

"It was one of those funny things," Detective Beresford said with an enigmatic smile. "First we got that picture of the theft equipment that disappeared from Marla Birch's apartment. So, we knew it had been there, but had no idea where it had gone. Then, out of the blue, we got another anonymous tip." Her bright eyes fastened on us.

"You did?" I said, confused.

"You don't say," Susan said casually. I turned to stare at her, suddenly suspicious.

Dot twinkled at Susan. "A few days ago somebody call our Crime Stoppers anonymous tip line and suggested that we check out a man named Bill Ellis, who worked near Ms. Birch's business. We checked out his home, and sure enough we found enough evidence to put him away for quite a while. He had one stroke of good luck, though," Dot continued, "because if the murderer of Marla Birch hadn't already been discovered, he would have been the prime suspect for that, too."

"Sounds like it worked out pretty well," Susan said, avoiding my eyes.

It had worked out incredibly well, I reflected. Mrs. McKenzie had been charged with all three murders, and with attempted murder in her attack on us. She had also, by her own admission, been planning to kill Ellie Meyers, the young redheaded girl at Harry's who had complained to us about Chuck's inappropriate behavior. Mrs. McKenzie had been violently obsessed with eliminating every woman

282

Chuck had flirted or slept with—so obsessed that she had imagined liaisons where they didn't exist. Where would it have ended?

Even without her confession, there had been plenty of evidence against Mrs. McKenzie once the police had known where to look. The green jumpsuit we had seen Mrs. McKenzie bring back to Harry's had actually had traces of Harry's blood on it, in spite of being laundered. With her medium height and stocky build, she would have fit into it easily and passed off as just another worker. Then all she had to do was strip it off, bundle it up, take it home and throw it in the wash. I shivered.

"Hey, what's wrong with you?" Susan demanded. "We need to get out of these costumes and get over to the guys' bagpipe thing."

I shook the dark thoughts out of my head. This was a happy day. "The bagpipe thing is going to be on this stage," I said. "They're setting up the mic's now."

"Mic's? Since when do bagpipes need microphones?"

"I don't know, but I have extra earplugs in my purse if you need them."

Susan rolled her eyes. "I brought mine, believe me."

We headed back to the dressing area, where Anne took a group picture of us and then began helping us out of our costumes.

"Ladies, I'm so proud of you!" she exclaimed. "I was just approached by a manager at Redvue Mall. She was in the audience. The Mall will be hosting their big International Festival in August, and they're looking for traditional music and dances from around the

283

world. After seeing your performance today, she's invited us to come perform!"

We all zaghareeted, squealed and clapped.

"Guess we won't be turning our sticks in anytime soon," Susan said with a grin. "That's good, because I've really been starting to enjoy it."

"I'm glad to hear that," said Anne, "because they want us for a twenty-minute slot. This piece was only five minutes long, so we need to add more dances and do a lot more practicing."

There was more laughter and a few good-natured groans as we processed this information.

At that moment, a loud wailing sound blasted our ears, dying off in a drawn-out squawk. The bagpipers were warming up.

Susan and I hastily finished dressing and made our way back to the stage area. Tara, John and Dot were sitting together, and we scooted into chairs beside them.

"I didn't know you guys were bagpipe fans," Susan said.

There was some hemming and hawing about this, and it turned out that they were mostly there to support Detective Dave McGirk at his surprise retirement party, which was going to happen right after the performance. His wife, two daughters and son were hiding around a corner and in some secret spot a large cake had been hidden. Quite a few officers were scattered around, trying not to be too noticeable.

Susan and I discreetly inserted our earplugs as a group of eight bagpipers and several people carrying different types of drums took the stage. The stage was barely big enough for them.

They were led by Detective McGirk, a large, burly man with red hair now turning grey. He was resplendent in a regal-looking kilt and jacket covered by gold braid. A tartan cape swept over his shoulders. He carried a tall gold staff, apparently to help the band keep the beat.

I recognized a few of the songs, such as 'Scotland the Brave.' There were fewer sour notes than I had heard on previous occasions—with all the extra practices, the band had improved! Thank heaven for earplugs, though. The background of the stage acted as a huge amplifier, but in spite of the ear-splitting volume, the people in charge of the sound system were still using the microphones to get as much noise as possible blasting into the speakers.

"I'll bet people can hear them all the way in Tacoma," Susan whispered in my ear during a break between songs. We had lent our spare earplugs to people in the neighboring seats. Tara and John had brought their own. Others who weren't so lucky tried various methods to cover their ears without seeming to do so. One man checked his wristwatch, feigned surprise at the lateness of the hour, and scooted away to safety. Several crying children were also taken out of the audience.

Once the show was over, Detective McGirk turned to lead the group offstage, but Michael and Jim stepped out of line to stop him. With a huge grin on his face, Jim scooped up one of the microphones.

"Ladies and gentlemen, we'd like to present you with a special surprise in honor of our leader, Detective Dave McGirk of the Puyallup Police Force. He's going to be retiring in a few days and we'd all like to thank him for his years of service."

285

While Jim was making this speech, a couple of Michael and Jim's buddies had hoisted a tartan-covered 3-foot-tall object onto the stage. Michael wheeled the thing to the front. Together, he and Jim lifted the tartan cloth.

"Oh, no," Susan groaned. Oh, *no!*"

My own stomach sank. A strangely-altered set of bagpipes sat on a framework of wheels. The 'bag' part of the pipes was hooked up to something that might have been an air compressor—I wasn't sure. The chanter was hooked up to a jumble of wiring that ended in a computer keyboard. Pipes stuck out from the thing at odd angles. Atop the tallest pipe sat a perky tam o' chanter. A large sporran covered the front of the bizarre assembly.

"They didn't," I said, sinking my face into my hands.

"Detective McGirk, we'd like to present you with the world's first fully automatic bagpiper—Sir Pipey McBaggins!"

"Hit it!" cheered Michael.

Jim threw a switch on the back of the monstrosity, and air began to hiss into the bag. An unearthly moan issued from the pipes as the bag continued to inflate. Then lights started flashing along the keyboard, which apparently relayed signals to the chanter. Something like a tune started from the chanter as the droning pipes continued to wail in a completely unrelated key.

Then the pitch started to rise. The bag seemed to be full, but it continued to inflate, and the pipes were obviously not up to the job of passing the air along. Michael and Jim looked at their creation in confusion as the noise rose to an anguished shriek.

Detective McGirk, who had been staring dubiously at the abomination since it had been wheeled out, now sprang into action. "Get off the stage!" he roared. "Everybody get back! Get down!" He waved his arms at the dumbstruck crowd.

Bagpipers and drummers dove off the stage like lemmings. The crowd scattered. Even Michael and Jim, with one last look at their beloved automatic piper, fled the stage. They hit the ground just as the bag exploded with an almighty bang.

Little pieces of tartan rained down as the pipes gave up a dying squawk. The automatic piper tipped over with a thud, and then a stunned silence settled over the area.

Everybody looked at everybody else to see if it was safe to get back up. Fortunately, no one seemed to be hurt. The only casualty was Sir Pipey McBaggins, lying in pieces on the stage. Fire sirens began to sound in the distance.

A local camera crew, who had been recording events at the festival, recovered their wits and zeroed in on the stage just in time to catch Jim and Michael getting shakily to their feet and examining their fallen creation. "Well," Jim said, in what was to become the favorite quote on the news for some time to come, "*that* wasn't supposed to happen!"

Chapter 35

The smell of barbeque wafted across Susan's spacious backyard. We had all gathered to celebrate Harry's freedom and the fact that we were all still alive.

The news for the last few weeks had been filled with interesting stories. 'The capture of the garrote killer' was right up there with 'Bagpipers accidentally blow up stage' and a humorous side story about how the Mayor was going to remove a controversial statute from his front lawn due to some 'disrespectful incidents involving inappropriate pieces of lingerie,' which the police had promised to investigate, but probably weren't.

"We didn't even scratch that stage," Michael said, munching his hamburger. "They're making it sound like we used dynamite!"

"You didn't get arrested," Tara reminded him. "Count your blessings."

"I can't believe you guys built another robot after what happened last time!" Susan fumed, remembering a brand new carpet that had been destroyed by one of the guys' previous efforts.

"It wasn't a robot," Jim insisted. "It was an automatic bagpipe."

Michael shot an accusatory look at Jim. "And it would have worked, too, if the air compressor had been regulated properly."

"You're just lucky that Detective McGirk spoke up for you," Tara said. "Considering his job, he might have thought it was a malicious joke instead of realizing it was just a stupid accident."

Michael and Jim hung their heads.

Harry and Camellia brought plates up to the picnic table and took their seats.

"What exactly was his job," Harry asked, "other than being a regular police officer? Did he have a specialty?"

Tara nearly choked on her burger as she laughed. "He was the head of the Bomb Squad!"

"That's perfect!" Camellia said with a chuckle. "He should be able to keep these two in line."

"We can always hope," I said.

Once the initial panic had died down at the festival, Detective McGirk's retirement party had resumed without a hitch. The cake hadn't suffered any damage other than being scattered with a few confetti-like bits of tartan, and friends of the McGirk's had appeared with gifts and dishes for a potluck. Michael and Jim had apologized profusely and volunteered to go to the nearest store and pick up several cases of soda to add to the feast.

"I've got more burgers here," called Jerry Lambert, who had been presiding over the grill.

Jim and Michael whooped and raced to the grill, but Susan beat them to it. Harry followed at a slower pace. Lady and Upchuck bounced around, hoping for dropped treats. I helped myself to another piece of Harry's famous dolmas.

"I'm so glad the police were able to prove that Jerry had nothing to do with the identity thefts," Camellia said to me in a low voice. "It was hard enough for Harry to find out that two of his employees were thieves—I don't know what he would have done if Jerry had been involved. They're such good friends. Did you know that Harry has brought him in as a full partner, now?"

I nodded. "How has the business been going?" I asked. "I've been worried that between the murders and the new publicity over the identity theft ring, customers might be avoiding Deerborne Florist. I didn't really want to ask Harry, though."

Camellia smiled. "He's actually had an outpouring of support from some of his previous customers, including the Nickleson's. He sent a letter to all of his clients explaining the security breach and warning them to check their credit records. He offered to help them clear up any problems. I think his customers appreciated his honesty."

"Of course," she added, "he's had to find replacements for Chuck and Bill Ellis, but that hasn't been much of a problem. He's also promoted those two young people, Peter Norberg and Ellie Meyers, to oversee some of the design work and accounting. It's been a rough time for him, but he's going to be OK. In fact, the Nickleson's were so impressed by his work at Kalina's wedding that they're hiring him to do the flowers at the One World Conference and the Viva Gala. It will be one of the biggest jobs he's ever done!"

My eyes widened. The One World Conference was a huge annual event arranged by the Nickleson's. Medical and technology experts convened at Viva Technologies to find solutions to health problems across the globe. The ending Viva Gala was the social event of the year, raising money for a kaleidoscope of health-related charities and research projects. For a smaller company like Harry's, it would be a huge job—and fantastic publicity! I felt my own face mirror the beaming smile on Camellia's.

As Harry swung back into his seat at the picnic table, Camellia threw one arm around him and rubbed her knuckles against his head with the other. "I'm so proud of you, baby brother!"

"Hey, watch the hair!" Harry joked. "At my age, it might not grow back. What brings this on?"

"Camellia was just bragging about your big new contract for the One World thing," I said.

Harry's eyes lit up. "I can't wait to get started on that," he said enthusiastically. "Jerry's already got some great ideas for it, and the

Norbert kid is turning out to have some real talent as a designer. I'm putting him in charge of the table arrangements."

"I heard you were promoting some of your employees," I said.

Suddenly Harry's eyes misted over. "They deserve it, the way they've stuck with me through all of this. Ellie's getting her degree in accounting, you know, and as soon as she gets her degree, I'm hiring her on as our full-time business accountant. She's been helping me figure out how to make up for what Chuck and Bill did to some of our clients."

"That wasn't your fault," Tara said, setting her own plate on the table. She looked at Harry with troubled eyes.

"It happened in my business," Harry said firmly. "If I can, I'm going to put it right."

Tara smiled at that. "That's what makes you such a great guy." Then she raised her eyebrows at him meaningfully. "Hey, what's this I hear about you having a new rose supplier?"

Camellia gave a deep chuckle, and Harry turned a little bit red.

"What's this?" I asked, interested.

"Oh, nothing," Tara said casually, "It's just that lately Camellia's been telling me about this lovely new organic rose grower who has some nice big curves and even bigger brown eyes…"

Harry turned an even deeper shade of red. I took pity on him. "So, Tara, where's Detective Harris?" I asked. "I know Susan invited him."

This time it was Tara's turn to blush.

"He's coming," Susan said, taking her own seat. "We just got off the phone. He got held up in traffic but don't worry—" here she grinned and reached over to pat Tara's shoulder—"he'll be here. He wouldn't miss it for anything."

Tara was still trying to figure out what to say to that when a cascade of barking broke out. Susan's neighbors had just pulled up in their driveway, and their Boston terrier had bounded out of their SUV as soon as the doors opened. Lady was streaking toward them.

For a moment, I was nervous that Lady had decided they were enemies again. Luigi Di'Ogee (wow, what a name!) was smaller than Lady and might come out of a fight with serious injuries.

I needn't have worried. As soon as she got close, Lady lowered her head between her front paws and wagged her tail. It was the universal dog code for "play with me!" Apparently the little dog's brave defense of Susan and Lady had cemented a canine friendship for life.

The black and white pug yipped happily, and together they raced around Susan's yard. Not to be left out of the game, Upchuck ran after them, part of a stolen hamburger still trailing from his mouth.

"My doggy heroes," Susan said wistfully.

For just a second I shivered, remembering the terrifying moments we had spent on this same lawn. Then I caught Tara's eye, watching me. She got up and wandered over to my seat as everyone else's attention was held by the frolicking dogs.

"Look," she said quietly, "you guys scare the crap out of me with all the chances you take, but—" here her voice faltered a little—"I can't tell you how grateful I am for helping me clear Harry. I'm just so sorry helping me investigate put you in danger."

I reached up and gave her a hug. "Look around you," I said, also keeping my voice low. "Everything's fine now. Harry's OK, and maybe even starting a romance with a rose lady—I hadn't heard about that. He doesn't have dishonest people working for him anymore. He's got a tight group of loyal employees now, and we know for sure that Mrs. McKenzie was planning to kill poor Ellie Meyers after she was done with us. There were probably even more women on her list. Camellia's happy because Harry's happy, and you're happy because they're happy. Even those ridiculous dogs are happy. All of that is worth a little danger."

Tara sniffed and swiped her eyes. Then she returned my hug. "Thanks," she said.

"Speaking of happiness..." I said, nodding toward the figure of Detective John Harris, who was walking across the lawn. Tara flushed again.

"Sorry I'm late," he said as he set a box full of gourmet cupcakes on the table. "I brought dessert."

Just then Jim and Michael, who had disappeared a few minutes previously, suddenly returned dressed in their kilts and proudly carrying their bagpipes.

Susan, who was in the process of inviting her neighbors over to the party, viewed them with dismay.

"Oh, boy," said Tara. "At least those shouldn't explode."

"Hey, dancers, who wants some music?" Jim roared. Michael whooped and played a few notes. The dogs stopped in their tracks and started to howl along.

I shrugged. After all, why not? Compared to everything else that had happened, bagpipe music wasn't that bad. They were outside, there were only two of them, and they weren't being amplified by microphones. If anybody called the cops, we could say that the cops were already here.

Susan strolled over to us after directing her new guests to the food. "What do you think?" she asked, raising her voice to be heard.

"Theoretically, it should be possible to dance to bagpipes," Tara shouted. "Actually that's kind of a catchy tune." She started an experimental shimmy as Harry and Camellia dissolved in laughter.

"I'm in," Susan yelled. She executed a few hip drops.

"Me, too." I wriggled out of my seat and started my own shimmy.

"Amateurs," said Camellia, "let an old lady show you how it's done!" She stood and performed a number of moves too quickly for me to even name them.

Tara grabbed Harry and hauled him out of his seat. He gingerly tried his own shimmy. Susan dragged her neighbors into the circle. They protested a little, but soon got the hang of it.

John Harris was left to me. "Come on, Detective," I challenged him. "Show us what you've got."

Everybody doubled up laughing as he started to dance.

In memory of Tuppence, who for 15 sweet years was our own beautiful 'Banshee.' We miss you, little one. Rest in peace.

57716448R00181

Made in the USA
Charleston, SC
21 June 2016